John Manuel

EVE
OF
DECONSTRUCTION

Also by John Manuel

The "Ramblings from Rhodes" series
of lighthearted Grecian travel memoirs:

Feta Compli!
Moussaka To My Ears
Tzatziki For You To Say
A Plethora Of Posts

The Novels:
The View From Kleoboulos
A Brief Moment of Sunshine

All of the above available from Amazon worldwide
in paperback or Kindle format
and from the publisher, www.lulu.com

More information about the above titles can be found on
John Manuel's blog:
http://ramblingsfromrhodes.blogspot.com
and from his website:
http://johnphilipmanuel.wix.com/works

*"When I was 5 years old,
my mother always told me that happiness
was the key to life. When I went to school,
they asked me what I wanted to be
when I grew up. I wrote down 'happy'.
They told me I didn't understand the assignment,
and I told them they didn't understand life."*

- John Lennon

EVE
OF DECONSTRUCTION

1. November 2012, Chippenham, UK

My name is Eve. Well, actually, it's Evanthia, sometimes Evanthoula or simply Anthoula, owing to the fact that my mother was Greek. From my earliest memories, however, I've been called Eve, since I was brought up in the UK, here in Chippenham in Wiltshire. I loved my mother so much. It's terribly painful to be doing what I'm doing, but there's no one else who can do it. I ought to explain.

Mum died last month. She was a good, hardworking, loving mother and she didn't deserve what happened to her. Ovarian cancer. I hate even saying those words. Still, there's nothing 'just' about the world we live in is there? At least she lived long enough to see me grow up and marry a good man, my Tom. I ought to be grateful for that. But these days sixty-one isn't old. She was still a young woman at heart and could have passed for someone ten years younger on a good day, when she'd taken the time to have her hair permed and coloured and done herself up a little. Put on a little eyeliner maybe.

I'm an orphan now at forty-two, my dear sweet dad Ian having left us back in 2002, an unbelievable ten years ago. He was only fifty-six. His heart just up and said one day, "That's it, I can't take any more of this, I'm stopping. Sorry, but that's how it is." Dad worked very hard as a furniture manager for a large "shed" as we seem to call out-of-town stores nowadays. For as long as I can remember he worked for that company. Never got rich, but always earned a good enough living for my parents to have a nice little life in a semi-detached house with a drive along the side, roses in the front garden and a half-decent family saloon in the garage. I had a swing hanging from the apple tree in the back garden. Dad put that up and how often he'd push me as I swung back and forth on it as a little girl. Such wonderful days. All gone now.

He often brought his work home with him. I well remember as a teenager watching him on the sofa during the weekday evenings, Ercol and G Plan brochures strewn all around him, files on his lap and, in later years, a computer too. He'd be processing orders, planning his buying, deciding what lines were going to be put in the next sale, calculating the commission for his three or four underlings, all of whom he cared for like a father.

Took everything seriously did Dad. He was never slapdash about anything, even his appearance. He was born out of his time in a way. He always looked like he ought to have been an adult during the fifties, even down to his penchant for smoking a pipe, one of those with a curly stem, like the kind that Sherlock Holmes is usually depicted as smoking. His hair was always parted on the side and Brylcreem was always to be found in his bathroom cabinet.

Now I'm filling up. I can't help it. Dad went all those years ago and now mum's gone too. Neither of them lived long enough to enjoy a nice retirement together; to see their grandkids grow up and settle down. My kids were so very young when Dad went, only five and three.

And now mum's gone. Just like that. She went from feeling bloated and having a pain in her lower abdomen to falling asleep forever in just a few months. None of us had time to adjust to what was happening to her.

Eve Watkins is sitting cross-legged on her mother's lounge carpet, surrounded by paperwork from her mother's steel box file, a legacy from her father Ian, who had everything filed in its place for this very eventuality. Eve had always hoped that this day would never come. Yet come it has and much earlier than it ought to. In the box are all kinds of papers that need Eve's attention. The will her mother left appointed Eve as executor and she's already had to telephone umpteen charitable organisations to tell them that her mother's contributions will now no longer be forthcoming. She's organised and paid for a number of "originals" of the death certificate and spent hours on the phone dealing with solicitors, Probate, banks, the electricity company, the gas company, the water company, the insurance companies and the list goes on. She's wondering how anyone can find the time to grieve when they lose their second parent. She reaches over to her mother's coffee table and lifts a chunky ceramic mug to her lips and sips the hot coffee. She exhales audibly…

She was a very good cook, Mum, too. Although I never learned Greek from her, I did learn how to make some mean Greek dishes. I can make a Moussaka to rival the best of them, Briam - which Tom absolutely loves, is one of my specialities. Gigantes I do well too. I don't cook meat dishes these days, although in times past my Kleftiko drew many expressions of awe from guests at dinner parties. Funny how it went from having a few friends in for tea to being called a "dinner party". Such is the way the world has moved on I suppose. It's all about how you describe things these days.

I was born in April 1970, in Lamia, Greece. Not that I remember anything at all about all that though. Mum was never very forthcoming about what went on back then, except to tell me that my parents had to make the move to the UK to avoid starving. Things were so difficult that a relative here in England wrote to say that they'd keep a job open for mum in a taverna in Bath if my parents could pack up and come over. I really ought to have looked into my background before now, but somehow I've never found the time. I do know that it was during the time of the Colonels, or Military Junta, who ruled Greece rather harshly from 1967 through 1974. You know, I'm ashamed to say that I've never even really quizzed Dad about how he came to be out there and how my parents actually met. I can only assume that he was a bit of an adventurer and went off to see the world. He'd have been about twenty-four I think; yes, he would have been, since he was born in 1946. Mum definitely told me though, that it was one of her relatives, a cousin, who'd offered her work here in England. I suppose Dad knew that back here in the UK he'd find work anyway, since he was British, after all.

Why do we take so many things for granted when we're small? I grew up never asking about why my mum spoke with a foreign accent. I just took it as how things were. She was an avid reader though, I'll say that. She told me that she wanted to learn English right off the bat and not turn into one of those people who live in a country and can't understand it when they pick up a newspaper or visit a grocery store. Whenever I conjure up an image of Mum, apart from those of her working around the house that is, she's in her armchair in the front room reading an English novel. She worked her way through Jane Austen, the Bronte sisters and even Ian Fleming whilst I was growing up. So, although she did sound Greek, her English grammar was very good. I'm proud of her for that.

We never had contact, at least not that I was aware of, with any Greek relatives whilst I was growing up. It's strange how only now, at the age of forty-two, I'm discovering a burning desire to know about my mother's past, about my Greek relatives who must surely still be out there in Greece somewhere. Greeks are so family-oriented that they surely must also be wondering what became of Mum, their little Chrisanthi. Perhaps for some reason they simply lost contact. They didn't have e-mail in those days after all. I could have cousins, nieces and nephews, aunts and uncles. Here I am now, sitting on the floor of mum's house, estate agent's sign announcing the end of an era for me to all and sundry who pass, that my last root, my last anchor, is being pulled up, as if I'm being cast adrift on a choppy sea with no clear idea about what direction I'm going in.

I don't want to see this house go and yet I don't have any choice. I have no use for it and Tom and I have a home we're immensely happy in. It's too fraught with potential risks and problems to think about renting this out. Anyway, if someone else who I don't even know is going to live here I'd rather not still have any connections with the place. It would be even more painful than not ever coming here again. No, to sell is the lesser of two evils.

But there's just so much stuff. At least there is a charity store not far from here who have promised that they'll collect free of charge anything that we finally want to leave behind after the gannets have been and riffled through Mum's belongings and traipsed off with whatever they want. It's all so sordid isn't it. Can it really be that someone's whole life, all their hopes and aspirations, their dreams and plans, come to this? The only answer to that one is, 'get on with it - it's how things are'.

All this paperwork. Ah, here's all the legal stuff by the look of it.

Eve takes a sip from her now stone-cold coffee, yet doesn't seem to notice its temperature. She pulls out a wad of A4 sheets from a file in her mother's box of documents and begins scanning them with her eyes. The afternoon has been wearing on and it's now growing quite dark outside, since it's November and, as is so often the case during this most depressing of months, it's cloudy too. Eve rises to her feet and walks across to the light switch on the wall. As she flips it, flooding the almost dark room with an instant electric glow from the low-energy lamp hanging from the ceiling, she finds a document that she's never seen before.

Well, well, if it isn't my parents' marriage certificate. I've never seen this before. I can't stand all this flowery jargon, "Certified Copy of an Entry of Marriage Pursuant to the Marriage Act of 1949"…blah de blah.

"Marriage solmenised at…" Wait a minute. I thought they'd married in Greece before coming back here. This is a Certificate of Marriage right here in Chippenham. I was born in April 1970. It says here that my parents married in March 1973. I'd have been almost three years old! What's going on? I must be seeing things, but no, it's very clear. Perhaps I was born out of wedlock. That would have been something in the Greece of 1970, especially in a small tightly-knit community. Maybe that's why they fled to the UK, perhaps they had two reasons to come here, only one of which was economic.

Eve sits down again, this time on her mother's sofa. She's staring in disbelief at the legal document declaring clearly that her parents married almost three years after she was born. Her mind is racing. After reading that her mother was listed as a "restaurant worker" and her father simply as a "salesman" she sees something else that completely stuns her. Eve's eyes cannot move from one word that jumps out and bores into her consciousness. It cannot be, surely, yet there it is, in liquid black ink from the registrar's fountain pen…

This makes no sense at all. Surely I'm seeing things. Perhaps it's the stress of all that's happened in the last few weeks. No, it's there, clear as day in black and white.

Under the column "Condition" my father is described, as you'd expect, as a bachelor, but my mother is described here as a ... widow.

In March 1973 my mother would have been only twenty-two years old.

John Manuel

2. November 2012, Chippenham, UK

My name is Tom and I'm a lucky man. No, I don't have a stunningly scintillating career as an international jet-setter. In fact to earn my crust I manage a tyre depot, but it's a good steady job and it pays well. I have twelve staff under me and I like to think that I'm a good boss. Friends and relatives come to my depot when they need tyres and I'll always arrange for them to have a hefty discount. Gone are the days when a couple of tyres for your car were cheap. It makes my eyes water when I look at what people pay nowadays for a set of "boots", so there are worse trades for me to be in.

I used to play rugby. I like to think that I was a good scrum half; I even tried out for England once but didn't quite make the cut. Never mind, I had a good ten years at club level and I enjoyed every minute of it. It's how I met Eve too, so it was worth it for that alone.

Eve was a dark, long-haired beauty with that ever-so slightly European look. At first I thought "Spanish", but she turned out to be half Greek, which was really exotic in my impressionable mind. She was a trainee physio and she worked on me after I was carried off once following a fierce tackle. I could have complained that the tackle was against the rules, but then, I met Eve so I was grateful in the end. As outside on the pitch my team went on to be given a sound 35-10 thrashing, in the medical room I luxuriated in this girl's two hands working all over my right leg. What more can a man ask for? It was 1989 and I was twenty-two and she was just nineteen.

We married in April 1995 and spent a week on honeymoon in Tintagel, Cornwall. It was the best I could do at the time and, anyway, a honeymoon's not really about exotic locations and sightseeing is it. In 1997 along came our first child, our son Andrew, who's now a strapping great fifteen-year-old who's going to be a better rugby player than I ever was. He already plays for his school team and I'm dead proud of the boy. He is starting to discover girls now though, so I may be faced with the old birds and bees stuff before long. Mind you, the way kids are today he's probably already light-years ahead of me.

In August of 1999 we had our baby girl, Zoe. Eve said she really wanted a Greek name and I couldn't disagree. Zoe means life and she's certainly got plenty of that. She's thirteen going on twenty-one and it frightens me how much like a young woman she already looks. She's been having the "woman thing" already now for two years and is dead against me going into her bedroom or maybe the bathroom (which none of us ever locks, even now) if she's in there, without knocking first. I can be grateful for small mercies though. She and Eve are like sisters. She tells her Mum everything and has no qualms about Eve picking up her mobile phone and nosing through it.

Recently I've had to be supportive of Eve, though, because her mum only died a month ago. They were very close. Although to all intents and purposes Eve's a British girl, her mum has transmitted to her a deep family loyalty that I can only assume is a Greek thing. It must go back to Chrisanthi's heritage in the Greece of her childhood. I'm exceedingly proud of Eve because she wants to deal with her Mum's estate herself. Yes, I do help with some things, especially the brawn angle when it comes to taking furniture out of the house in preparation for it to be sold, but Eve is determined to carry out her role as executor and so I'm taking a back seat and waiting for her to ask me if she needs any help with anything.

Tom Watkins, Eve's husband of seventeen years, is driving home through the November murk. They live in a comfortable semi on a fairly new housing development just off the A4 Bath Road, to the West of their pleasant little country town of Chippenham. Tom's depot is in Melksham, so it's a drive of perhaps twenty minutes or so, occasionally more if the traffic's heavy, but it usually isn't. He's drumming his fingers on the steering wheel of his VW Passat and musing about his wife and the loss of his mother-in-law, whose house is on the other side of town, thus also a drive of some fifteen to twenty minutes from their home. He knows that Eve has been over there this afternoon to go through some more paperwork, but fully expects her to be home and for the smell of cooking to greet him as he opens the front door at somewhere around 6.00pm.

Andrew will be at rugby Team practice and Zoe probably in her room listening to that awful Eminem "music" which Tom can't abide, but feels he has to tolerate. At least it's usually on her headphones and not on the speakers of her bedroom stereo. Turning into their close he notices that Eve's Mini Cooper isn't on the drive.

Hmm, that's odd. She ought to be back by now. Hope everything's OK. Why is it that I always think that she's had an accident or something if she isn't where I expect her to be? Of course, I'd have heard if she had any serious problem. Stop worrying you idiot.

I'll call her on her mobile when I get inside.

Tom turns his Passat on to the drive and kills the engine. As he takes his keys out of the ignition the sound of Amy MacDonald dies too as the CD player fades to darkness. He grabs his briefcase from the back seat gets out of the car and doesn't look back as his fingers operate the plip-lock on his key and the car's four orange flashers blink a couple of times, accompanied by an electronic bleep that says the car is now locked.

He puts his front door key into the lock and lets himself in as outside the drizzle begins and inside the darkness of the hallway sends his right hand up to the light switch to throw light on the murk within. He calls out, "Zoe!! You up there?"

His thirteen-year-old daughter's voice drifts down the stairs, irritation oozing through every syllable, "No! I'm still over at Trisha's!"

"Where's your mother?" Calls Tom.

"Am I my mother's keeper?" comes the reply.

Tom tuts, enters the kitchen, drops his case on the dining table and pulls his mobile phone from his inside jacket pocket. He taps the screen a couple of times and places it to his left ear. It's ringing. The display reads "Eve" as it does so.

After about six or seven rings, his wife's voice creeps out from the device into his ear.

"Hello Tom, love. Sorry, I'm still at mum's."

"You OK? Nothing's happened has it?" asks Tom. Quite what "something" may have been he's not entirely clear about.

"No, no. Well, yes. Tom, I'm a bit, well, [a pause, and then] …who am I?"

"There's no drink at mum's house is there? What do you mean, 'who am I?' I'm not following you love. Why are you still over there when it's after six?"

"Tom, I found something. My parents' marriage certificate." She stops, unsure of how to continue.

"Yes, well, it's not as though we didn't think they were married Eve, is it? Why should that cause you any concern?"

"Tom, love. They were married in 1973. I was born in 1970."

"OK, so they weren't married when they had you. That's not such an unusual happenstance these days love. Look, can't we talk about this here? Why don't you just lock up and come on home? What say we get a Chinese tonight, you won't want to cook now will you?"

"Tom, that's not all. The certificate says that when mum married dad, she would have been only twenty-two. But the certificate says, under the heading "Condition" that she was a widow!! What does that mean Tom? What is it that she never told me during all those years? None of this makes any sense Tom, none of it!"

Tom's now also confused about what his wife has told him. But feels he must offer reassurance.

"Look, love, I'm sure there's going to be some perfectly rational explanation. Why not just lock the house up and get yourself back here. I'll call the Peking Sun and get some food ordered and we'll talk over a bottle of wine and some prawn crackers."

"But, but… who am I Tom? How could I not have been told all of this? Why was it kept from me? I've got to know. Mum and Dad are both gone now, so who can I ask?"

"Darling, look. It's far better to talk about this face to face. Get yourself home, now, OK?"

John Manuel

3. November 2012, Chippenham, UK

Tom is watching anxiously as his wife's Mini Cooper turns into the close, its windscreen wipers swaying rhythmically this way and that against the thickening drizzle. He can see them in the yellow sodium glow of the streetlamps. It's 6.30pm and totally dark. Puddles are scattered randomly across the pavement and the tarmac surface of the road. Tom's eyes follow his wife's car until it stops behind his on their driveway and its lights die. Just before Eve gets out he spies their cat Frazzle, sitting on the dry paviors under his car's engine and displaying that body language that cats do when they're quite disgusted with the weather.

Tom watches Eve spring from the car and sprint for the front door. What started out as drizzle is now morphing irrevocably into steady rain. It's typical November weather. Once inside the door Tom is there to greet her and take her coat, which he throws onto an available hook in the hallway and then he turns to give his wife a hug. She willingly accepts his bearhug whilst holding a sheaf of paperwork between their chests.

"Wine open?" She asks as she extricates herself from Tom's arms and walks into the lounge. As she flops on to their loose-cotton covered off-white sofa, she receives her answer, as there on the coffee table is an open bottle of chilled white and two glasses.

Tom says, "The Chinese will be here any time. They've got a youth on a moped now to do home deliveries, good eh?"

"As long as it doesn't mean you pay more for the privilege," replies Eve.

Tom's trying to gauge his wife's mood. He wants to know how to proceed with this conversation without stressing her out any further. He decides against reminding Eve that there would be a cost in petrol involved if he had to drive the mile and a half or so to the Chinese to collect the food. He asks:

"So, have you got the Marriage Certificate there?" he points with his eyes to the paperwork that Eve is still clutching to her chest. She looks down and realises that she's holding the files in a vice-like grip. It's like there was a gale blowing in the lounge and she wouldn't want any of the papers to be blown from her grasp. She still has her leather jacket on too. Tom gestures to her to let him have the files while she removes the jacket. She complies.

Swopping the files for the jacket with his wife, Tom then walks out into the hallway to hang it up. When he returns Eve is taking a first swig from a full wine glass and peeling off sheets of paper from the wad which she's laid on the table before her.

"There it is, you read it. Am I seeing things, Tom? Is there or is there not a huge bombshell right there in black and white?" She thrusts the certificate at Tom, who accepts it as he sinks into an armchair. She takes another sip and then cradles the wine glass in both hands as her husband picks up his, then sips at it while frowning his way down through the details on the sheet in front of him.

"Well, first and foremost, it seems genuine and from this we have to accept that your mum and dad probably had you out of wedlock then. But that's no big deal. Anyway, who's going to find out about this now, after all these years? I don't see why you need to worry about that love, I really don't."

"Tom, that's not it. *Read it* properly, love. It says that mum was a WIDOW when she married Dad. A *widow* at twenty-two? Who was she married to before? Tom, am I stupid or is it just possible that my Dad, my lovely Dad who I worshipped throughout my whole life isn't really my birth-father at all? Where does that leave ME?"

"OK, look, love, yes it's a puzzle, yes it's a bit strange. But I don't see that it need change anything. It didn't ought to make you suddenly go into 'crisis' mode over who you are. You had a wonderful upbringing with two loving parents. Why not let sleeping dogs…"

"TOM! NO! I can't. Surely you must understand that. A person can't just tell herself how to think; how to feel. From the instant I read that certificate over at Mum's I felt different. I felt like my anchor had been severed and I was adrift in a sea of unanswered questions. My identity, who I really am, is at stake here. Surely you…"

Eve is interrupted by the slamming of the front door. Their son Andrew appears in the lounge doorway, still in his rugby kit under his duffle-coat. His hair is plastered to his head from the rain outside, which can be heard drumming like a brush on a snare drum on the front windows. His sports bag is slung over one shoulder. He looks from one of his parents to the other, notices their facial expressions and says:

"OK. Bad time. I'll take a shower."

"No, Andy..!" Starts Eve, but too late, her son is bounding up the stairs and, as he passes his sister's door on the landing on his way to the bathroom, he gives it a thump and yells "Snot pants! You in there?"

Tom looks at Eve and tries to establish eye contact. He's trying to think of what to say to keep his wife from, as he sees it, overreacting to this new information, but he can't quite frame any words. He reaches for the wine bottle to pour a top-up for each of them when the front doorbell chimes.

"That'll be the Chinese," says Tom as he puts down the bottle, gets up and walks out into the hallway.

4. Chippenham 2012-13

Tom thinks I'm overreacting. I know he means well, but he doesn't get it. Of course, the first thing he wanted to know was why the hell I didn't know the year of my parents' wedding all throughout my childhood. I suppose that was a fair question.

There is only one answer. I never asked and Mum was always a bit evasive if I ever did get near to things that happened in the distant past. I always put that down to her unpleasant memories of how tough things were before they came here from Greece, or back here in Dad's case. If Dad had lived longer then I suppose I may just have asked whether their pearl wedding Anniversary was due or something. But then, I do remember that both Mum and Dad used to say that they didn't go in for all that kind of stuff. Just a simple card to eachother and a meal out somewhere would always suffice and - call me stupid - but I wasn't ever really that interested in how long they'd been married anyway.

I do remember that on the odd occasion when I'd quiz Mum a little, she'd say something like "Evanthoula mou, why you want to go back into all that stuff? It was bad back then, but your father is a good man and he saved me! That's all you need to know, moro mou, isn't it?"

She didn't seem to want to address her Greek past. I never had any Greek relatives to visit all the time I was growing up. Dad's family more than compensated anyway and Mum seemed to be comfortable with that, so why shouldn't I have been? Even the mysterious 'cousin' who's meant to have found Mum a job in a Greek Restaurant here in England never materialised in my life. Perhaps he or she died young too, I really don't have a clue. I've always been under the impression that perhaps Mum's Greek family didn't approve of dad because he wasn't Greek, or more importantly Greek Orthodox. I suppose too that, reading between the lines, Mum didn't have much of a family anyway out there by the time I was born and thus it was no great wrench for her to come to the UK, where she was fairly sure of a better quality of life.

Ah well, what to do now is the big question. I'll have to hope that Tom comes round and begins to understand that, while I may have left it a bit late, having lost both of my parents at only 42 years of age, I do need to find out some stuff about my past. I have to know who Mum was married to before and there must be ways of finding out.

There must be.

As the next few weeks fly past, Eve is more than occupied with the affairs of her mother's "estate", which consists mainly of a few thousand pounds in a bank account and the house and its contents, which Eve eventually manages to prepare for sale, much to the relief of her estate agent. It's a nice little place and ought to sell quite quickly, despite the fairly depressed market at the moment. *"A well-maintained, traditionally built property, dating from the 1960's, with a rear aspect opening on to a private, well laid garden with mature apple tree…"* says the estate agent's spec sheet for the house.

Now that Eve has sorted out the Probate and finished dealing with all the charities and utility companies, the bank and a credit card company, so many of which want an "original" of the Death Certificate, she's realising that her physiotherapy business, which she runs herself while consulting with a couple of private health clubs and municipal sports centres, is suffering a little. Time to fill that appointment book again. After all, two growing kids and a mortgage to keep up with mean that Tom's salary, although pretty good, doesn't stretch the whole way nowadays.

February 2013 arrives and she realises that she's still got this void deep in her soul. Her feet have barely touched the ground and now she's finally beginning to feel the emotions of grief over her mother, coupled with the deep unease about her real roots. The estate agent has called to say that they have an offer on the house. It's not the asking price, but much to Tom and Eve's relief, it's above the lower threshold that they'd set as an acceptable minimum.

For a couple more weeks Eve is dealing with the estate agent as the delicate process of agreeing the sale proceeds to a completion. She and Tom sign all kinds of paperwork for the estate agent, for the solicitor and for the buyer's solicitor. Someone arrives to do an energy survey, something that was entirely new to Tom and Eve, not having been involved in buying or selling a house for over fifteen years. A few odd potential spanners in the works are finally ironed out, things like who's responsible for the fence between Eve's Mum's property and the land that it backs on to. There had been a potential issue with the drains too, which finally got sorted out to the satisfaction of the buyer's solicitor.

By the time they have a completion date Eve is mentally exhausted and Tom is trying to buoy her up. Andrew and Zoe just get on with their own lives in total oblivion to what their mother is enduring emotionally. On one occasion during the weeks leading up to the completion date being agreed, Andrew had asked his mother how much money the family was due to inherit. That seemed to her to be the limit of his interest in the whole affair. As he'd entered his teens he'd seen less and less of his grandmother, sadly in Eve's view, because she would insist on patronising him and treating him like a small child. This fact was made very evident by the paltry sums of money she'd slip the children when they did deign to go and see her. Andrew had decided a year or two ago to cut his losses, despite remonstrations from Tom and Eve.

One Tuesday morning, when Eve's diary is clear of physio appointments for a change, she calls up her old school friend, still her closest girl friend.

Fay Trenchard is a silver-spoon girl whose parents were very well-to-do, hence Fay has never really needed to do much with her life apart from play with horses and find a plum-in-the-mouth man to marry when she's ready. That aside, she's always been close to Eve and they were inseparable for years at senior school. Now both in their early forties and Fay having indeed found a racehorse trainer for a husband, they still do coffee at least once a week. Granted, this habit had suffered for a few months while Eve dealt with her mother's estate, but it's now back on track as the Winter of 2012-13 draws toward its inevitable end as it makes way for another Spring.

"Costa Coffee, fifteen minutes?" Asks Eve.

"Sounds like a plan," says Fay on the other end of Eve's mobile phone.

Half an hour later, Fay and Eve face eachother across a table, hot Mochas in front of them both. Fay speaks:

"Can't believe it's been a couple of months since we did this Evie.

What's the news?"

"Well, we've got a completion date of March 8th on mum's house, so that will be a load off our minds."

"And the other business, resolved or not?"

"I haven't had time to do anything about it. But I must, Fay. I have to find out what happened back then. I have these nagging doubts, this feeling that maybe my dad's not my real dad after all. I know it's all probably rubbish and they just probably had me before they got married, but my mum was definitely born in March of 1951 and the marriage certificate, a British one, dates from March seventy-three, when mum would have only been twenty-two. How could she have already been a widow at that age? I know I have Greek blood in me, through mum of course, so I can't help feeling that the answers may be out there in Greece somewhere. My knowledge of mum's youth is sketchy at best. She just never talked about her younger days, her time before dad came along. I've always assumed that dad was an adventurous traveller who met mum in Greece and then brought her back here. I suppose I always had the idea that dad had lived out there a while and that they married out there, but I'm ashamed to say that it's all a fog to me, I know so little about it."

"Well," replies Fay, "at least these days we have the Internet. I'm sure you'll be able to turn up all kinds of stuff if you go Googling, Evie. You'll probably find there's a simple explanation to the whole thing. Who knows, maybe you'll turn up a few Greek relatives that you never knew you had. That'd be rather exotic, yeah?"

"You sound like Tom now Fay. If he's said 'there's a perfectly rational explanation' once since last November, he's said it a hundred times. He thinks I ought to leave the whole thing anyway. 'What you don't know won't hurt you' is another of his favourite sayings lately. But it's not that simple. Can you understand that Fay?"

"I think so Eve. It's difficult for me because I'm just a boring old English girl whose past is all laid out behind me. No mysteries there. All rather dull really. You, on the other hand, my girl, you are beginning to sound to me like you have a book in you, waiting to be written. 'All About Eve' would be a good title, wouldn't it?" Fay smiles at her own inventiveness and sips her Mocha. She stares at her friend and waits for a response. Eve is looking at her friend but her mind has gone off somewhere. She's imagining small Greek villages and what life may have been like for her mother as a young girl growing up in a tiny village on a Grecian mountainside in the 1950's and 60's.

Just how different was that world from the UK during that era? She wonders.

5. SORONA 1960's

Far up in the hills above the town of Lamia, in central Greece, sits the windswept village of Sorona. It lies only about thirty kilometres up in the hills from Lamia, but for all the chance most of the village residents have of ever going there, it may as well be Athens, Rome or London. To make the trip from the village down the slopes to the 'big' town would involve a perilous "Jerusalem to Jericho" expedition along twisty-turny dirt lanes that from time to time afford the traveller tantalising glimpses of the metropolis far below before mercilessly turning the weary wayfarer away as it bends and ducks behind yet another hill or rise in its convoluted course. To make the trip would invariably involve walking the whole way or perhaps riding on the back of an ass or donkey. The adjective 'Biblical' naturally springs to mind. At least from the village there is a grand vista affording anyone who has the time to appreciate it an uninterrupted view of the majestic shallow valley plain that drapes across the country of Greece from Karpenisi to the West through Lamia to the Malian Gulf and twinkling Aegean Sea to the East.

In the Greece of the early 1960s, one could imagine that one were in the England of the 1900s. Sorona is a village that, in another few short decades, would be the type of place to elicit sighs of longing and whimsy from shorts-clad, baseball cap-wearing tourists clicking away with their iPads, digital cameras or mobile phones. Yet in 1963 it's a subsistence village, where the lives of the inhabitants are lived and lost amongst labour and toil on the land and among the animals that they tend and live off of. The bread ovens in the streets will one day be props up against which spaghetti-strapped women will drape themselves while their partners or husbands say "Great, hold it like that! Perfect!" Click.

Today, in the summer of 1963, those ovens are worked continuously to provide hot meals for hungry labourers and their wives and children. Women ceaselessly pack them with wood and then, after use, clear out the ashes before the next session. The idea of electricity being supplied to every private household is a distant dream. The interior walls of the old stone houses run with water during the short, yet bitter winter months and exhibit a creeping, black mould by the time that Spring comes. In summer at least they do provide some respite from the relentless heat outside, as long as the shutters and doors remain tightly closed whenever possible. Many of these village dwellings don't have many, if any, windows anyway. Those that do exhibit very small ones, with wooden frames that continuously need re-painting and invariably have warped and pulled away from the apertures into which they were fitted eons before, thus allowing the bitter wind to whistle into the house when it blows in January, cold enough to cut you in half.

The 'road' that leads up to the village from the plain below enters the village from the side and the village slopes steeply upward from low left to high right. Immediately on entering the village it empties out into the central village square. All streets, or rather 'lanes' lead off from there. At the far left of the square, or 'platia' is the Byzantine church with its bell tower, which chimes continually on the hour, even during the night time, as if to remind the residents of how brief their time on this earth is, and often at other times when there's a religious festival or observation, or when someone in the village has died, for example.

Life expectancy in 1960's rural Greece is pitifully short compared to North West Europe. Yes, there are wizened old women sitting on doorsteps, their headscarves ever-present around their visages, their gnarled, arthritic hands resting on wooden staffs cut from olive trees and worn smooth and shiny by continuous use as their owners gaze at nothing in particular. More than likely their minds are seeing the streets of their youth, when they ran around their mothers' aprons and danced in the square during the *paniyiris*; days that to them seem to have only been just a moment before. Yet by and large one can expect to survive into one's sixth decade, if one is lucky, here in a Greek village in this particular era. One of the main reasons for this is the fact that the nearest doctor is three villages away over some very rough terrain. Here one can die of something that would be easily treated in, for example the UK, where an ambulance would arrive in minutes to whisk the patient off to the nearest hospital. Three or four decades hence, in the 1990's, a helicopter transfer service will be introduced to many of the more remote Greek villages and islands, but here in 1963, well, you can easily die of appendicitis, or perhaps from a stroke or heart attack that could be dealt with quite routinely, were the patient in a position to be taken directly to hospital.

On the other side of the square from the church, perched high above the square, is the main taverna-cum-kafeneion of the village.

This establishment is called *"To Steki"* [The Hangout or Meeting Place] and its proprietor is Minas, who is married to Panayiota. Minas is a short, thickset man with a good head of thick, white hair. His top lip hasn't been visible for many years, since it hides itself under a generous white moustache, which in turn hovers perpetually above a mouth that usually exhibits a wide smile, one that reaches all the way to his sixty-year-old eyes. Those eyes are framed by deep laugh-lines that lend credence to the theory that one's face becomes set in such a way as to reveal one's personality the older one becomes. If this theory is true, then anyone meeting Minas for the first time would judge him to be genial, happy and generous. They'd more or less be spot on.

His wife Panayiota is of similar height, ten years his junior and always dressed in drab brown clothes, the front of which are probably several shades darker than the rest, owing to the fact that she wears an apron twenty-four seven, since she spends her entire life in the kitchen of their establishment, creating Elliniko coffees for the old men of the village 365 mornings of the year. Thus the sides and back of her skirts and jumpers are probably faded by the light, to which the chest and lap areas are never exposed. Panayiota has shoulder-length wavy hair that's now more grey than brown. If she were to be running this Kafenion thirty years later she'd be able to keep its original colour by applying it from a bottle, but such a luxury is not available to one such as her here in 1963.

And so we have a picture of Sorona, a fairly typical and totally non-descript Greek village in 1963, the village where Eve Watkins' mother, Chrisanthi was born and raised.

*

"Chrisanthoula!!! Get back in here now!! It's time you got yourself ready my girl!!!" The voice of Kyria Sofia Katsandadis is anything but soft and dulcet. When Sofia shouts the whole village pays attention. She never fails to use this method to gain the attention of her children, the oldest of which is 12-year-old Chrisanthi. There are two younger children, each one separated by a mere 12 months in age. Both are boys, Giannis and Dimitris.

Sofia's mother Tassia has just died, much to her husband Petros' relief. He and his mother-in-law never saw eye to eye, in fact they hardly ever saw each other at all as, over the years during which Petros has been married to Sofia, he's grown more and more irate at his *'pethera'* and her interfering ways. Of course, he was never good enough for her daughter. He was always a disappointment to his wife's mother. Petros, on the other hand, always maintains that Sofia's parents should have been grateful he'd taken her off their hands. Not that he hadn't loved his wife when they were first brought together by the arrangement between their two families all those years before, but Sofia had been one of three daughters born to her parents, who never had a son. He'd gallantly agreed to accept her with a very modest dowry, though he could have held out for much more, but she was pretty, he was desperate for sex and the parents just didn't have anything else to give.

Petros knew that it was never worth the risk of trying anything remotely physical with Sofia before their wedding night. The shame it would have brought on the families had it come out, or worse still had she become pregnant, which Petros thought until he was almost 25 could occur simply with heavy petting, would have been unbearable. They had married in 1950, when Sofia was just turning fourteen. This was nothing unusual in the rural Greece of the time.

In Sorona the villagers subsist, as have generations before them, on farming. They all grow their own olives, vegetables and keep goats and sheep, which prove to be their source of milk, clothing and meat. Since mains electricity, which by now is pretty general in Lamia, the town which they can see hundreds of metres below them from their vantage point on the mountainside, has yet to come to the village, in 1963 they are still lighting their homes with oil lamps and drawing water from the local spring and a few wells. Every house has a system for trapping the rainwater that falls in the winter months and channelling it into rock cisterns hewn out centuries before by their ancestors. Once the summer has dragged on into August though, the spring and the wells receive more and more visits by villagers with drums and bottles, buckets and barrels. Often it's the children who get sent to collect the water by their hardworking parents.

Sofia's mother died yesterday, Wednesday August 14th 1963, aged forty-three, a fairly average lifespan in these parts for the 1960's. The funeral will take place at three o'clock this afternoon. Here in Greece it's the norm. Someone dies one day, they are buried the next. All through the night various women from the family have been sitting with the body and much wailing has been carried on. A funeral director from another village supplied the very basic coffin and Tassia has lain in it, with the lid propped up against the wall outside, for all to see and some to kiss on the forehead. At approximately two thirty the pallbearers, all close family members, arrive to carry the coffin, still open, to the church for the funeral service.

This is why Chrisanthi's mother Sofia was calling her home. She is a girl who is always running around, she hardly ever walks anywhere and she's hardly ever within her mother's line of vision, which is why, even though she's still only twenty-seven, Sofia's developed a foghorn-like quality to her voice, borne of perpetually shouting to get her daughter's attention. Since the girl is always somewhere within the village, it usually has the desired effect. The fact is, since this method of gaining their children's' attention is one that many women in the village have adopted, there are certain times of the day when a chorus of housewives' voices can be heard thundering across the rooftops in their quest to get their children to turn up at the back door when required. Of course, if the call is for mealtime, the results are usually much better than on other occasions.

Chrisanthi runs into the open front door just in time to avoid crashing into the first pair of pallbearers. She deftly avoids her mother's attempt at clipping her around the ear and dives into the cupboard beneath the bed to retrieve her dress for this sombre occasion. By the time the whole family is ready to go the church, Petros, Sofia, Chrisanthi and the boys all look like they're going to a funeral. 'A result,' thinks Sofia, who'd borne Chrisanthi, her first child, when still only fifteen.

Inside the church the priests start up their droning chant whilst the attendants pass along the rows of mourners with a taper to light the candle that each one holds in their lap. The attendant lights the candle of the mourner nearest to the aisle and then each mourner, in turn, lights his or her neighbour's until the entire row has a lighted candle before them. The priests drone on, evidently wanting to make sure that the appropriate measure of piety and sympathy is achieved to make the fee seem worthwhile. Sofia whispers to the children about just how mad she'll be if any of them allow melted wax to drop on to their garments. In a village like this one, which well reflects the lifestyle and financial status of thousands across rural Greece, no one wears jewellery and no one has any expensive clothes. Their daily garb is drab in colour and rough in texture. Yet the robes worn by the priests are opulent to say the least, with flowing black skirts and a brightly coloured silk stole, with embroidered crosses all over it, draped across the shoulders of the one taking the lead. Their stovepipe hats adorn their heavily bearded faces as they invite the audience first to stand, then, after a couple more moments of further chanting, to once more be seated - and so it goes on for the best part of half an hour.

One or two latecomers enter the church by the rear door, kiss the icon which is handily positioned under glass on an angled and gold-plated lectern just inside the door, cross themselves and find a place toward the rear of the gathered throng. Some have lighted cigarettes still cupped in their palms, so that they can take a crafty drag when another chanted prayer is under way. Others have flicked their stubs away at the moment when they entered the building.

After what seems to 12-year-old Chrisanthi like an age, but is actually about forty minutes, the priests signal that it's time to proceed to the cemetery. Waving his gold censer first this way, then that, the lead priest proceeds down the aisle immediately behind the coffin, once more hoisted aloft by four men of the family, all dressed in the only black suit, in fact the only suit, that they own and keep for occasions just such as these. The immediate family follows and gradually all of the assembled throng empties out into the paved churchyard, through the gate beneath the bell tower and along the street. In rural Greece it's unusual for a church to be situated among the graves in the graveyard. No, the graveyard is a couple of hundred metres outside the village perimeter and virtually the whole village is now walking slowly and sombrely behind the priest as he carries on waving his censer around as he steps slowly and solemnly along through the narrow village alleys following the open coffin.

Once at the grave site, where the gaping expectant hole yawns between two huge mounds of yellow earth, into both of which is embedded a long-handled shovel, the head priest stations himself at one end of the pit and gets going again on another round of chants. The congregation slowly fills every available space from the graveside back through the maze of marble headstones and some strain to catch a visual of the action. Finally, the coffin, still lidless at this stage, is lowered into the waiting grave by a rope and, once it reaches the bottom, off the priest goes again. Before the lid can be dropped into the grave, hopefully to land in the right position, he ceremoniously bends to pick up a handful of soil and throws it down on to the deceased, soiling her immaculate white lace and making dust marks on her pallid skin. Whilst he carries on, demonstrating nothing if not stoicism in the face of the extensive ritual that he is duty-bound to follow each time one of his flock surrenders to the inevitable, two grave-diggers grab each of them a shovel and begin vigorously shovelling for all that they're worth, throwing the dry earth down into the hole on top of the now mercifully closed coffin. The lid, though, has not been secured, merely placed atop the coffin at the last moment. In a few short years the body will be exhumed and the bones transferred to an ossuary.

Chrisanthi is losing the will to live herself as the ritual continues all the time that the grave is being filled back in. In fact, the work is so vigorous and done with such gusto that the two who began it are, after several minutes of working up a decent sweat in the August heat, relieved by two others with barely a break in the rhythm of scooping up a shovelful of earth and jettisoning it into the steadily shallowing hole. For the first time in the entire afternoon, the young Chrisanthi decides that things are looking up, for one of the two men now shovelling, his short sleeved shirt allowing her to marvel at how his muscles are rippling with the movement of the work at hand, is none other than Stathis Stefanos who, at twenty-eight, is fully sixteen years her senior.

For reasons that a twelve-year old girl would be hard put to explain, she feels herself warming all over with a red flush. It's hot enough anyway in August, yet she feels as though she's just put her head into the stone oven that sits in the street outside their house's front door. Her entire body feels like it's exuding liquid through the skin and her groin sends to her brain sensations that she doesn't fully understand. Chrisanthi may be twelve, but as yet she hasn't begun to experience a woman's cycle. What's happening right now in her abdomen is about to change all that. She has the sudden realization that she's developed an ache in her stomach and knows that she ought to run home. But she remains rooted to the spot, unsure of which will be worse, her father's wrath at her having bolted before the funeral finished, or her mother's anger at the fact her undergarments will be soiled in some way that she as yet isn't certain of how to understand or explain.

Stathis had served in the military and also been away at sea for a number of years, before returning to his home village to care for his parents. Chrisanthi, from the moment she first set eyes on him, knew she was going to be his wife.

*

The Stefanos family is well respected in the village. They have more olive trees than most and the largest herd of goats for several villages round about. Stathis is the oldest son and, after getting away to see the world, has finally decided that he could do with a nice young wife to share his bed with and to give him children. He has no shortage of options in that direction.

It's September now and, since it's mid-morning Stathis is sitting with his Elliniko in the village kafeneion with the older men of the area. Minas and Panayiota are flurrying this way and that. Giorgos the baker walks in, a cloud of flour drifting along behind his head. He smells of fresh yeast and baking bread, which makes Stathis' lips smack with hunger. Giorgos has been up since several hours before dawn, when he prepared the wood to light the oven before making the dough and kneading enough of it to prepare enough loaves to feed the village for another day. His work is done and his young daughter is now manning the shop as the women of the village filter in and out for their daily *psomi*.

After calling a greeting to each and every one of the dozen or so old men seated at the tables, the baker casts a glance at twenty-eight-year old Stathis and grabs a box of backgammon from a pile near the doorway, before making his way over to his friend's table. He's a rugged, bearded man of thirty-seven who looks sixty. His hair is already salt and pepper and receding rapidly. The distance from his bushy eyebrows to his hairline is already several inches more than it was ten years ago. For all that, he still cuts a handsome profile and there are women in the area who'd be very happy to look across the pillow at him in the morning. Well, they *would* if he was ever likely to be there when they woke up, which, of course, he wouldn't. His wife died a few years ago and he's had the empathetic pity and the patronage of the whole village ever since. His wife's dying had done more for his profit margins that all the hard labour that she'd put in when she was alive.

Slamming the backgammon box down on the table with gusto, he rocks Stathis back and forth by the shoulder with a strong, flour-covered hand and says "*Gia Sou palikari.* Let's see if you can beat old Giorgo today, eh? Not likely I know, but you won't give up trying, right?"

While the two comrades set up their game, Minas brings Giorgo his Elliniko and a glass of water.

"I don't know why you bother, Stathi," says the kafeneion owner, "You'll never get the better of him, he's invincible."

"If there was ever someone who liked a challenge Mina, it's me. You ought to know that." Replies the younger man. "Besides, I'm learning from the master, so sooner or later I ought to be able to get the better of him. Positive thinking!! That's the only way to tackle life!"

"Aaach!" says the kafeneion owner as he retreats back to the sanctuary of his chair near the old cash register, where from a glass ashtray on the tabletop a curl of blue smoke rises from his ever-present Assos cigarette.

Giorgos and Stathis shake the dice a few times and make their opening moves, all the while cocking an ear to the conversation that's going on among the old men of the village around them. These are still debating heatedly the events following the assassination in May of political activist Grigoris Lambrakis. Since then the political situation has been steadily de-stabilizing and a Greek likes nothing more than to discuss politics. As the discussion becomes ever more excited, with old civil war rivalries once again being referred to, Giorgos looks across the table at his younger friend and says, "Will our country ever be able to hold its head up in this world of ours and say, 'Look, we Greeks invented democracy, so see - here's how it's done?'"

Stathis exhibits a wry smile and throws the dice from his cupped hand. He wants to keep out of it. He was born in 1935 and so was approaching and entering his teen years during the major part of the Greek civil war. He well remembers still how it tore his village apart. Men that were once field laborers together donned khaki and began shooting at eachother, hanging one another and raping or torturing eachother's wives. To many Greeks the memory of their bloody and bitter civil war is a thing of shame and even worse to recall than the years of Italian and Nazi occupation. Stathis keeps his counsel whenever those times come up for discussion. He looks at the baker and says:

"You know what, Giorgo? I think it's time I got myself a wife. I'm twenty-eight now and I quite fancy being a dad.

"I'm gonna get my old man to have a talk with old Katsandadis. If I play my cards right I might be looking at that young Chrisanthi; you know, Petros and Sofia's daughter. She's a bit young yet, but with negotiations going the way they usually do, she'll be just ripe for the picking by the time the two families get it all ironed out. What do you think?"

"I only wish I were in your shoes Stathi. There's not a young virgin in Sorona who wouldn't be willing to take your hand, you're too good-looking for your own good. HAH!! GOT YOU AGAIN!!"

Stathis stares down at the backgammon board in disbelief.

*

September of 1966 rolls around in Sorona. The villagers are excited because the first ever electric cables have ascended the mountain and reached their streets and, although as yet there are no private homes with electricity, there are a few shiny, bright new street lamps attached to poles in various parts of the village, thus dispelling the impenetrable darkness of the night hours.

Following months of conversations having taken place over coffee at the Kafeneion, plus various family conferences at which the ins and outs, the benefits and the drawbacks that the uniting of the two families may bring or incur have been discussed, it's been agreed that Stathis Stefanos will marry Chrisanthi Katsandadis in the spring of 1967.

Once the engagement becomes public knowledge in the village, many young women enter a deep depression over having lost their chance to share a bed with their idol, to them the best looking and most eligible bachelor in Sorona. As is so often the case, it polarises the young unmarried female population. Some congratulate Chrisanthi, who'll be just sixteen when she gets married, and take every opportunity that comes their way to talk with her in whispered giggles about what her wedding dress will look like, whether her cooking will please her new husband and how she's going to handle the wedding night. Others, well and truly put out by the news, shun her and act as though she had been personally responsible for ruining any chance that they may have had of finding happiness. Groups of young girls gather under the tree in the platia, their headscarves covering most of their long locks while they share their feelings of pique or pleasure, depending on which side they decide to take in the matter.

Plans are under way in earnest.

Chrisanthi's parents, Petros and Sofia, although not rich, have managed to prepare a very acceptable house for the young couple to move into. As the spring of 1967 draws near, they spend every waking hour making preparations and every spare Drachma on making sure that no shame will be attached to the family when the wedding day dawns. Appearances must be kept up, whatever agonies may be expressed in private about the expense.

Greek Easter will fall on Sunday April 30th this year. Thus the wedding is set for Saturday 6th May, since Orthodox tradition forbids marriages from taking place during Lent. The couple got officially engaged in front of the whole village back in October and that was when they exchanged rings of simple gold bands, which they've been wearing on the third finger of their left hands ever since. During the wedding these same rings will be withdrawn and then placed on the corresponding finger of their right hands, where hopefully they will remain until their deaths.

John Manuel

6. Eve, Spring 2013.

I'm going to start and I'm going to start today. Fay is right, I ought to be able to get somewhere with the Internet, surely. And I do seem to remember aunty Effi, a woman who used to come and see mum when I was small. They'd drink Greek coffee in the conservatory while I played on the floor. I've been thinking about her on and off since mum first became ill. I'm pretty sure that she wasn't my real aunty, but because she was also Greek she and mum had something in common. Now, somewhere in what's left of mum's things I'm sure there's an old address book. I put it aside so that I could go through it some time and make sure that there was no one who ought to know what happened to mum who hadn't been contacted.

It's a Tuesday on a brisk, breezy March morning. Candy floss clouds are rolling across the sky like dried up tumbleweed bouncing along a Western movie town's main street. Their backdrop is a scrumptious azure blue, the kind that you only get in the UK on days when the humidity is unusually low. The sun is going in and out, bathing Eve's kitchen table one moment in a brilliant, dazzling yellow glow, the next leaving it in subdued shadow. The kids are in school and Tom left for work an hour ago. Eve's diary is happily light of appointments for today and that's why she's been secretly planning for a while to get started on her search into her mother's past, to find out what happened in the years leading up to and beyond April of 1970, when Eve was born.

Eve places a hot mug of filter coffee on the coaster beside her laptop, all the while staring at the screen. She taps a few keys and is soon looking at the Google homepage. Behind the laptop's screen is a cardboard box, with all kinds of paraphernalia poking out of the top of it. There are envelopes exhibiting by their faded colours that they have been around for many years, a couple of photo albums put in an appearance and numerous suspension files all bulge with papers that add up to the six decades life of one widow, now no more. Bills and policies, correspondence and memories, all jostle for position in that box. It's all that's left to prove that Chrisanthi Anderson, née Katsandadis, actually lived, actually walked this earth for the most fleeting of moments and was gone. Also laying beside Eve's left hand is her birth certificate.

Eve knows that a good place to start would be with that address book, which she also knows is stuffed into the box beneath a sheaf or two of rubber-banded envelopes. However, she first wants to see if she can get anywhere by checking out some Greek websites for records of births, deaths and marriages. She makes a mental check of what she actually knows. It isn't much.

My birth certificate is one of those smaller square ones, it's always sufficed until now, but it doesn't carry anything like as much information as Tom's, or even those of our kids. All mine says is, "Name and Surname, Sex, Date of birth, Place of Birth and then there's a brief statement signed by the Superintendent Registrar in

50

Chippenham. I know I've been stupid, but it's only now, looking at it that I see that the date at the bottom reads 1973, when I know that I was born in April 1970 and it actually says that anyway a little further up, under 'Date of Birth'. I don't have a Greek one for some reason, even though this one says that my place of birth was Lamia, Greece. I know that my parents came to the UK after I was born and I now know that they only married on 24th March 1973. Beyond that, what else do I know? Zilch. Dad and mum are both gone now and so I can't ask them and, anyway, if they'd wanted me to know what really happened then I can only presume that they'd have told me. Maybe they just thought it best to leave it all in the past.

Or, on the other hand, suppose they thought that if I knew the truth then it would upset me. What if mum had a Greek husband before dad and what if I was the natural daughter of that man, whoever he was? Their marriage certificate definitely says that mum was a widow at twenty-two.

The answers must lie somewhere out there in Lamia, Greece.

Not sure of what to type as she stares at that ever-blinking cursor in the Google search field, Eve decides that first she'll dig out that address book. She gets up and walks around the kitchen table to the box and begins pulling stuff out from the top and placing it on the table. When she's already lain there three photo albums and as many ripped and bulging, elastic banded suspension files on top of those, she draws out an old-fashioned address book, trimmed with lace on the front cover. She opens it to the title page, where it reads, in Greek:

Belonging to Chrisanthi
February 1974

Eve would have been approaching four years old when her mother acquired this book. Could Chrisanthi speak any English back then, having only lived here about three years? Eve concludes that she must have been able to, since she'd apparently worked in a Greek restaurant right from the off as it were. Plus, having taken up with and married an Englishman, it stood to reason that she'd have learned fast. Eve could not remember, too, a time from her earliest memories when her mother hadn't spoken to her in English.

The book's pages are guillotined so that one can flip it open to whichever page of the English alphabet one is searching for. The next problem Eve encounters, though, is that she can't quite remember the mysterious Effi's surname. When had she last set eyes on her "aunt"? It must be at least twenty years ago, but, yes, she does remember having gone to her house once. It was in Batheaston if she remembers right, Elmhurst Estate was it? Eve flies around to the laptop on the other side of the table and types "Elmhurst Estate, Bath" into Google. Sure enough, a list soon drops down beneath the search field confirming that she'd got the name right. There's no way she can recall the house number, but she does decide that if she were to go there she'd be quite sure she'd be able to identify the house.

But first, there'd be nothing lost by trying under "E" in the address book.

But no, there's no mention of Effi by her first name, just a few old distant family members of Ian, Eve's Dad. Eve recalls the branch of the family whose name was Easthope, none of whom she's seen or heard of in decades. Aunty Clarice immediately springs to mind. She was always very sweet to Eve when Eve was a small child and the memory of a family outing to Weston Super Mare sands springs instantly to her mind. She can even hear her dad's cry of "Yeah!!" as he hit the tennis ball for six when they were all playing French cricket. There must have been about twenty of them. 'When was this now?' Eve asks herself…

Ooh, must have been around 1980 or thereabouts, over thirty years ago. We always seemed to end up playing French cricket on family outings. I enjoyed those days. It seemed as though I was destined to be a child forever and others were cast to play the part of adults, old folk, big girls and big boys. There was Mr. Crouch in the local general store where I'd have to go and fetch dad's tobacco. There was the King William pub where dad played skittles every Tuesday evening and, just on the odd occasion, he'd take me with him. Not during school term though, that would never have done, I wouldn't have got up in time for school.

I still remember when Mr. Crouch converted his shop to a video rental store. Dad was livid as it meant he'd have to go further afield for his tobacco.

Eve catches herself descending into a reverie and pulls herself up, mentally. She crosses to the kitchen noticeboard, where suspended by a bulldog clip from a metal hook are her car keys. She's on automatic pilot as she drifts down the hall, grabs a coat and handbag and walks out the front door. Within five more minutes she's driving along the A4, past Corsham on her way west.

'No time like the present' she thinks as she accelerates a little more once she's on the open road. She's going to Batheaston.

Twenty-five minutes later, Eve signals right on the London Road at Batheaston and, after letting a few vehicles come on in the other direction, she drives into Elmhurst. The road soon rises as it becomes a quiet suburban access way and the link-houses that begin to drift past the window of Eve's Mini are ex-council houses, virtually all of which have now been purchased by their owners and personalised with privet hedges, hydrangea bushes and wrought-iron gates across once open driveways. At the top, where she enters Catherine Way, she has to wait a while and think. Is it left or right here? She decides with some confidence in her memory that it should be left and so drives on slowly. Eventually she sees a house to her left, a little below the level of the road, but it seems to be familiar to her. Even though the last time she'd have seen it she'd have been a lot smaller than she is now. Strange how everything looks smaller when you go back after decades of absence. Walls that you thought were too high to see over you could now quite easily sit down on.

She decides to drive on past, find a place to stop that doesn't block someone's access and walk back. A hundred yards further along the street, she kills the engine and sits, staring out the front windscreen, asking herself, 'what the hell am I doing? Moments ago I was about to go surfing on the net to see if I could find information about Greek marriages, births and deaths and all of a sudden I'm sitting here in a street I haven't been to since I was a toddler. How old must Aunty Effi be now? Was she older than mummy? I don't really know, but assuming she was about the same age she'll only be in her sixties.'

All things being equal, Eve decides that 'Aunty' Effi would very likely still be living in the same house. She doesn't rightly remember how they lost touch, but she's fairly sure that there hadn't been a falling out. It probably had more to do with the fact that both women were raising young children and neither could drive. It's just the way things go when you don't live in the same street or one nearby. She's going to do it. She steels herself, opens the car door and steps on to the road. Without looking back she presses the car key and the vehicle responds with an electronic peep and flashes its directional indicators.

Arriving at the three concrete steps leading down toward the short path to the front door of the house she believes to be the right one, she turns and, without faltering, descends and approaches the doorstep, where she immediately presses the doorbell. She can't allow herself to hesitate. The desire to find out as much as she can about her mother's life as a young woman and thus her own early history is now becoming, as she finds herself mentally admitting, all-consuming. She has to know, whatever it takes.

Eve stares at the white PVC neo-Georgian door and its brass urn-shaped knocker. To her right there is a hanging basket with some fledgling bedding plants hanging from the horizontal rectangular concrete door shelter above. Beside the front door on the well-swept concrete front step is a small stone dog with a bone in its lichen-covered mouth. Looking to the left, she sees a front window that is dressed on the inside with lined curtains, framing a hycainth plant in a pot on the windowsill. The plant is in full bloom and Eve is almost lost in a memory of how she loved the smell of the hyacinths that her father used to grow when she was small. He'd always have several in pots around the house from the late winter into spring, as he also adored their fragrance.

Almost lost in this reverie Eve at first doesn't notice that a woman has opened the front door in response to her ringing. She jumps slightly from embarrassment at making eye contact with a portly woman who wears glasses, from the arms of which hang the ends of a cord that extends around the back of her head, testifying to the fact that she needs these glasses at regular intervals all through each day of her life. She's wearing a black cardigan over a black woolen long-sleeved top. Her pleated skirt is in some dark colour and her feet sport a pair of Marks & Spencer comfy slippers. She has a newspaper and a pen in her free hand, while the other holds the front door open. The extent to which she has opened the door makes Eve hope that this is a welcoming person, someone who's open and at ease with new acquaintances. The woman is quite evidently in her sixties, her hair supporting this conclusion, cut short as it is almost in a man's "short, back and sides" and now displaying more grey than the jet black that it once was. Her facial features are strong, with deep eyes and the characteristic Greek nose, deep creases running down from the corner of each nostril to either side of her mouth, which to Eve's delight, is smiling broadly.

"Can I help you?" The woman asks, the "h" in 'help' carrying just a hint of the "c" that makes it slightly guttural, thus betraying the woman's Greek origins.

"Aunty Effi? It's me, Evanthoula, Chrissi's daughter. It's been a long time."

For a moment the woman hesitates, taking in the facial features of the younger woman standing much taller than her on her doorstep. Then the eyes betray recognition and she exclaims,

"*Aach! Panagia Mou!* Little Anthoula!! My, how you've grown. Come in, please, come in!" She reaches out both arms for an embrace, kisses Eve enthusiastically on both cheeks and then stands aside for Eve to enter the hallway and once having closed the door she passes her younger visitor and leads her through into the dining room, which is graced with a large window affording a superb view down across the valley below, at the bottom of which the A4 London Road threads its way into the city of Bath. The other side of the valley, several miles away, is green with fields and woodland, above which the huge expanse of blue and white sky complete a very acceptable backdrop to the brightly decorated and smartly furnished room. Nevertheless the furniture and trimmings display evidence of the Greek origins of the resident. The wood of the heavy dining set is dark and polished and lacy white doilies grace most surfaces. The ornate lamp hanging from the ceiling is also something which Eve would have ripped out and thrown away years ago, but the room is nevertheless well dusted and smells fresh. This woman is diligent around the home; of that there can be no doubt.

Effi now continues, "*Then to pistevo!!* How come you found me after so many years? The last time I remember seeing you, why you must have been not even a teenager. How beautiful you have become *Anthoula mou*. And how many children do you have? Do you have a good husband? Is he a good provider? How long have you been married and where do you live? You have your own house yes?"

So many questions that Eve is feeling a little bombarded, having quite forgotten the Greek penchant for extracting the kind of personal information which the British would leave until they have developed a much deeper friendship before revealing. Before, though, she can choose which of the questions to begin answering first, Effi adds another,

"…And how is your mother? I'd so love to see Chrissi again. I do hope she is well."

The expression on Eve's face following this last question gives the answer that Effi instantly understands. "Oh, no. Please tell me no. What happened?"

Eve struggles with her feelings, all the heartache flooding back. It is, after all, still only months since her mother died. Her eyes fill up as she starts:

"It was all quite sudden. We didn't really have much time to prepare. Ovarian cancer. It was only months from when she felt unwell to …well, we lost her last October. I'm so sorry to have to tell you this Aunt Effi."

The older woman slides an arm around Eve's shoulder and says, "Come on, let's go into the kitchen and I'll make us a coffee," her voice only betraying the merest hint of a once strong Greek accent. Eve complies gratefully.

Half an hour later, Eve having finished the first *Elliniko* that she'd drank for many years and enjoyed it, the conversation hasn't flagged for a second. Effi is now fully up to date with Eve's family and has expressed a desire to see Eve's children. Eve has assured her that they won't be losing touch again and that, sure, she can come over and have Sunday lunch with her, Tom and the kids some time soon. Eve has yet to ask about Effi's history. The main purpose of her visit hasn't even been addressed.

"Anyway, tell me about you, Aunt Effi. How has your life been? You seem to have a very nice home here. Are you alone? Is your husband still alive? What about your children? I'm afraid that my only memories of you don't seem to include any of your kith and kin. I just remember you and mummy chin-wagging over Greek coffee while I played on the floor. It seems like a few moments ago. Yet for some reason I knew how to find your house, so I know now that you haven't ever moved. I must have been here a few times though when I was little."

Effie proceeds to fill Eve in on her life since they'd last seen eachother, some thirty years ago. She, like Chrisanthi had married an Englishman, Alex. Their marriage had produced two sons who were now both living in other parts of the UK. Effi goes out to Athens a couple of times each year, yet cannot bring herself to move back there, her life here suiting her in ways that she can't always explain even to herself. She'd never want to live in a different country from her sons anyway. She and Alex divorced ten years ago citing irreconcilable differences. She doesn't see him these days. She's not even sure where he lives any more. She does, though, know that he remarried an Englishwoman.

Her social life is essentially TV-based these days. She doesn't go out much but she has very good neighbours and occasionally goes to the local pub with one or two couples she knows on the estate. She spends her days keeping house and telephoning her sons as often as she thinks they can spare her the time. Eve gets the impression that she wishes they had more to do with their mother. If only they realise what they have, she thinks. She has to depend on one or two good neighbours to take her shopping once or twice a month.

Eve decides after more than an hour of catching up that she needs to get to the point of her visit. Effi it seems would happily go on chatting all day, but it's almost 12.30pm and Eve does have a booking to work on someone's leg injury in Trowbridge at four. Before that she ought to get something done about the evening meal for her hungry horde. She looks for a way of introducing her quandary to her mother's old friend.

"Aunt Effi," she begins, "There's a particular reason why I decided to come and see you after all this time." Before her host can perhaps be offended, she hastily goes on, "Not to say that I didn't want to see you again anyway, of course. You've been on my mind a lot since mum became ill and then we lost her. I can only apologise for not getting to you before she went. There just seemed so much to do, so little time for so many important things, important people. I hope you understand."

"You're an only child *Evanthoula mou*. Of course I understand. There was obviously a lot on your shoulders toward the end. Don't worry, I'm just so glad that you came now. But what is it? What do you want to ask me?"

"Well, how do I start? I suppose the beginning's as good a place as any. When I was going through mum's things at her house after the funeral, when we were getting the house prepared to put it on the market, I came across my parents' Marriage Certificate. Aunt Effi, I was born in Greece in April 1970. I'd always had the belief

59

that my dad as a young man had been a travelling sort, who'd ended up in Greece, met my mum, married her and then brought her home here. I knew that things weren't good for them in the small village where my mum came from, and that somehow they knew someone in England who had written saying that mum would have a job if they came here. Dad was sure to find something, he was a resourceful, hardworking sort after all, but the marriage certificate is dated March 1973, almost three years after I was born. That didn't bother me unduly, but what really threw me was that my mum's status, or 'condition' I think it says, was described as 'widow.'

"Aunt Effi, what I'd like to know is how much mum told you about her past. Maybe you can't help at all, but..." Before Eve can continue, her mum's old friend's face betrays an expression that tells Eve that there may just be a bombshell waiting behind it. Fearing something equally unsettling, she asks, "Aunt Effi, what is it? You look like you've seen a ghost."

"Oh, Evanthoula mou, I always assumed you knew. It never even crossed my mind that you wouldn't. Ian was never in Greece. He ate at the taverna where your mother worked back in the first couple of years of living here. That's how they met. Did your parents never tell you this?"

"No," Eve replies, "they didn't".

7. Eve, Spring 2013.

Eve is sitting in her car; she has yet to start the engine. She's feeling quite numb about the news. Her mother's old friend 'aunty' Effi has confirmed that there is no doubt that the man who raised her as her father, Ian, who's now been dead and gone these eleven years, was not her biological father at all. Effi always knew that the pair had met *after* the young widow Chrisanthi had arrived in the UK. Chrisanthi was still only twenty years of age and already a young widow with a small child to bring up.

Eve is torn about what to agonize over first. Does she try hard to imagine how life must have been for a young Greek girl with no English to arrive on these shores in such circumstances, the only support she has in the world coming from someone who knew someone she knew? Or does she focus on her own bombshell, the fact that the man she knew and loved as her daddy was not her real father at all. She decides on the latter of the two.

What the hell is going on? Something like a year ago my life was great. My mum was alive and living a very independent life just a few miles away, happy in her little house, despite having lost Dad.

Dad? I know he loved me as his own. I know that to have given his best years over to looking after mum and bringing me up ought to make him what any sane person would describe as a real father, yet, well, here I am now with feelings I can't understand. Now, in what seems like the twinkling of an eye, my mum's gone, I find out that my parents married after they had me and that my 'Dad' isn't my father after all. My life is deconstructing before my eyes. What else is there, waiting around the next corner for me?

How can just a few words on a piece of paper and a comment from an old family friend make such a difference to my state of mind? How could Mum and Dad have thought it right to keep this from me all through my childhood, my life! What WERE they thinking?

Surely Tom will understand now why I need to find out what happened. Surely he'll realise that I need to know. I need to sort it all out. I can't think of anything else.

Eve looks at her watch and sees that it's already two in the afternoon. She needs to move some if she's going to get tonight's meal prepared and then get her kit and be in Trowbridge for that 4 o'clock appointment.

*

It's just after six and Eve hears Tom's key in the front door lock. She can't understand why, for some inexplicable reason, she's nervous of her own husband coming home from work. Her Tom, to whom she's been married for almost eighteen years, is coming into the home completely as per usual and she's anxious about seeing him. Their son, sixteen-year-old Andrew isn't home - again. He's probably still hanging around in town with his mates from school.

He'll probably fly into the house like a SWAT team making a hit from a helicopter at the stroke of seven when he knows that his mother will be placing the meal on the dining table. Thirteen-year-old Zoe, Andrew's sister, is up in her bedroom, also as per usual. She's listening to some boy band on her MP3 player while at the same time texting with her school friends, her fingers tripping across the face of her mobile phone like she was born to it. She ought really to be doing homework, but she'll wing it again and hope that the teachers won't notice when she hands it in tomorrow.

A family rule that Tom and Eve have always tried to keep to is that of the whole family sitting down together to eat their evening meal on weekday evenings. They hardly see either of the kids during weekends, so at least they can try and keep the familial bond going over the dinner table.

Tom enters the kitchen, where Eve tenses ever so slightly as she busies herself over the hob. Steam is rising from a pan full of pasta and hanging in front of her momentarily, before being sucked up into the hood, along the duct and into the cool evening air outside. Tom steps up behind his wife and slides his arms around her waist.

"How'd it go today? Do anything interesting? Session go OK in Trowbridge this afternoon?" He asks these questions while gently parting the hair at the base of Eve's neck and planting a kiss there, making his wife genuflect a little.

"If you don't want stodgy pasta, you'd better give that a rest young man!" His wife replies. Then she continues, "Yes, thanks. Everything went OK. In fact, I went to see an old friend of Mum's this morning too, and you?"

"Spiffing, sweetie, simply spiffing!" Tom has a strange habit of breaking into what he thinks is "posh person's" English without any warning whatsoever when he's searching for adjectives. "In fact, landed a new deal today with a local van fleet to fit all their tyres for the next three years. They've got six Peugeot Boxers and three Transits, not half bad. Probably get the staff to bring their own wheels to us as well. So yours truly is feeling a bit proud of himself.

"So, who was the old friend then? Anyone I'd know?"

"Probably not. We lost touch with her when I was still in my early teens. Mum used to spend a lot of time with her, though, when I was small, because she's another Greek woman, and they used to revel in their memories of the 'motherland' over Greek coffees back then. I think at one time they used to see eachother at least twice a week."

"What brought that on then? Did she phone or something? Has she just lost someone? Why did you end up seeing this person after no contact for so many years?" Tom retreats to the table and flops himself into one of the dining chairs. He picks up a raffia coaster and twirls it between his fingers.

Eve feels herself coming over all hot and bothered. She can't help hearing Tom's words of just a few weeks ago, when he'd advised her to drop the whole 'finding out about the past' thing after she'd told him about the marriage certificate. She decides to carry on finding something to do on the worktop or hob, to avoid turning to look at Tom as she continues,

"Actually, you know that box of Mum's things that I still have to go through, you know, to decide what to throw out and what to keep?" Eve can almost 'hear' her husband nodding, "Well there's an address book in there."

"And you found this person in there? That's nice. Trouble is, you might find a dozen others too, then you'll be busy, eh?"

Eve decides not to tell Tom that Aunt Effi wasn't in the address book, well, not under "E" anyway. She just goes on…

"Her name is Effi and she's probably only a year or two older than Mum. Anyway, I thought it would be only the right thing to go and see her. There's no way she could know that Mum's gone and they were very close at one time. She lives in Batheaston, so I just decided to surprise her."

"I'll bet you certainly did that. Did she recognise you. I mean, you're a bit bigger than you were last time she saw you."

"Careful, matey!"

"You know what I mean. Bigger as in all grown up. Don't put meanings into my words that aren't supposed to be there."

Eve knows what Tom meant. She's just trying to keep the mood light. She goes on, "She did take a moment, but soon realised who I was. She was really pleased to see me. You know, she hadn't changed all that much from how I remember her either. A bit greyer perhaps, slightly fuller of figure, but I knew it was Aunt Effi right away as soon as she opened the front door. Get four plates out will you love?"

Tom gets up, dropping the coaster on the table, and opens the eye-level crockery cupboard to his wife's left and extracts the required number of plates. He knows that he's expected to lay the table and so carries on finding knives and forks, place mats, drinks glasses and condiments to arrange on the dining table.

"It was hard telling her what had happened to Mum, especially as she'd asked me all about my life, my husband, my kids, my work and all that stuff. Before I could come round to the subject, she asked me how Mum was and said how much she'd love to see her again."

"Awkward, eh?"

"Yes, very. I just had to tell her as simply as I could. You can imagine she was pretty surprised and shocked. After all, Mum was younger than Effi."

"Does she have a family? I mean, husband, kids?"

"She does have two grown up boys, but she is divorced. Has been for a long time now." Eve hesitates, not much, but enough for her intuitive husband to know that there's something else, something under the surface. She still keeps her back to him as he arranges stuff on the dining table behind her.

"Evie, love. Best come out with it. You talked about something else I presume? Did she drop a bombshell on you? Is that it? Something about the past? Come on love, out with it."

Eve mentally curses her husband for knowing her so well. She turns to face him, tears welling in the corners of her eyes. He notices right away and moves to stand immediately in front of her, both hands coming to rest on her shoulders, before he lifts his right and gently wipes the tear from the corner of her left eye. He knows that whatever it is she's going to tell him, this won't be the time to chide her. He waits, an expectant look on his face, a look that says, it's OK, come on, tell me and I won't react unreasonably.

Eve struggles with the lump in her throat, but eventually manages to go on. Amidst deep intakes of breath, together with equally deep shrugs of her shoulders, she says, "You're going to be mad with me. You're going to say, 'why don't you just leave this, Evie?' I know you will."

"Eve, I promise, I won't, OK? Just tell me what she told you."

"You know my Dad was British and my Mum Greek." Tom adopts the kind of expression that says, 'now tell me something I DON'T know', "well, as I've always told you, I thought that Dad had been a bit of a Bohemian traveller when he'd met mum. You know, travelling Europe on a shoestring, that kind of thing. After all, it was the hippie era and everyone thought that by the time the

1970's were in full swing, the Russians and the Americans would be throwing nuclear bombs at eachother and we'd all have had our chips." Tom still struggles to bite his tongue and simply keep eye contact with Eve, expectant. He's not the most patient of people in such circumstances.

"British boy sees beautiful young Greek girl in some far-flung corner of that enigmatic country, falls head over heels for her, they marry, he brings her back here with a young baby in tow, me of course. Then they settle here and bring me up. End of story."

Eve grabs a piece of kitchen roll from the dispenser on the wall behind her, signalling that both of them may find it a better idea to sit down at the table before she goes on. They both do so. Tom resumes playing with the coaster to keep himself calm while waiting to hear what it is that's upset his wife so.

"Look, Eve," Tom says, "If it's about this issue of the marriage certificate, well you know I already know that now. But you're coming to something else, aren't you?"

"Tom, it's not just that they married after they had me. Aunty Effi knew my mother very well. Mum used to tell her a lot of stuff, you know, private and personal stuff. Well, she told me for sure that Dad was never in Greece, at least not at the time when it mattered. He only met Mum after she'd moved to the UK, Tom. She came here in 1971, when I was a baby. They married in 1973 because they only met when Dad used to go to that taverna where Mum was working. You know what that means, don't you?"

Tom's face betrays his full understanding of the facts, at least, of the facts that Eve knows so far. He longs to repeat his words from some months ago, to tell her that it's all water under the bridge and that nothing would be gained by dragging it all up now, all these years later. She has a loving husband, a pair of pretty smart kids, OK she's lost her parents, but she has a good stable life. He also knows, though, that his wife's emotional state after learning these things is something he can't control or regulate.

They still have both of Tom's parents too, Cyril and Freda, who still live up a path bordered with tea roses in their hometown of Reading. They're both around the seventy mark, but thankfully both still in pretty good health. Tom was their only son and yet they'd tried hard not to spoil him. When he was little they'd always make sure he spent time with his cousins on weekends, when the family would get together. Of course, with Tom moving West with his job and getting married to Eve, he hardly ever sees any of his cousins nowadays, but always on high days and holidays he and Eve are sure to visit Tom's Mum and Dad and occasionally they drive down to Chippenham and spend the weekend with Tom, Eve and the kids. Cyril and Freda are cruise fanatics and right now, in March of 2013, they're somewhere among the Canary islands, or maybe Madeira, strolling the decks of a liner and enjoying the milder temperatures of the region.

It's amazing how much can flash through your mind in a few milliseconds. Tom had momentarily reflected on all of this while searching for some way of pacifying his wife.

All he can do though, in response to Eve's question, is nod.

"The man I always called Dad *wasn't* my dad, Tom. Of course I'm grateful to him for what he did and I know that he legally adopted me when he married mum, so to all intents and purposes he was a wonderful father, but he wasn't my *birth* father. My birth father had to have been Greek. That means that I'm 100% Greek, not fifty as I'd always believed before now.

"Tom, I probably have relatives out there even now who can tell me what happened to my real father. I've got to find out. I have to know!"

Tom looks at his lap and then raises his head back up to make eye contact with Eve. He grabs hold of her hand and squeezes it. Much though he'd rather tell her to drop it, not to rock their cozy little life's boat, he says, "OK, love. OK. Look, why don't you just start a gentle search on the Internet, hmm? Everything's on there somewhere isn't it? If there is anything, anyone, that can help then I'm sure you'll turn it up there. I won't keep on at you to leave it any more, not if it means that much to you, all right?"

Eve's gratitude for Tom's shift of opinion extracts a smile among her tears. She leans forward and they kiss, right at the precise moment when their boisterous teenage son Andrew, bursts through the kitchen door and shouts,

"EVERYBODY FREEZE! THIS IS A YUK RAID!! PARENTS KISSING!! YUK FACTOR EXCEEDS RED ZONE!!"

8. SORONA May 1967.

It's Monday May 1st in Sorona. The margaritas are just beginning to pass their best on the hillsides and the young baby goats and sheep, born during the chill winter months of January and February are already half as big again as they were when they dropped out from their mothers' bellies on to the cold ground. The lush green of the hillsides will soon begin to turn pale, then to yellow, as the dry summer months draw on.

The winter in Sorona was hard. Winters in the uplands of mainland Greece usually are. There is invariably snow and often it hangs around for weeks on end. Usually, come March, it's confined to a few North-facing lines in the undulating ground, where the still low sun doesn't reach the hollows until the arrival of late April or May. The wind has howled through the gaps around everyone's windows and doors and hessian has been stuffed into every reachable aperture to keep out the frigid winter air while the months of January and February pass, too painfully slowly for most villagers. The huge piles of logs that rest against the exterior walls of each dwelling have been decimated to a fraction of their pre-winter size, thus auguring the arrival of the warmer months. There is not a house in such a village as this that doesn't have a *tsaki* - a log fire in a fireplace in the corner of the main *saloni*, or living room.

Despite the vast difference between the temperatures of mid-winter and those of the summer in an upland village, the villagers tend to wear pretty much the same clothes the year round. The prime reason for this is that they can't afford a different wardrobe for each of the two main seasons. Most of their outer garments are of rough linen or woven goat hair or wool. They're usually dyed a dark brown or black and the shirts and blouses are of tan, coarse linen too. Occasionally someone will sport a white shirt, but that's often the only contrast with the prevailing colour scheme of the villagers' attire. More often than not, white shirts and blouses are reserved for special occasions, or at least church on Sunday when, even in the 1960's virtually the whole village will attend and listen to the rituals played out by Papa Mihalis, who in essence is the village patriarch, since everyone accords him favour and respect, at least in public.

Greek village life here in the 1960's could as well be the village of the Britain of the 19th century, so little has changed for thousands of years. While in the UK and America the woman of the house has a vacuum cleaner and a washing machine and every home has hot and cold running water, not to mention electric light, here in Sorona in 1967 all such things are nothing more than a pipedream. In fact, most of the women here are not even aware that their counterparts in Western Europe and the North American continent have such miraculous labour-saving devices at their disposal. Most of the residents of this village don't even know that television has been invented. The more well off have a radio, but no one has a wireless because no one until recently had any electricity with which to power it. For the villagers of Sorona it's especially strange, because from most parts of the village there is a view all the way down the mountainside to the town of Lamia, probably no more than 15 kilometres away. Of course, the road that leads that way is anything but straightforward or even surfaced with anything other than rocks and dust, or in wintertime mud, but for the villagers who exist with oil lamps for light and who still visit wells for water, to be able to gaze down to the town that glows after dark with electric street lights and the dancing of vehicle headlamps is a kind of continual taunt to the poor people of the hillside above. At least there are about a dozen electric street lamps in Sorona's tiny thoroughfares now, ever since the summer of last year. Some villagers still demonstrate a deep distrust of such things however, expressing their views that they'll all soon fry from some imagined electrical surge that will electrocute the entire population.

Yet, for all of this the community is strong. In a Greek village like this everyone looks out for everyone else. No one ever worries about where their toddlers are playing. The idea that anyone could be lurking who might want to do them harm is anathema. Crime as yet is a phenomenon that they don't have to be concerned with, well, apart from the odd disappearing goat, or perhaps the occasional feud that develops between a couple of families that is. Sometimes problems arise over who owns a particular olive grove, or where the boundary is between two parcels of land. This is because all title deeds have been verbal for centuries. Everyone just learns from their parents who owns this pasture, whose olive trees they are or whose family owns that building.

In Sorona, as is the case in myriad Greek communities countrywide, the word of the priest is law. He can get away with liberties that no one else would ever dream of. He hardly ever pays for his drinks in the kafeneion, or food in the taverna. If there were public transport vehicles up here, like buses for instance, which as yet there are not, he'd never have to pay a fare. He can commit minor, even quite major misdemeanours and, if you were to quiz a parishioner of his about how he can be allowed to do such things and still be called a Christian minister, you'd get the response, "Well, he's only human, like the rest of us. God understands and forgives."

Papa Mihalis has a generous girth, which means that he hasn't actually seen his own private parts for a decade or two. At least, not without the aid of a mirror that is. That's not to say that he hasn't put them to some use. Although he does have a longsuffering wife and a couple of children, it's no secret among the flock that a couple of other bairns in the village (and the odd neighbouring one too) bear a striking resemblance to the great man. It seems that his pastoral work often extends to helping frustrated women appreciate that their duty to God is to help their local spiritual leader satisfy his purely natural needs from time to time. Plus he often explains anyway that he's doing this merely to help them in their hour of need. How wonderful it is that their God is so forgiving. How self-sacrificing is his earthly representative that he will do whatever is necessary to keep his parishioners happy.

Taverna *O Meraklis* is along the lane a while from *To Steki*, slightly off from the main village square. It's reached by climbing a handful of steps from the street below and thus, when one is seated on the terrace one can look down at passing pedestrians, which basically means everyone because all but one or two locals don't possess a motor vehicle here. Stathis takes a sip from his Greek coffee and stares across the table at the Papa.

"I'll be thirty two in a couple of months Papa Mihali, I've taken long enough. She should be a good bet for a clutch of children though, young Chrisanthi, eh? Sixteen years old, pure and fertile I'd say. Bit of a looker too fortunately. Got to admit too, the house her parents are supplying could be a lot worse. All in all, I'm looking forward to a very warm bed and a very quiet life from here on in."

"I should think so too, Stathi. Your life's been anything but quiet up until now. I wouldn't be surprised if you weren't already a father, going by the tales I've heard you telling after you've got a few Ouzos down you of an evening."

The wedding of Stathis Stefanos to Chrisanthi Katsandadis is only five-and-a-bit days away. Preparations are going on in earnest. The bakery is especially busy making cakes and *Bombonieres*. The latter are sugared almonds, the use of which at weddings dates back thousands of years. These are especially fiddly to make, so Giorgos the baker has enlisted the help of a couple of village girls to work along with his daughter in this task.

Young Chrisanthi, by no means the youngest virgin of this village to be wed, is now getting very nervous about what to expect following the ceremony. She and her family, plus a few friends have begun preparing the house in earnest and this week they'll be preparing the marital bed. Stathis will have to inspect it and give it his approval before well wishers arrive to sprinkle money and rice across it, unwittingly paying lip service to ancient gods of fertility. Sometimes, if there's one available, a babe in arms will be 'rolled' across the bed before the wedding too, once again in the belief that it will ensure the fertility of the union that's soon to take place between the sheets. Some hold the belief that the sex of the baby used in this ritual will also determine the sex of the firstborn of the couple.

As it's now May the temperatures are very suited to the comfort of those who'll be attending and participating. This is just as well because the men will be in very heavy suits, the only ones they own and which only see the light of day if someone is born, someone gets married or someone dies in the village.

Saturday, May 6th dawns and Stathis is at his parents' home, sitting in his bedroom in nothing but his coarse briefs, awaiting the arrival of the various honoured guests, friends and family, who will attend the dressing of the groom. He has chosen his old friend Giorgo the baker to be his *koumbaro*, or best man. So, before he can be dressed, he will appear in the salon amongst the packed horde in the house, all singing the wedding song in low tones, where Giorgos will whip out a cutthroat razor and shave his good friend. Giorgos stands ready with a hot towel over his left arm and the sharpened razor ready in his right hand. Before him on a small wooden table sits a bowl of soap, which has been whipped into a thick foam that Giorgos will smear all over Stathis' face before beginning the shave. Sitting in the bowl at the ready is a horsehair shaving brush. This ritual is carried out to demonstrate the trust and fidelity that exists between the two men. No man would willingly submit himself to be shaved by someone he didn't like, or even worse, was at enmity with, using a cutthroat razor.

Meanwhile, across the village in another house, Chrisanthi and Spiridoula, her *koumbara*, or maid of honour, are looking over the clothes that the *koumbara* has laid out for her friend. Again, as with the groom, women from the family and village have been arriving for some time now to assist in or observe the ritual of dressing the bride. The soles of her shoes have writing all over them. The reader would discover that it's a list of the names of all of Chrisanthi's unmarried friends. Those names that are worn away or are no longer legible by the time the bride takes them off are believed to be those who'll soon be married themselves.

In the Stefanos household, once Giorgos has put away the razor and wiped his friend's chin clean of foam, various members of Stathis' family begin to take turns at dressing him. One will put on his socks, another his shirt, someone else his trousers and so on until he is ready to leave for the church. His parents of course, although not too good healthwise these days, participate, his mother tying his tie whilst tears flow freely down her cheeks and then his father goes behind his son and offers the jacket, sleeve holes at the ready, for Stathis to slip on over his white shirt.

Something similar goes on in the Katsandadis household and finally the bride is ready to walk to the church, taking care to follow the tradition of casting a glance over her shoulder as she walks away from her family home, to ensure that the offspring of the marriage resemble that side of the family.

Later that evening, after interminable rituals and traditions have been observed throughout the entire wedding ceremony, the village lets its hair down in the square.

In the corner a ragtag collection of musicians, all playing traditional instruments, some homemade, manage to belt out a sound that is much more powerful than one would have expected just from looking at them. Chrisanthi's young peers stand in one corner giggling, some of them even getting the chance to dance with the boys, most of whom are gathered in the opposite corner and all of whom are competing to boast about which of the available girls he is going to take as his bride when he's good and ready.

The priest holds court at a table laden to breaking point with roasted lamb and pork, various traditional vegetable dishes and a more than respectable collection of bottles, most of which are by now empty. Papas Mihalis' face is a deep shade of red, borne of the effect of the gluttony he's displayed, along with the ongoing problem he now has with his blood pressure, something of which he's blissfully unaware. He casts surreptitious glances at various members of the fair sex as they whirl past him in the dances, which have been going now for a couple of hours and show no sign as yet of coming to an end. As long as the musicians have their glasses replenished when required, they'll play on for quite a while yet.

Stathis and Chrisanthi hardly know eachother really. Not that this should have a bearing on whether their marriage is a success. In Greek village life no one separates, no one ever divorces. The shame that it would bring upon the families would be too much to bear. No, if a couple isn't fortunate enough to come to love eachother with the passing of time it's no big deal. The husband will simply discreetly cast his oats around whenever he has the opportunity and his wife will resign herself to a life of domestic servitude. At least she'll be provided for, while at the same time cooking, cleaning, washing and nursing her spouse through thick and thin. Most of the customs in 'modern' Greece are hangovers from the centuries of Ottoman (and hence Muslim) rule, as is the cuisine.

Of course, Stathis has spent a few evenings and passed a few social occasions in her company, but never have they yet been alone, it simply wouldn't do. Chrisanthi, whilst the village revelled in celebration of her nuptials all around her, has passed the evening first with musings over how she'd lusted after her new husband when she was a girl of twelve, when he'd taken his turn shovelling earth into the grave at the funeral of her grandmother four years ago, and latterly by growing increasingly anxious about what is going to happen when they arrive in the bedchamber alone, just her and this big masculine, bear of a man. She's never ever been physically very close to any man except her father, when she's been cuddled by him or sat in his lap to have him tell her stories. Now, as she approaches the time when her husband will take her hand and lead her amongst much raucous laughter to their new home together, she is beginning to feel extreme nerves and no small degree of fear. This time there will be no one to turn to. There will be no other shoulder to cry on if things go awry. Her mother Sofia, still only thirty-one herself, but going on sixty, will be elsewhere, tending to her own husband's needs, tucking Chrisanthi's two younger brothers into their beds for the night.

The time finally arrives for the bridal couple to go to their new home together. They have danced the last dance and been well rewarded with bank notes, which have been pinned on their clothes by the well wishers around them as they danced. They set out in procession from the plateia to the street at the far end of the village, where the newly finished house awaits them. It's perched atop an escarpment that sweeps down to several miles of olive groves in a secluded valley below, thus making the front of the house one storey higher than the rear, which looks out on to a terrace which takes full advantage of the view. The entire village walks in procession with them, all the while women plucking any blossom that comes to hand and rushing forward to throw them over the bride's head.

After just a few short minutes they arrive at the door of the house, where they turn, accept the good luck calls from those accompanying them, then turn back to enter the house. Stathis is already eager for the rest of the evening's events to begin. His young child-bride, however, couldn't be more anxious. When they reach the bedchamber, he turns her to face up at him and he sees that she is crying. All of a sudden it dawns on him that she is indeed a young child, just turned sixteen. Momentarily he feels uncomfortable himself, before her beauty plays its part in him overcoming the feeling and tearing at her clothes.

She closes her eyes and decides to let whatever is to be simply be. She tells herself that whatever happens, she'll probably awaken still alive the next morning.

And she's right. She does.

9. SORONA May 1967-January 1970.

The weeks since the wedding have passed quickly and Chrisanthi now feels much better. After the mauling she'd received in the marriage bed she'd found her husband to be quite remorseful the following morning and since then he'd been very attentive and affectionate around her. He didn't need to explain to her something that she's soon come to understand as one of life's lessons, which is learned only from experience. A man, when he gets aroused, isn't the most subtle or patient of creatures. She's yet to really come to enjoy the experience of sex, since her husband has yet to take the time to consider her feelings in the process, yet she already sees in him a weakness that he is as yet unable to tackle. She can sympathise with the fact that he is unable to restrain himself.

Yet at all other times he now makes great efforts to be kind and considerate. He talks to her while she goes about her household duties, all the while reassuring her that she is indeed showing all the indications of becoming a good wife. Her domestic skills are generally pretty good. Her cooking still needs some work, but her mother is continually offering her help and advice and she is slowly getting the hang of things. So far, Stathis is finding his mother-in-law quite tolerable, even likeable in fact. After all, they are much the same age.

In the daylight hours he's gone from the house at the crack of dawn. He has animals to tend to, markets to travel to and from, fruit trees and olive trees to cultivate. At certain times of the year he works long hours turning over the soil in the citrus and olive groves in order for the winter rains to be able to penetrate soil that, if left unbroken, forms a concrete-like surface which won't absorb the water. Unbroken soil will cause rainwater to simply run off as if it were a solid surface, which it is. The rains that come throughout the winter and that eventually peter out in May or early June must be allowed to get to the roots of trees that are going to endure the long summer months, all the while their fruits developing for the succeeding winter harvest. Olives will be gathered from November through January, oranges, grapefruit and mandarins right through until March. There is the constant drudge of recovering as much manure from horses, mules and sheep as is possible. This is then spread across and dug into the ground that will hopefully be producing the vegetables that will be put on the tables of the village homes throughout the year, each vegetable and fruit in its season.

Some of the men of the village are gone for several months during the summer, as they have relatives working on fishing boats going out from the small fishing harbours dotted around the bay just east of Lamia and so, lured by the promise of a wage and some of the catch, which will be salted and carried home at the end of September, they go.

Chrisanthi is respected in the village, something that to her is still a novelty and also cause for some degree of pride. It seems that to be the wife of a Stefanos gives her a stature that she hadn't anticipated. She is soon behaving much more like a woman several years her senior, as she mixes with other wives and goes about the village making visits to the bakery, interacting with the other wives who exchange favours like sewing and garment repairs, recipe tips, for example.

Of course, there's the chitchat too. The first year rolls around and there's still no sign of Chrisanthi falling pregnant. By the time that the summer of 1968 arrives more and more of the other women are saying things like "Everything all right, is it Chrissy? You know, between you and Mr. Stefanos that is? You are 'pleasing' him, yes?" The inference is clear. They think that if the bedroom proceedings are going according to plan, then surely Chrisanthi's belly ought to begin expanding sooner rather than later.

This summer, as she walks the narrow streets, she can't fail to notice that people are talking behind the backs of their hands, carrying on discussions that they quickly abandon once they see she is approaching, whereupon they'll greet her merrily and stare up and down her body in the search for any physical clues about her corporeal state.

No one, of course, is unkind to her. No one means her any harm. She is well liked and that's no surprise, since she has a very likeable personality. Her inherent humility soon returned once she became aware that the initial respect that had come her way was quite short-lived and pales into insignificance when compared to expectations of the patter of tiny feet.

Stathis has said nothing, at least not to her face. He has however, already begun to hear jokes in the kafeneion to the effect that perhaps he's not up to the task. Some of the more bawdy of his neighbours, the Papas included of course, have jokingly expressed a willingness to step in and do the necessary if he'd like.

It's the way of the world in a small rural Greek community. A couple gets married and they are expected to swell the family to three almost instantaneously. The pressure can be extraordinarily strong. For a young fecund girl to be wed and not pregnant a year after marriage is all that's needed to set tongues wagging and theories flowing throughout a community. It's fuel for endless speculation and as such very welcome among the more idle of the local inhabitants. Some will simply opine that it's early days and no one ought to be drawing conclusions about the couple as of yet. Others already make it known that God is withholding his blessing and there must be a reason for this. The more senior and hence even more superstitious of the women suggest remedies that betray their slavery to traditional beliefs that have their origin deep in pagan rituals from times long past. Some of these busybodies suggest mainly harmless things like eating more pomegranates, a fruit long believed to be a symbol of happy times, prosperity and fertility. The worst though to a Westerner most innocuous suggestion relating to these is to tie some of the fruit to the bedpost.

Others are a little more forceful in their desire to be helpful. Old Paraskevi, who is eighty-five if she's a day, insists that the problem is no cactus. Many Greeks believe that the best way to ward off *'to mati'* the evil eye, is to have a spiky cactus growing as near to the front door as one can. If there is no available patch of soil, owing to the fact that the residence is either simply too small and near to the street, or perhaps due to the fact that the door opens on to the traditional *avli* (courtyard), then a pot fashioned from an old olive oil can will suffice. Paraskevi is physically hunched these days and when she smiles, which isn't often, she betrays a distinct lack of many remaining teeth. Those that do still grace her mouth have long since abandoned any attempt to stay white. She's perpetually dressed in black from head to toe, her skirts always dusting the floor as she hobbles along and her head is never seen without its scarf, wrapped tightly around her face and knotted under her wrinkly chin.

Paraskevi knocks Chrisanthi's front door one morning at the crack of dawn. The young wife, already busy working under the light of oil lamps in the kitchen following her husband's departure for the fields, wraps a coarse gown around her still slim and curvy body, opens the door and sighs as she gazes down at the old woman's face. Suspended from the hag's right hand is a large rectangular olive oil can, its top already cut away. Rattling around in the can is a cutting from a cactus plant, one of those with spikes as long as your little finger. This type of cactus is often planted in spots where people want to prevent goats getting through. They're quite lethal.

"Got no soil. Young Stathis won't have any problem bringing you some of that. But you need to get this in position my girl. Best way to stop the evil from getting in. That's why you haven't fallen yet, mark my words." These comments are accompanied by the vigorous wagging of a gnarly forefinger from the old woman, who may be misguided, but means well. Of course, to women of her generation, it simply doesn't do for a young wife not to fall pregnant the instant she's wed; in fact, even earlier as long as the bump doesn't show until a respectable time after the nuptials.

Chrisanthi replies, her patience not at its best at this hour, "I'm not having that anywhere near my door, Kyria Paraskevi! When I DO have a baby, I don't want it getting impaled on those spikes the first time it toddles out the door! It's downright dangerous!"

"Listen, my girl," replies her would-be protector, "You may regret not doing as I say in times to come. Why haven't you grown plump so far, eh? No protection from the *Mati!* That's your problem." She spits three times in a further attempt to keep the hex at bay.

"Look, and not that I believe in that stuff anyway, but what's that?" Asks the younger woman, pointing to a circular blue, white and black charm hanging from a black cord on the wall near the doorpost, "If that's not doing its job, then I don't think a cactus will do any better."

A few moments later the old woman is shuffling back along the narrow street, her feet barely rising more than a millimetre or so from the compacted earth, mumbling to herself about how foolish and ungrateful are the younger generation nowadays.

Chrisanthi is already chopping vegetables at her kitchen table, cursing the fact that she isn't yet with child. She curses even more the fact that she doesn't really want to be. The trouble is, what options does a young girl in her circumstances have? You don't really grow up in a small village like Sorona with any hopes and expectations other than that your eventual husband will be kind to you, that he'll maybe be a good provider. In this culture, where most of the village girls are married and frequently already looking after more than one child before they turn twenty, that's just the way it is.

For someone like Chrisanthi, the fact that a thousand miles further West, in countries like the UK, France and Germany, girls of her age are living in apartments and taking part in love-ins, going to university or college, perhaps deciding not to marry, at least until after they've lived a little, holding down jobs and making life-choices like not to have children at all, this is incredible, unbelievable, the stuff of dreams. In this community, a young girl has one sole purpose, to become someone's wife and produce the next generation. If she can extract some fleeting moments of pleasure and satisfaction now and again as she navigates her way through her few short decades, then she'll have had a good life.

The winter of 1967-68 had passed, bringing with it the usual months of snow, biting wind and frosty windows for weeks on end. A few more streetlamps are installed so that now the main street is flooded with a yellow glow should the occasional villager be slapping his hands against his forearms whilst wending his way home from an evening spent arguing over politics at the Kafeneion, or maybe Taverna *O Meraklis.*

Kyrios Minas, proprietor of *To Steki* Kafeneion, is extremely proud that his establishment is the first in the village to be connected to mains electricity and he has wasted no time in having a real wireless shipped up from Lamia in order to ensure a full house every morning while the local men listen to news about the deteriorating political situation in the country. In December of 1967 the King himself had fled the country after a disastrous decision to sack the government a few years ago led to the Colonels' coup the previous April. Now there seems to be a witch-hunt going on as anyone deemed to be either a communist or simply an opponent of the new regime is being rounded up, imprisoned or exiled. Thousands had been arrested in the months following the coup and an atmosphere of gloom now prevails in Sorona, such as is reflected all across the country.

It seems inconceivable, but even the great musician Theodorakis is in prison. His music is banned from being played anywhere. He served 5 months in gaol and is now exiled to a camp somewhere on the Peloponnese, awaiting further banishment and probably exile.

"What is going on?" asks Giorgos the baker, as he sips at an Elliniko one morning in July 1968. "What did we have all that fighting for after the war, eh? I still remember with pain the days of the civil war. It was horrible Stathi mou, horrible. You were young I know, but you remember a lot about it too, right?"

Stathis stares at his friend. "You know something Giorgo? I don't want to know. It's all so much crap and they're all out for themselves. As far as I'm concerned, as long as the world out there doesn't come up here to Sorona, I'm finished with it. I've got my animals, I've got my trees and crops, I'll keep my mind on them and leave all the making sense of such things to people who think they are wiser than I am."

"What about your wife?" Asks his friend the baker, "You didn't mention her."

"No need to read anything into that Giorgo. Chrisanthi was a given that's all. She's a good girl and I reckon I did all right marrying her. My belly's never been so satisfied. I reckon she's learnt to be a better cook than my own mother. Don't tell either of them that I said that though."

"No sign of any developments there yet though?"

This remark evidently finds its target with Stathis, but he goes on the offensive. "Look, Giorgo, you and I are friends. Have been for a long time. You know how old my wife is? She turned seventeen this month. I've seen quite a lot of this world; I've seen how young girls like her are living in England, in Canada and other places. She's just a kid. I'm very glad to have her, don't get me wrong. In fact praise God the families agreed, because she's the best looking girl in Sorona as far as I'm concerned. But she has plenty of years yet and I for one don't want her losing her looks and her figure before her time. Look at her mother, Sofia. She was a looker once. She's only thirty-two now and it's all going south, if you know what I mean. Women, once they're married, so often seem to give up. They've got their man, they no longer have to put on a show. They go to pieces. Fact is Giorgo, they can't keep up appearances once they have their first child because they don't have a minute to themselves for the rest of their lives. I'm not one to talk, I know. I'm just as much trapped in our culture as the next man, but I've seen women in England, for example, married ten years and still looking like they ought to be on the cover of a posh magazine.

"You don't often see that in a Greek village like ours. So I'm happy to give it a few years before I get my wife all blown up like a balloon just so my neighbours and family can have the satisfaction of seeing the next generation coming on."

The baker hasn't much to say, he stares at his friend and waits for him to go on, which he does.

"Tell you something else Giorgo, something I'd not usually say here in the village, owing to the fact that it wouldn't go down too well. If I had the choice I'd be off out of here in no time. Trouble is, I don't. My home is here and we don't have any real wealth to speak of. What we have is in stone and earth. But given the choice I'd like nothing more than to take Chrissy off to see some of the world. I'd like to show her off to people I've met in other countries. Let them see what a beautiful young Greek girl looks like. I know I sound contradictory, having just said that the rest of the world can leave us alone here. But what I said holds true too because I have to say that I'm mature enough at thirty-three to know the things I can't change.

"I have a good life, simple though it might be. I've been lucky enough to have seen some of the world before settling down, so I can accept this life with gratitude. When I was on the ships I saw things that you wouldn't imagine my friend. Beggars without limbs, blind men in gutters in India. Oh yes, I know where my bread's buttered all right. To have a beautiful young girl like Chrissy to cuddle up to in bed at nights is pretty much all any man really can ask for and I've got it."

Stathis, of course, is only too aware that his close friend no longer has anyone to share his bed with. His wife died some years ago of something that would have been treatable had they been living in a rural community in the UK. Here, though, the nearest doctor at the time was a few villages away and there were no means of communication other than someone riding an ass at full pelt from one village to another. By the time a doctor could make the trip to Sorona, Giorgo's wife had died.

Giorgos has his daughter Voula as some compensation, but she, although a good-looking girl, will not marry as long as she has her father to care and housekeep for, not to mention the bakery to run beside him. Though she is still only fifteen, he has tried to encourage her to look for a husband, even had discussions with other families regarding various possibilities, but he won't force her to marry against her will and her will is that she stay with her father. He is, however, very fond of Stathis and would never take offence at anything the younger man might say.

Giorgos' face tells Stathis that it is time to change the subject. Stathis has made his point. He won't be cowed by village speculation, however much it may be getting at him inside.

*

In the summer of 1969, despite the horrors of torture echoing throughout the country and despite many of the country's luminaries in the world of the arts and literature having been sent into exile, the general consensus about the rule of the Junta is remarkably upbeat. The rest of the world still looks on with disapproval on the non-democratic government of the country that invented democracy, but only in political circles. In business circles however, the large scale infrastructural works and a very acceptable degree of foreign investment has meant that Greece's economy is doing pretty well thank you very much. This won't last though, but for now, that's the situation which prevails.

Much of this goes unnoticed in Sorona. The only appreciable changes that have come to the village are a properly-surfaced tarmac road winding up the mountain from Lamia far below, village-wide street lighting and electricity in many more of the homes. Quite a few houses now have a wireless and several even have telephones. Most of them have no one to call, but it's a status symbol, so that's all right then.

Stathis and Chrisanthi have been married just over two years and still there are no signs of the patter of tiny feet. Stathis stalks around the village broodily and his mood in public is such that no one dares raise the subject any more. Even his good friend Giorgos the baker keeps off the subject of children. Chrissy is now quite overwhelmed by well-meaning village women and their superstitious suggestions as to what should be done to remedy the situation. She's taken to wearing a clove of garlic on a string around her neck, but this is more for the benefit of others than because she thinks it'll do any good.

In private neither Stathis nor Chrissy are that bothered, but this is subtly beginning to alter as Stathis now does occasionally think in his quiet moments that perhaps there is something wrong with either himself or with Chrissy. It has to be said that she's never looked better physically. She's eighteen now and has blossomed into a strikingly beautiful young woman. Looking at her now, her husband concludes that she really was still not quite 'formed' when they'd married, but, oh how grateful he is that they did.

Yet, despite his professions that "it'll happen in its own good time" he does wonder now and then how to broach the subject of perhaps making the trek into Lamia to see if there are any tests that can be done to determine whether there is a problem somewhere. Their bedroom relations are certainly not the problem, that's for sure. In fact, in the past twelve months or so Chrissy had learned so much about how to make both hers and her husband's experience in the intimacy of the marriage bed more fulfilling that it has added to Stathis' concerns about why she hasn't fallen pregnant yet.

When they'd first wed, the young Chrisanthi had begun married life with absolutely no idea about what was supposed to go on between a man and a woman. This had led to quite a long period in which she had simply submitted to whatever was required of her until the whole thing was over. Despite his greater age and experience of the world, Stathis didn't know either how to improve things and couldn't bring himself to talk it over with his young wife. Fortunately though, Chrissy herself had begun to change her attitude toward the whole thing and decided that, much as with many things in life, it's all about your attitude towards it. From then on things had improved in leaps and bounds.

The summer wears on and the village continues to subsist on watermelon and figs, on strawberries and pomegranates, on tomatoes, onions, aubergines and cucumber. On special occasions a goat or a sheep is slaughtered and meat is added to the diet until the entire carcass has been exploited to the full. There is twine, hair and wool for new clothes, which are still produced in the couple of looms that clatter and clack in a couple of village houses during the evenings and early mornings, when the summer heat is not quite so oppressive.

Before long the days are shortening and the temperatures are dropping to something like the level when one can work outside for hours without suffering from heat exhaustion. November 1969 is upon the village and it's time for the olive harvest to get under way in earnest.

Once the work is under way the village is almost completely deserted during daylight hours, except for a few old folk, but even some of these make their way to the olive groves to try and contribute in some small way to the work. Older women find a rock or a log to sit on and mind the picnic hampers, which are packed with rough village bread, some homemade, some courtesy of Giorgo the baker, Feta cheese, bottled water and Retsina. Every able bodied villager, both men and women, together with some of the children, often work from dawn until dusk for several weeks to get the harvest gathered in.

Men can be seen up in the boughs of the more mature trees with tenon saws, some of them double-handled, sawing the central boughs off to give the tree light and help it to breathe. These saw away, working up a sweat, until the bough they're cutting tumbles to the ground below, accompanied by the sound of a cry to those beneath of "*prosexete!*" - 'look out!'

Those on the ground are using batons made of olive wood, usually cut to about a foot in length, to thrash the boughs that have fallen in order to get them to release their reluctant fruit, which falls into the nets which have been spread across the ground all around whichever tree is being worked on. The men standing on the ground use three and four metre long whips of willow or maple to agitate the higher branches and they cause a virtual rain of olives, which come hurtling like hailstones on to the women and others who are working below. These largely ignore this inconvenience and concentrate on the job at hand. Others of the men work on the fallen boughs, cutting them into smaller, more manageable sections and, once these have had the olives stripped from them by those with the batons, more tenon saws are employed to cut logs for the hearth from the larger diameter branches.

At the perimeter of each olive grove is a motley collection of mule-carts, ready to haul either firewood back to the village, or olives, stuffed into hessian sacks, to the mill several kilometres away. It's a bucolic scene of industry and dedication. Occasionally someone strikes up with an old traditional folk song, to which often a choir of voices will also sing along. It's a joyful time of year, even though the work is brutal and the days are long. Once the villagers get the olive harvest into full swing, they hope for dry weather. At this time of year it's not guaranteed. The need is for the fruit to be harvested, packed into sacks and shipped to the mill without it being rained on, at least not too much, which can result in the olives rotting in the sacks where they lie. This can be disastrous and does occur now and again.

Before the work began, the priest had made the trek out to the groves in all his robes and regalia, to bless the trees and the harvest. No one would start the work until Papa Mihalis had done his thing. Usually, too, once the harvest is complete, the whole village has a feast in the *plateia*, when trestles are laid out, a spit roast is barbecued and there is music and dancing to celebrate the success of the gathering in and the making of the precious oil.

This year, however, this is not to be.

Partway through the harvest this year, Chrisanthi is found at home one mid-morning preparing a hamper for her husband. She'll make sure that there is plenty of bread and cheese within, along with green apples from their own tree near the house. She's feeling happy and with good reason. The distance from the house to the olive grove where the village folk are working today is about two kilometres. The grove contains something approaching two hundred mature olive trees and is in the bottom of a wide, shallow valley, which isn't visible from the village. The walk from the house to the valley will take Chrisanthi about half an hour. She sets out in the crisp sunshine, her scarf tied around her chin and her mood as light as the breeze, which is as light as anyone could wish for on this kind of day, the kind of day when it makes just about anyone glad to be living and breathing. There are buzzards soaring on thermals high above and hooded crows circling lower down, making their "caw caw" sound as they drift along the valley. Sparrows hop around the narrow street that Chrisanthi follows away from the *plateia* and around the gently curving hillside toward the edge of the village. Village cats study the small birds with longing, their heads almost on the ground and their back legs practicing a stationary walk in preparation for a hoped-for pounce.

As she walks she finds herself humming an old tune to which she often dances the *Kalamatiano* when the village holds a *panayiri*. She almost feels like dancing herself as she walks, she is so happy with her lot in life. She's the happiest she's been since she married Stathis. With the village being so deserted, she does actually skip, like the way she used to when she was a small child. Then gazes to her left and right, anxious in case there may still be eyes watching her from behind lace curtains in small windows. Her face has never looked more radiant, with her full red lips, which have never seen lipstick and never really needed to, slightly parted to reveal her perfect teeth, still unaffected by age and lack of dental care. From around the edge of the headscarf wisps of her almost black hair tease her forehead and eyelashes and she occasionally sweeps her free hand across her face to clear it of a hair that sticks. Her cheeks, displaying radiant young teenage skin are rosy and her dark eyes sparkle in the November sunlight.

Rounding the hill that eventually brings the olive grove into view, she gazes ahead to see where the folk are working. She soon sees a knot of people toward the far end of the valley, still probably five hundred meters away. It's odd though, because they don't seem to be working, but rather standing in a circle around something. What can be going on?

As she draws nearer to the group of her family and friends, Anastacia Loukas, wife of Tassos who runs the *O Meraklis* taverna, spots her and breaks away from the group. Walking briskly, even slightly hurriedly toward her good young friend her face gives away the fact that something is wrong. Something has happened.

"Oh, Chrisanthoula *mou!*" Anastacia cries, extending both arms out to her friend. Chrisanthi reads into her friend's body language quite correctly that there is something that Anastacia really doesn't want Chrisanthi to see.

"What is it? What's happened?" Chrisanthi anxiously asks. "Why are they all standing around like that? What are they looking at?"

Almost in response to her enquiry, a bloodcurdling groan rises from the other side of the tightly packed circle of bodies. Chrisanthi makes as if to run forward, but her slightly older and stronger friend restrains her with both arms, "Please! Chrissy!! Wait…" But the younger woman writhes in her clutches, breaks free and runs toward the others, where she forces her way through to the front to see what they're all looking at.

Lying on the ground, his body twisted into a grotesque shape that instantly tells Chrisanthi that this is something very serious, is her husband, her Stathis. He is stretched out across a huge olive bough and his face lays upward, his body arched so that his legs and arms dangle downward at each end of his torso. The expression on his face is one of complete and utter agony and shock. There are two men, one on each side of him, trying to move him from atop the bough without causing further pain or damage to his broken body. These are instantly joined by Chrisanthi, who lets out an earsplitting wail as she falls upon her husband's face and cups it with both hands. She kisses his face several times and cries,

"Stathi *Mou! Agapi mou!* What happened, what's going on!?"

Anastacia, together with another woman from the village tries to drag Chrisanthi away, but she won't let go of her husband's clothing. She's hampering the efforts of the two men to help her husband.

Stathis tried to speak, but a small trickle of blood creeps firstly out from the corner of his mouth. He looks in his wife's eyes and whispers,

"*Agapi mou. Agapi mou* Chrissy. I haven't told them. I left it to you, just like we agreed." His words are barely louder than a whisper, but at this moment all have fallen silent as they share the pain of the couple before them.

Chrisanthi turns her head to the throng. "Has anyone sent for a doctor? What are you all standing around for? Fetch a doctor!!"

"Chrissy," answers Tassos the taverna owner, "we have sent young Stergo on a mule, but it'll be hours before the doctor can get here, always assuming that Stergo finds him at home or in his surgery. You have to let us get Stathis on to a cart, so we can get him back to the village. Now, please, Chrisanthoula, come away and let us get on with it."

Reluctantly, the young woman does as she is told and stands up, allowing Anastacia to place a consoling arm around her shoulder. Her skirt is wet around the knees from kneeling on damp, soft earth. Anastacia guides her a little further away and tells her what took place.

"Stathis was up in the tree. As you can see, it's one of the largest and oldest. Probably this one's a couple of hundred years old. It was certainly there before I was born. He was sawing out the middle boughs when his foot slipped on the damp trunk. He fell backwards and landed straight on that huge bough that he'd only just cut and let drop minutes earlier. No one was watching him until we heard the thud. Oh Chrissy, I'm so sorry. I'm sure that he'll be all right. He's strong."

Chrisanthi looks away, tears almost blinding her eyes. She looks toward where the men have finally lifted her husband's broken body away from the huge gnarled bough on to which he'd fallen. Stathis had groaned a few more times, each utterance piercing the hearts of those around him. Then he falls eerily silent. They lay him on to the back of a cart, the bed of which has been hastily cleared of olives and sacks. They stand back and stare at him. He doesn't move.

One of the men starts, as if to reveal his anxiety that they may have lost Stathis. He lifts the young man's arm and feels the wrist. He places an ear to Stathis' mouth and, after what seems like an age, lifts his head, stands erect and shakes his head.

The procession of pathetic and distraught villagers makes its way slowly toward the village of Sorona. At the front is a rickety cart, on which lays the body of the young Stathis, cut down by a cruel accident during the olive harvest at just thirty-three years of age. The cart's wheels rattle over the uneven surface of the dirt and stone lane. Buzzards still circle above in the afternoon sunshine, but the mood of these people now is such that the brightness of the day is an affront to their sense of decency.

Immediately behind the cart staggers Chrisanthi, young wife of the deceased, barely eighteen years old and already a widow. Walking close beside her, with a protective arm around the young widow's shoulder is her older friend Anastacia. Behind them follows a motley group of men and women, the men with their caps in their hands, the women dabbing at their eyes with coarse handkerchiefs. It's like a funeral procession already.

As they enter the outskirts of the village, something comes to Anastacia's mind. She ventures to ask her young friend a question.

"Chrissy *mou*. I hope you don't mind my asking, but I overheard what poor Stathis said to you before he ...before... Well, I thought he said that there was something he hadn't told us. Something he'd left to you. Please tell me to mind my own business, but was there something you were going to tell us?"

Chrisanthi looks up through eyes blurred with excessive crying at her dear friend. She gulps back a few efforts to speak over her choking throat, then succeeds in whispering,

"Oh Stasaki *mou*. How can I tell everyone now? How can I tell them that I'm four months pregnant?"

John Manuel

10. Eve, Summer 2013.

Seated at the kitchen table, coffee at the ready and laptop open before her, Eve opens the Google search page. What to type in, that's the question. She sips from her mug of coffee, then puts it down and types 'Greece births deaths and marriages".

She's momentarily pleased to see an extensive list drop down below the search field. Then she's a bit perplexed while she wonders where she should go first. Clicking on a likely web site she begins reading all about Births, Deaths and Marriages in great detail under the heading "Greece - Civil Registration", but soon finds that this site deals mainly with records dating from the 1940's backwards.

Nope, she goes back to the Google search result and scans down the list for another site to try. Off she goes into another web page, furrowing her brow as she scans down the many lines of small print, before rubbing her eyes with both fists and sitting back in her chair.

What exactly is it that she wants to find? She grabs a small pad that she's got beside her on the table and writes, "Who was my mother married to in Greece?" She places the pen down beside the pad and reads her own words.

She mutters aloud to herself, "Yea, that's it. That's the crux of the whole thing. My birth father's name and date of death. I know mum was from Lamia, or at least, the Lamia area." She types into the search box again, this time "Lamia Greece death records".

Not very helpful. The best she can do here is to go to a site that says it can help you find a grave, but the list is endless and the names gobbledygook. What was her mother's maiden name? No, wait, would that be her widowed name or the name she had before the first marriage? Eve reaches into a plastic file and pulls out her parents' marriage certificate again. There, where her mother's name and surname are written, it says she was called Chrisanthi Stefanos. Maybe there's a clue right there.

Stefanos. Was that her birth father's surname? She'd have to set out with the belief that it was.

The doorbell rings, momentarily making Eve jump; she's been so wrapped up in her thoughts. She rises from the table and trots along the hallway to the front door. Opening it she's quite pleased to see her best friend Fay standing there. They share a genuine hug of affection and Fay follows Eve back into the kitchen, closing the front door from behind her.

Eve has already told Fay about her visit to her mother's old friend "Aunt' Effi. That visit had been back in March and it's July now. Eve has telephoned Effi once or twice since, but they haven't yet made arrangements to meet again, despite Eve's intention to invite her mother's friend over to Sunday lunch some time. Somehow the weeks just fly by.

Once Fay has a hot mug of filter coffee encased in her right hand, fingers through the handle, the two women talk for a while about all kinds of trivia, how the children are doing, what Fay's husband's latest successful horse is called, what cups it's won and so forth. They compare clothing, makeup, fingernails and talk about recipes. Finally, Eve tells Fay what she'd been trying to do when her friend had turned up at the doorstep. They talk on for a while about the best way for Eve to find out what she so needs to know. Fay then makes a suggestion.

"You know what Evie? We ought to go out there. You and me. Out to that place, what's it called again? Narnia? I got that wrong didn't I." they both affect a short laugh.

"Lamia. It's a town on the mainland in Central Greece, quite near the Aegean coast. I've studied the map."

"Great, fine, so you're ahead of me. Is it easy to get to? Doesn't sound like it's on the tourist trail."

"Dunno, but why don't I Google airports in Greece for starters?"

Eve does as she'd suggested and they're soon studying their options. There is an airport apparently at a place called Nea Anchialos, which is near the town of Almiros, but it doesn't look very big and it's not likely to be the kind of airport that charter flights make use of. They trawl the package holiday sites, only to find that the vast majority only offer flights to the islands. Where they do have mainland destinations it's only either the Peloponnese or Halkidiki, both of which are nowhere near Lamia. Half an hour goes by and they've found nothing very helpful.

"Looks like we'd have to fly into Athens and hire a car," says Eve. "It can't be that gruelling a drive up to Lamia from there, surely. Hang on." She types 'hotels in Lamia, Greece' into the search field.

"A result!" Declares Fay, who is as rapt by the laptop's screen as is her friend. There, before their eyes is a web page displaying five or six hotels in Lamia or the surrounding area. "Be easy, Eve. Book a couple of flights, get us a car, drive up to Lamia and check into a room we've pre-booked on-line. I'm up for it, aren't you?"

"I think we should think about it a bit first, Fay. Of course I'll do it if it proves to be the best thing. But perhaps I ought to persevere on the Internet first for a while." Fay just waits, sips her coffee and studies her friend's face for a moment. She knows Eve very well. Sure enough, Eve adds, "Would be fun though." They both exchange knowing smiles.

"You think Tom would mind? Can he handle the kids?"

"Oh they'd be fine. They'd like nothing better. Probably try and get their father out of the way and have a party or three. He'd probably be happy to scoot off to Reading to stay a few days with his parents anyway. They're always saying that they don't see enough of their son. Typical parents I suppose." Eve pulls herself up short. Her own words have brought a lump to her throat as she remembers that she hasn't got parents any more and one of the ones she did have has turned out not to have been a blood relation. The reason for all this speculation is thrown into sharp focus.

Fay rubs her friend between the shoulder blades in a gesture of support. "Evie," she says, "OK, so I was getting a bit enthusiastic like this would be a jolly or something. But if you need to do this then you'll need someone to give you moral support along the way. You can't do it alone and I doubt Tom would be as keen to help as I am, right?"

"Thanks Fay," replies Eve. "Look, why don't I carry on a while longer on-line? I'll give it a couple of weeks. If I don't get anywhere by then, then maybe a trip out to Greece would lay some things to rest. Even if we don't get anywhere out there, at least I'll probably feel better for having tried."

Fay stays a while longer and then decides to leave her good friend to it. Eve is soon back before the laptop on her own, frantically typing all kinds of things into the search field, trying to find something that will help her find out about her mother's last years in Greece before she came to live in the UK, already a widow, carrying a young child, at such a young age.

After another couple of hours Eve realises that her quest is going to prove extremely time-consuming when she glances up at the clock on the kitchen wall and sees that it's approaching four o'clock in the afternoon. At least the kids are amusing themselves, since they've just broken up for the summer break. School's out and so are her two children, most of the time.

She has a couple of hours before Tom gets home and so reluctantly closes the computer and gets up from the table to start thinking about an evening meal.

Six o'clock in the evening comes around again and the sound of Tom's car on the drive tells Eve that he's home. No sign of the children yet, but that doesn't worry her unduly. Her daughter Zoe has texted to say that Trisha's mum is cooking for her this evening and then they're off to see a movie later. Andrew is notorious for not texting, but he always turns up if he's hungry. Eve knows that if he wants to eat at home then he'll be in that front door by a quarter to seven. If he's not here then, she muses, he won't be home tonight until late. Their family mealtime plan takes a battering during school holidays. As it happens, tonight she doesn't mind at all, because it's time for her and Tom to have another talk about what she's trying to do. He has been more supportive of late, but Eve knows her husband well enough to realise that, if she gets too obsessed by this, his patience will run out.

She hasn't made a lot of progress with the Internet. The sites that she thought might have proven the most useful were in Greek and she can't read her mother's native tongue, despite having understood some of it quite well when she was small. Having had a very traditional British father, she really only remembers speaking English at home right from a very early age. The only memories that are vivid of hearing her mother speaking Greek were on visits with Aunty Effi.

'Aunty Effi. Yes, Effi. Perhaps it's time for another visit,' she thinks to herself, as Tom arrives in the kitchen, his shirtsleeves rolled up and his tie hanging loose below an opened neck button due to the summery weather.

Eve kisses her husband and in that instant makes the decision to put the little chat that she'd planned on the back burner.

On a baking hot afternoon in Batheaston, Eve is sitting with her mum's old friend out in the back garden on the decking, with a view across a verdant valley to Little Solsbury Hill to the West. To anyone who's lived in the area for a few decades, this flat-topped hill was always known as Little Solsbury, although since the famous song by Peter Gabriel brought the hill to the attention of the world at large in the 1980's, many who are not so familiar with the area (including Google Maps) simply call it Solsbury Hill. Such is the manner in which folklore and local customs evolve.

Eve sips through a straw at a glass of delicious homemade lemonade. Effi still makes it in the manner in which her parents used to back in Rhodes when she was a little girl growing up. They've exchanged the usual pleasantries, kissed on both cheeks and now, with the drinks sorted out (Effi has an Elliniko in a tiny cup and saucer before her on the teak patio table), she speaks to her younger visitor.

"How have you been Evanthoula mou? Are you dealing with what you've learned OK? I know it must have been a shock to you.

Since you came I've often sat and wondered how I'd have reacted. I'm glad you've come again and, don't worry, I know that with a husband and two teenage children, it can't be easy for you to find time to ask me over. I'm not offended. You work too, yes? I don't think you expanded on that last time we talked."

"Yes, I'm a physiotherapist. It's actually how I met my husband. He used to play rugby and I was the attending physio at a match when he was carried off injured. Love blossomed over the quadriceps, you could say! I hadn't fully qualified in those days, but, well, here we are now, married eighteen years with two growing up kids to worry about. He's a good man. I don't think I could have done better."

"I'm glad for you Eve. You know what we so often say in Greece. 'Many years, good health and prosperity'. A good family life, regardless of how well off one may be, is to me the real prosperity. Anyway, I presume you're still eager to learn more about your parents and your own history, right?"

"Well, of course. You're quite perceptive, Aunt Effi. You appear to be the only real source of information I can turn to so far. Recently I've been trying to find out stuff on the Internet, but it's really hard. When I do get to a site that may just be what I'm looking for, it's in Greek. The first question I want to find an answer to though is, was my mother's maiden name Stefanos, or was it the name she took from her first husband? You know, like here in the UK some women when they're widowed or divorced revert to their original family name, so I was wondering if my mum had done that too."

"I'll tell you what I know child. It's time after all. I'm only sorry your mother isn't still around to help you. I'm sure she always had your best interests at heart. You ought never to doubt that. Maybe had she lived she'd have found the courage to tell you the whole story. So I hope you don't judge either her or your father too harshly."

"I can honestly say that I've never had any feelings like that. Since I found out this anomaly in my past I've spent a lot of time thinking, obviously. But it's all to do with my confusion about who I really am. There's this burning going on inside my heart that I can't put out. Truthfully though, I have no feelings of anger about either of my parents. In fact, I'd so love for them to be here now so I could thank them for the life they've given me. I just need to know, that's all. I can't seem to move forward with my life until I have this resolved.

"I really loved my Dad and when I analyse what I know now, it doesn't really change that love, but rather is adjusts it. Do you know what I mean?"

Eve doesn't need an answer from her host to this question. She receives an expression of the face that gives the answer she needs and so continues. "The head works one way, the heart another. I feel so deeply grateful for all that my father did for me. No one could have had a better Dad and no one could have loved his daughter more than my Dad did me. But there's this void. I know that he... Well, let me rephrase that, "I'm convinced that he was totally unselfish because he took me on along with the woman he'd fallen in love with. I was the baggage that came with the package, but he shouldered it willingly and - apart from the fact that it's not his DNA in my cells - he was a real father in every sense.

"Aunt Effi..."

"Evanthoula, I think that nowadays, simply 'Effi' will do, *agapi mou.*"

"Yes, OK, I'll try. Well, Effi, how can I put it? There's all this stuff going around in my brain. There I am, working on someone's knee joint, flexing it back and forth and all the while my mind's somewhere down an imaginary street in 1960's Greece trying to envision what my family would have been like. What did they do for a living? Did my Mum and real father have many relatives? Surely there must be some of them still living out there now, maybe wondering what became of my mother after she left and went to the UK. Surely she'd have kept in touch with some of her family? I have no recollection of any of them, but that doesn't mean that Mum didn't maybe write sometimes. She was only sixty-one when she died. Perhaps her mother is still alive! It is possible after all."

"So, you'd like to tap my brain as much as you can. Well I'm happy to oblige, I really am. To be honest, it'll do me good to go back over all those nice times with your mother. I have very fond memories of our friendship, Eve."

Eve riffles in her handbag and draws out a notepad, the reporters' kind with the ring binding at the top, and a ballpoint pen. She says, "Do you mind if I write some things down? I'm not going to remember everything if I don't."

"Be my guest. But before we start the interrogation," she smiles here to be sure that her visitor understands the gentle joke, "how about lunch? I have fresh bread, some Feta cheese and Kalamata olives. There's a shop down on the London Road in the village that's run by a family with a Greek name. They keep me well supplied with the few things I need to remind me of home. I even have a drop of Retsina in the fridge. Can I tempt you?"

"Any tzatziki? Sorry, that's cheeky isn't it?"

"I do have tzatziki, so that's settled then is it? Just hold on here, compose some questions for me if you like, while I get something sorted and bring out a tray."

Fifteen minutes later, Eve, who's been enjoying the warmth of the summer sun on her face and arms, is amazed to see the feast that her host has assembled on the tray that she carries out from the kitchen door and sets down on the table. Effi places side plates, paper serviette and cutlery in front of Eve, then lays out Tzatziki, hummus, Feta cheese in sugar-lump-sized chunks and pierced through with cocktail sticks, a dish of very appealing black wrinkly olives, some freshly cut bread from one of those loaves that we'd perhaps call olive bread, lightly dusted on the crust with flour, a couple of glasses and a bottle of Retsina on the table between them. Eve is impressed and suddenly, also, ravenous.

"Tuck in Evie *mou*." Says Effi. Eve obeys, loading her plate with something from each of the items on offer. Effi pours the resin wine into a "dumpy" glass, much the same as the kind of glass in which Retsina is usually served while dining out in Greece. After a mouthful or two, Eve is ready to begin.

"I suppose I'd just like you to tell me the story of how you and my Mum met from the beginning. If I think you've left anything out I'll interrupt, if that's OK? *All* the details too please, everything you can remember."

"Right, *loipon*, well, I was working part time in the Acropolis Taverna in Bath. This would have been 1971. Savvas was the boss and he was a good man to work for. On Saturdays we'd have a couple of musicians in and the place would be packed. The English guests would book their tables for eight o'clock or nine, they'd turn up, eat, tap their fingers to the music and watch as Savvas and his teenage daughter would do the occasional dance, applaud, pay their bills and leave at some time around eleven, just when the Greek regulars would start turning up. A lot of Greeks lived in Bath at the time, as they still do, although these days I don't get out much and so I don't know many of them any more.

"In those days probably every Greek in the city knew everyone else. It was quite a community. Lela waited tables and lived just off the London Road in Grosvenor and one evening she told me that her cousin was coming from Greece. We all knew that Savvas was looking for another junior to man the bar and wait at tables. He was a purist, old Savvas. Greek restaurants should have Greek staff, he'd always say. One or two of our crew were from Cyprus, but that was OK, they were still Greeks in language and culture after all.

"I still remember the first time your mother came to the taverna. She arrived at about seven in the evening. It was a Monday, I remember because it was the one and only day in the week when we didn't open, except for private functions. Lela came in through the door as we were doing a big clean. Once a month or so we'd do that. We'd all go in on a Monday and give the place a really thorough going over. Floors, tables, windows, kitchen, everything. Lela came in with this young girl in tow. I say 'young girl' but I wasn't much older myself. But she was stunning. The men, Kyriakos, Grigoris and Lefteris were all mesmerized when they set eyes on her. She was very timid and didn't speak any English. I'm quite sure that if she hadn't been Lela's cousin she wouldn't have got the job. But Savvas knew that her looks alone would do the place no harm and he was right. He took her on for a very small wage, which she accepted because she was staying with Lela while trying to get started in Britain and so didn't need to earn a fortune. She didn't have a lot of choice anyway. I don't know whether she'd have been allowed to stay for long in the UK, as all that official stuff didn't really concern me at the time."

Effi pauses while Eve jots furiously on her pad and Effi herself needs to charge up her plate with Feta and bread. After chewing on an olive, spitting out the pit and spreading some more hummus across a slice of bread, she continues.

"Chrisanthi learned English impressively fast. She was a bright young woman, much brighter than me, although I was already married to Alex and so I spoke English, at least, high street English, at the time.

"I tell you Evie, it didn't take long before the male clientele increased quite a lot. There were men who'd come in every Friday or Saturday for a souvlaki, just so they could study Chrissy. Not many of them had the courage to say anything to her, but you could watch their eyes and you knew what they were thinking.

"Your 'father' Ian, was a lovely young man. He'd have been in his mid-twenties and all the staff knew him. He was a regular who often asked us about life in Greece. He'd never been but loved the music, the food, and the history. He had a couple of Greek acquaintances at his place of work, which I think was a furniture store on the London Road. It's odd because he wasn't one of the trendy types. He seldom came in with a group. He was much more kind of conservative, with a small 'c' I suppose. But he had more guts than most of the trendy types. He would engage Chrissy in conversation. It was obvious that he fancied her. I have to say that I think it didn't take long before she was drawn to him too. You know Evanthoula, I think it was because, more by accident than intent, he was mannered more like the young Greek men from back home. The only other person that would come in with Ian quite often was this older Greek man who worked with him. Adonis was his name and I knew him too, though he lived in Chippenham, not Bath. In fact, as you know, that's where your 'father' was from too."

Eve's face betrays the fact that she's currently totally entranced by this tale. She's hearing stuff about her parents that she's never heard before. It's as if her life is filling out in front of her.

"Go on," she says, "How did they actually get together then? And did you know about me? I must have been about eighteen months old at this time."

"To begin with, we none of us knew that Chrissy had a baby. I think she was worried that we'd disapprove somehow. Only after I began to socialise with her did she begin to open up. That's when I began going round to her cousin Lela's place in Grosvenor on the occasional Sunday afternoon. The first time I went, *agapi mou*, there you were in one of those playpens on the sitting room floor. You had a piece of cardboard which you were merrily tearing to pieces and shoving some of them into your mouth. You were such a sweetie. In fact, you won't remember this, but I asked if I could pick you up and I did. I bounced you in my arms for a while and coo coed with you, you were such a sweet child.

"That's when your mother told us about what had happened to her. It was so tragic. I hope you're ready for this, because it's going to be hard to tell you, although you have a right to know."

Eve suddenly notices that her eyes are rimmed with tears. She's anxious about what's to come, but knows that she has no choice. She has to know. She has to hear what Effi has to tell her.

"I didn't tell you all of this before because I didn't know how to if I'm honest. Plus it was the first time I'd seen you for so many years and I didn't know what you wanted to hear. I didn't know how much you were really in the dark. Of course, I understand now.

"There's a box of tissues in the kitchen. Hold on, I'll fetch them." Eve doesn't remonstrate. She knows that she's going to need them.

"The essence of the story is this. Your mother married her first husband in her home village a few years before she fell pregnant. They lived a rural lifestyle..."

"Hold on, Aunt, sorry Effi. You said 'village'. I always thought that Mum was from Lamia, which if I understand right is a town. But you said 'village'. Is that important? Do you know the name of the village?"

"You know, I really don't remember right now. I did know once. It may come back to me. But it was a little way away from Lamia, up in the hills I think. I'm not from that area so I don't know a lot more than that. But I did know the name of Chrissy's village. If and when it comes to me I'll tell you of course. Shall I go on?"

"Please."

"Well, as far as I can recall, your mother and her first husband were married a while and there was no sign of any offspring right away. She used to tell me about all the superstitious ideas that the fellow village women would suggest to try and make sure she conceived. Although I love my home country, there are things about our traditions that I don't miss. The unbearable pressure that's put on newlyweds to have their first child is one.

Evie, it seems that when they eventually knew for sure that you were on the way, they kept it from their friends and family until they were absolutely sure. A doctor had to come from another village quite some way away to confirm it. Your mother had to make up all kinds of stories in an attempt to put the busybodies off the scent each time he came to see your parents. When they decided that it was time to tell the villagers and family, it was the olive harvest. Your mother told me that just when they were going to announce that she was expecting you, your father died in a horrible accident in the olive groves. He fell from a tree and landed on a huge sharp bough. He died before they could get him back to the village."

Eve isn't sure how to assimilate this news. Her whole conception of what she is, where she came from, is being blown apart before her eyes and ears and the tragic nature of this tale is also making it hard for her to breathe. Rushing through her mind are all the feelings of how her poor mother must have felt. To suffer such a terrible loss at such a pivotal moment, what inner strength her mother must have had to summon in order to survive. Eve doesn't even have the insight into the customs of close Greek rural communities of the time to further deepen her understanding of what was now facing her mother. What life choices would she have to face, a pregnant teenager, now widowed? Who would want her? How would she live in a place where there was no chance of state aid or financial support?

'And…' thinks Eve, "if my father hadn't died, would that mean that I'd have grown up in a small village in central Greece? What a monumental effect my father's death had on my entire life.'

While Eve sits in the warm summer sunshine quietly sobbing, Effi decides it would be a good time to make a cup of tea. She's lived in the UK long enough to know when a cup of tea brings immeasurable comfort. While Eve contemplates all that she's learned so far, Effi quietly clears away the lunch things and takes the tray back into the kitchen, where she puts away the things that ought to go into the refrigerator, places the rest in the sink and fills the kettle.

What? How? Why? I think I'm in danger of going crazy. Can all of this really be the background to my conception, my coming into this world? I'm a Greek girl and I don't even speak the language. I could have right now been married to a Greek goatherd, making my own cheese and washing clothes in an open-air kitchen. I might have had a couple or three dark-haired children running around my heels and perhaps never have trained to be anything in life apart from a simple housewife. I'd have been Greek Orthodox too. Would I have entered into an arranged marriage, decided on by my parents and those of the man I ended up having as my husband?

I'd never have met Tom; I'd never have known my 'Dad' Ian at all. I wouldn't have Andrew and Zoe and I'd never have heard of Fay. What kind of life is it in a Greek village these days? I don't even know how much of the modern world and its gadgets and conveniences there are in a Greek village, or would have been when I was growing up.

Because of one brief moment, one tiny slip of a foot in an olive tree, everything changed. My real father died and I was there, still developing in my mother's womb.

Effi places the tea tray on the table, on it there's a bone china tea set, a milk jug and a few shortbread biscuits on a small flowery china plate. 'How strange', thinks Eve. 'I wonder if in Greece now, in my mother's home village, they ever drink out of such cups as these?' She realises, it dawns on her, that from this moment on she's going to have to get right to the very bottom of the whole thing. If she doesn't her life will continue to deconstruct before her eyes, she herself will look like she's deconstructing before the eyes of her husband and children. There will not be from now on a single waking moment when she's not preoccupied with thoughts about what her alternative life may have been if it weren't for that one fateful moment in an olive grove back in the 1960's in deepest Greece.

"Sorona!" Cries Effi, pouring hot steaming tea from the pot into Eve's cup.

"What?" says Eve, suddenly shaken from her reverie.

"Sorona, it's the name of the village your mother came from. It was up in the hills above Lamia."

11. Sorona, April 1970.

The Papas is seated at the dining table of a couple in the village. He sips at a glass of Metaxa, clutched between his fat fingers, many of which are encircled with fat gold rings, which the husband has set before him. The bottle too is on the table. It's late in the evening and the electric lights are on, still somewhat of a novelty to the villagers. In fact, some of the older residents have refused to have them in the house, declaring that this kind of thing is only a hair's breadth from the destruction of the world as we know it. It can't be natural, they exclaim, and so continue to light their oil lamps and set them upon their wall brackets and the tops of their sparse items of furniture, fearful that the Devil is taking hold of their beloved neighbours.

"I have heard from the person I know in Patra," says the priest. I think it can be arranged. It will be up to you, though, to make it very clear to her that she has no choice in the matter. This will be the only way that you're going to be able to raise the funds to send her to England. You did say that that was where your niece was living, right?"

"Yes, yes." Replies the husband of the couple seated across the table from the priest, "We correspond from time to time and she has told us that she would be willing to have the girl come and stay with her. She works for a Greek and he's told her that there may be a job going if she can get there within a few months."

"It is for the best you know." Replies Papa Mihalis. "She'll starve if she stays here anyway and there are many more opportunities for her over there. Let's face it, she won't ever find a man to take her now anyway if she remains here. You know that too, don't you? She's soiled goods, now." The priest doesn't demonstrate the most sensitive of attitudes towards the feelings of the couple he's addressing. Get the thing done, that's his attitude.

The woman's eyes fill with tears and these begin to roll down her cheeks. Her husband turns to her and says, "He's right Sofia. No use getting all upset. There is no other way. This cash will solve the problem and Chrissy will thank us for this in the years to come, see if she doesn't."

Six months have passed and Chrisanthi, together with one cardboard suitcase in her left hand and a bundle, which is in fact the young Evanthia, or Evanthoula as she's already being affectionately called by her teenage mother, all swaddled up and clutched close to her mother's chest by her right, is standing in the tiny street outside her home, the house where she and her late husband Stathis were going to build a life together, waiting for the baker, her husband's lifelong friend Giorgos Spinadis, to come and collect her in his van. There are still precious few motor vehicles in Sorona and so, when Giorgos the baker offered to take Chrissy to the airport in Athens, some three hours away by road, the family accepted the offer gratefully. The distance to the airport at Glyfada is over 230 kilometres from the village, so it's going to take the baker the entire day to get his young charges safely there and then make his return, yet he refuses flatly to accept any contribution toward the expense of the trip.

"This is the last thing I can ever do for my dear friend," Giorgos had told Chrissy's parents when he'd made the offer. "If I can help his poor young wife to get out of this backwater, maybe find some happiness somewhere else in the world, then it will have been worth the effort."

Hours later, as the van chugs along the main roads skirting the metropolis of Athens, the young Chrisanthi is staring agape at all that surrounds her. She has never even been down the mountain to Lamia, leave alone as far away as this. How can there ever be so many buildings, so many roads, so many vehicles in the world and she had not known about them? How can these people survive without the earth beneath their feet? Do they ever see a bird, a goat, a hare or a fox? What strange existences these people must be leading.

Then, after what seemed like an interminable voyage, during which she's been bounced every which way by the hard suspension of the baker's van and the uneven roads they'd traversed during the greater part of the journey, they eventually turn on to the approach road to Athens International Airport, at Glyfada. Mercifully, the baby has slept virtually the whole way, except for a half an hour or so when Chrissy had discreetly fed her as they trundled along, exposing a nipple in such a way as not to distract her benefactor or let on quite what was going on. She needn't have worried, since Giorgos is a father and well remembers his own dear wife when she would feed their daughter Voula many years ago.

The moment arrives that both the baker and his young passenger have dreaded. It's time for the apprehensive young girl, her baby and suitcase to go it alone. Giorgos can't even come through the glass doors with her, as he can't leave the van where it is for a moment longer than it takes to see her safely out of the door. After a genuinely fatherly hug, and two affectionate cheek-kisses, Giorgos grabs Chrisanthi's hand and presses a wad of Drachma notes into it, saying, "Now you be sure to eat something my girl. Keep your strength up. Now just follow the signs once you get inside. You'll be just fine, you hear me?"

The months that have passed had been necessary for Chrisanthi's parents to organise a passport for their daughter, as well as tie up certain other matters. This document now clutched in her hand along with the handle of her suitcase, the baby in the other, Chrisanthi takes a deep breath and marches toward the glass doors, above which the sign says in huge Greek letters, 'INTERNATIONAL DEPARTURES.'

12. Chippenham August 2013.

There's been some rain, but generally this August is proving to be fairly average weather-wise in Chippenham. The first couple of days of the month were the hottest of the year so far, with parts of the UK seeing temperatures in excess of 30°C, very unusual. Eve and Tom are planning to use this mid-August Sunday morning for a long walk. They're in Tom's car at around 11.00am, driving down to Limpley Stoke, near Bath, where they're going to park up and walk the canal to Bradford on Avon, take in a pub lunch and then walk slowly back to the car. Both children have plans for the day and so they're off of Eve and Tom's hands.

The sky is mainly blue, with wispy white clouds drifting across the expanse posing no threat of imminent rain. It's around 25°C, so it's perfect for a good walk on an English summer's day.

For several weeks now Eve has been trying her best to keep her feelings in check. Tom eventually parks up on Winsley Hill as there's an easy place to access the canal, right next to a stone bridge, from there. Eve has been straining to keep her words until they're walking in step, arm in arm along the canal towpath. Car locked, and walking boots laced up, they set off, wearing light tops and long shorts, Tom feeling well and truly happy with his lot in life. The canal sweeps around a long gentle left hand curve and they're soon walking with woodlands to their left and the River Avon close by below them and to their right. Narrowboats chug sluggishly past on the flat, green surface of the canal and those aboard always wave at people on the towpath.

Tom and Eve wave at one couple as they slide gracefully past atop a gaily-painted narrowboat and Eve takes a big swallow in order to begin.

"Tom, darling…"

"I was wondering when you were going to bring it up again. Crafty minx." Her husband's quick response momentarily alarms Eve, until she sees that he's turned his face to her and is grinning widely. He slides a hand around her waist as if to reassure her that it's safe to raise the subject and so she presses on.

"You know you told me months ago that you wouldn't mind if I went digging around on-line to see if I could find anything out about my parents?"

He says yes, he remembers that he did. She goes on, "Well, I've been to see mum's old friend Effi again and she told me a load of stuff that I never knew before."

"Like what, Evie?"

"She knows how my real father died and why mum came to the UK in the first place." Before her husband can interject, she presses the advantage, "Tom, she even knows the name of the village that my birth parents came from. I always thought they were from Lamia, the town. You know that anyway. But Effi says that in fact they were from a village up in the hills above the town. It was called

Sorona. You know what this means, don't you love?"

"Sounds expensive to me," replies Tom. "And didn't we agree that you could go searching on-line. What's with all the visits to this woman?" Tom's mood is changing. Eve can sense it. She's already gone off at too fast a pace, but it's no good worrying about that now.

"Doesn't make a lot of difference, love, does it? What matters is that I've found out stuff. I know where my real dad was from and that ought to make it quite easy to... Well, not maybe 'easy', perhaps 'straightforward' would be a better word, but to see if I still have surviving relatives out there. And Fay said that..." Eve is motoring like she has no brakes.

"Eve, look. Look, I'm not trying to be difficult, OK? Whatever you feel you've got to do, well, if you really have to then you really have to. All I'm saying is, for goodness sake think hard before you go opening more cans of worms. Doesn't that make sense? I mean, what if you go and turn up stuff that's even more perplexing than what you already know. What will it all accomplish in the end?"

"Tom, what can be more perplexing? I already know that my real father wasn't the "Dad' who brought me up. My real dad died when mum was four months pregnant. Can you imagine that? He died in a freak accident in the olive groves when they were harvesting olives. I was already growing in my mother's womb. Surely you see what that means Tom, love.

"Imagine if that hadn't happened, if my father hadn't fallen on that day. I could never have..."

"Evie, Evie. Listen, please. Where's all this going to take you, eh? You have a loving husband. You had two loving parents. I know, it's tragic that you've now lost both of yours, OK ...all three of yours if you like, but hell Eve, we don't deal the hands, but you were dealt a pretty good one compared to many, right?

"I only worry that you're going to upset the balance, rock the boat, if you like, of our family life, of our family's happiness. The kids have already said that for the past few months they feel you've been somewhere else. Andrew says his kit's been wrong when he's gone to play rugby at school on more than one occasion, things missing, you know. Zoe says she talks to you but you often don't even hear her. It's like you're somewhere else entirely.

"To be honest, love, I too have seen a change in you. You often look at me and it seems to me that you're not really looking at me, you're seeing something else, I don't know what, like you're looking right through me, but it puts me on edge. Am I registering here?"

These words hit home and Eve stops walking, turns to face her husband full on, drops her hands, then emits a huge sigh.

How can I have been so stupid? Who was I fooling thinking that I could keep all this to myself and not let on. Why are we women so transparent? Have I really been putting my family, the three people I love most in the world, through this stuff and not know it somehow? When was Tom going to tell me all this? No wonder he was so keen for us to do this walk today. He'd been planning to tell me this while at the same time I'd been planning to spring my news on him.

Doesn't he realise, don't they realise, though, that it's not like I have a choice. Something inside is driving me along here. I can't go on with my life from here without knowing where I came from. Don't they understand that this discovery, starting from my parents' marriage certificate, changes who I am? Changes my whole perception of what makes me ME?

"Eve, wave, for goodness sake, or they'll think I've abducted you and call the police or something!" Tom is holding her shoulders and tilting his head toward the canal beside them. Yet another rented narrowboat is gliding by and three children and two parents are vigorously waving and calling to them. Any second now and they'll think something's going on.

Eve returns to the here and now and immediately raises an arm to return the greeting. It seems to work, as the family continues sedately on its way, eagerly seeking for the next people that they can greet along the towpath.

"Eve, Eve. What's to be done with you, eh? Surely you know how much we all love you. We all want what you want. It's just that lately things haven't been the same and you're the only one who doesn't seem to see it. We've all been tiptoeing around you, hoping that this will soon pass. The trouble is, it hasn't and it's getting worse. I hate to say it, but it's becoming an obsession with you. That's why..."

Eve now flies back at her husband. It's time to fight her corner, she thinks.

"An OBSESSION! Whoa there, Tom! Give me a break. Cut me a little rope here, will you? Have you ANY idea what it's like to have such a bombshell dropped on you at forty-two years of age? It's all right for you, you had a stereotypical British upbringing. Roses along the garden path, Sunday roast, real BIRTH parents. What if YOU'D suddenly found out that your Dad wasn't your dad. Your real father fell out of a tree leaving your mother a widow before she was twenty! A PREGNANT widow. It's not like they just moved house, my mother was forced to move countries!"

"OK, OK, OK," replies Tom, "Sorry, all right! But try and keep your voice down Eve. There are people about. Let's not create a scene here."

"I'll create a SCENE where I bloody well like!!" Shouts Eve as she turns and marches back toward the bridge a few hundred yards away in the direction they'd come from. Tom's at a loss, as so many men are when their wives reach this pitch. He decides to follow her and keep quiet until the opportunity arises to talk again with some degree of privacy. Warm sunny weather brings out the crowds and Tom hates having a heated discussion somewhere where others gaze at him and Eve from afar, judging, commenting behind the backs of their hands. There are walkers, some with dogs, at regular intervals all along the canal path.

Eve reaches the bridge and stops. She stands, facing the canal, arms folded tightly across her chest and head slightly down, as though she's studying something on the algae-covered surface of the water. Secretly she herself now regrets her outburst, but can't bring herself just yet to be conciliatory to her husband. Tom reaches her side and stands facing the same way. A couple of minutes pass and Tom does something he very rarely would admit to. He prays to whoever may just be up there, 'Give me strength. Give me the right words, pleeeease?'

After another couple of minutes, during which Eve struggles with herself for having been so quick to lose her temper, Tom says, "I can see fish."

"Where? I can't see them? Where, Tom?" Replies Eve, and the tension is released. Tom stretches out an arm and points,

"There, see? I don't know what they are? Perch, Trout, Carp?"

"Well, they're not goldfish, at least that's for sure."

They both smile and momentarily lock eyes, Tom now slides an arm around his wife's waist, silently signs off with his prayer 'Thanks! If that was you!' and says, "Evie, I'm sorry. I…"

"No. I'm sorry. I shouldn't have gone off like that. You're right Tom…"

"No. I'm not right. I shouldn't have said it was becoming an obsession. I…"

"Never mind that now. I only wish I'd known sooner what I'd been putting you all through. I don't know what to say to my own kids now."

"Oh, they'll be fine. Don't say anything." Drawing his wife even closer, he continues, "Eve, look. Maybe I have underestimated what all this means to you. But you have to take us with you. You can't go on with this without keeping us in the loop. You know what I mean?" She looks up at him and nods a smile. "I want regular bulletins. Whatever you learn, tell us right away, OK?"

"I've just been so scared, Tom. Scared that if I told you all the things I feel, the things I've been thinking about, what I may want to do, no… have to do to get this all resolved, you'd snap at me to give it up."

"I know and it's my fault. We men are from a different planet after all. We think, you women feel. I read that somewhere."

"I don't know about you, but I'm starving."

Tom realises instantly what this means. They're fine with each other again and they need to get that pub lunch down them. They turn and set off at a vigorous march back along the towpath, arm in arm.

John Manuel

13. 1972.

Ian Anderson is twenty-six. He's had a couple of girlfriends it's true, but experienced he isn't. He was always the slightly boring one at school, keeping his head down, avoiding trouble, but as a consequence managing to avoid a lot of the fun too. His grades were always good enough without being exceptional. He decided against doing the sixth form when a friend of his father offered him a job on the bottom of the ladder in his well-established furniture store on the London Road in Bath.

"Play your cards right son, work hard, know your trade and you could be earning good money, time you're in your twenties," the man had said. And he'd been right. With his parents' approval (they knew their son well enough to know that he was never going to be a luminary, but he was nevertheless exceptionally diligent and honest) the sixteen-year-old Ian had begun as a 'gofer' at Halton's Furniture Emporium, London Road, Bath in September 1962.

Now, in the summer of 1972, Ian is already deputy manager of his branch and has a Morris Marina, courtesy of the firm, to show for it. He works with an older man called Adonis, his boss and the store manager, which is why he's begun to develop an interest in all things Greek. Adonis is married and has a couple of boys. He's very genial and has taken Ian under his wing. He's also fiercely proud of his own country, but not so much that he'd want to go back there to live.

One thing every ex-pat Greek wants to do though is find *to steki* where he or she can hang out with fellow Greeks, or even - at a push - Cypriots, with whom residents of the mother country have a kind of love-hate relationship, a bit like the English and the Welsh. If there's a taverna anywhere within a forty mile radius of a Greek's home, especially if it's one that puts on a bit of live music on a Saturday night, then that Greek not only knows about it but will be there as often as is humanly possible. There they can get to know others from their *patrida* and exchange stories about home. They can indulge in nostalgia to their hearts' content. Adonis suggests to Ian that it's time he experienced how to really have a good time. No one in the world knows how to enjoy a good time more than a Greek does, so he tells his younger impressionable friend.

Ian doesn't need much persuading. Having recently moved out of his parents' home into his very own two-up, two-down house on a new estate on the outskirts of Chippenham, for which he is now the proud holder of an endowment mortgage, he senses the need to improve his social life. Well, to begin one at all would be a start.

Adonis says that, as it's a Saturday, they're both going to a taverna. There'll be Bouzouki music, decent Greek food and dancing. Ian will find out how to enjoy himself, he'll see.

"What time are we setting out?" Asks Ian of his friend, over their afternoon cuppa in Adonis' office at the store.

"Well, as it's half an hour's drive back here to Bath from home,

I'll be outside your place and toot my horn at around ten. That OK?"

Ian's not sure he heard right. He says, "Ten? Like, ten o'clock. In the evening?"

"What's the matter Ian, you got to get up early tomorrow? Tomorrow's Sunday, you remember?"

"Yes, but, well, I thought you'd say seven thirty or something."

"Listen, Ian. You gotta lot to learn. We don't finish work in Greece before nine in the evening. The night is time for *to kefi*, the good time, fun. The English, they all come to eat at seven thirty. Then they go home at ten thirty, maybe eleven. Got to be tucked up in bed before midnight, yea? We turn up when they leave. That way they don't mess up when we're dancing, with their pathetic attempts to do the steps that always pull and push us about like crazy. No Ian, trust me, OK?"

Ian decides that he ought to trust his friend. And they are friends. Adonis thinks a lot of his young deputy and this makes for a good working relationship between the two. He has seen during the time that Ian has worked under him how conscientious the younger man is, how he strives to do everything with integrity. It's one reason why he is glad to have Ian rather than another Greek.

At eleven fifteen later that same evening, the two men walk into the Acropolis Taverna in a small backstreet in the city of Bath. Bouzouki music and thick blue, smoke-laden air greet Ian's ears and nose simultaneously. Already the place is half empty as the earlier full house of English diners have left and those that remain are studying their bills to decide who pays how much in each table party. Gathered around the bar at the far end is a steadily growing knot of Greeks of both sexes, chatting, clinking glasses and all of them puffing vigorously away on their cigarettes, thus thickening the already thick air of the place.

Ian doesn't smoke. Before long his throat is sore and his eyes are stinging. Following a ten or fifteen minute interlude, during which his boss has slapped several backs and had his slapped in return, not to mention kissed that many people on both cheeks that Ian's lost count, they repair to a table in the corner with two other Greek men, both of which are considerably older than either Ian or Adonis.

Most of the conversation is carried on in Greek and thus Ian finds himself sidelined somewhat. This isn't intentional, it's merely a side effect of having entered a little piece of Greece a couple of thousand miles outside the country's actual borders. His fellow diners, or rather, drinkers, are genial and often turn to him, slap his back and clink their glasses with him, but they can't bring themselves to make the effort of switching to English for more than a few seconds at a time.

As the ashtray on the table slowly fills to overflowing, Ian finds himself mesmerised by two things. One, the Bouzouki player, whose hands he finds himself studying with some degree of awe as the musician navigates his way through song after song. There are only two musicians, the Bouzouki player and a man behind a keyboard, yet the sound emanating from the two large washing-machine-sized speakers either side of the 'band' is that of a full orchestra of drums, bass, guitars, keyboards, all of which lend support to the star of the show, the Bouzouki itself.

The other thing that has Ian mesmerised is the young female waitress who relentlessly cleans tables, takes away empty glasses and returns with refilled ones, or bottles of Ouzo, Metaxa or whisky. He has arguably never cast eyes on a more beautiful specimen of the fair sex in his life. She has large, deep, brown eyes and a perfect bone structure. Perhaps if there were any criticism possible of her facial features it would be that her nose is slightly, how would Ian put it, strong, yet it nevertheless seems to still lend support to the description that he finds himself mentally using to describe this very slim and well-proportioned siren - perfect. The nose is a Greek nose after all, that's what adds that air of the exotic to her.

She's dressed in a white short-sleeved blouse and a black pencil, knee-length skirt. He can't help but study the skin at the top of her chest and nape of her neck as it becomes visible above the last button that's fastened on the front of the blouse. He can just discern the shape of her bra beneath the dress as she moves around the room and he's intoxicated. Whenever she's not actually in the kitchen, he can't take his eyes off of her. There's something about her too. Something else. She's sad, he can feel it. She's got some reason to be down, he just knows.

The night wears on and, largely because of the presence of this young girl, he doesn't mind the fact that, to all intents and purposes, he's alone in a crowd. Adonis and his friends have been up and down to and from the dance floor for several hours now and Ian, glancing at his watch is surprised to find that it's after three o'clock in the morning. The place is still buzzing with people who, with the exception of Ian, are all Greeks or Cypriots, as if he'd know the difference anyway. The time is flying as he continues to study this girl. The others around him can see what it is that he's doing and so they decide that it won't do him any harm if they just leave him to it.

By about four o'clock, the body count is starting to decrease and, finally, the object of Ian's undivided attention is standing alone at the end of the bar, puffing at a cigarette and watching the dancing. Three men remain on the floor, two of which are on their haunches vigorously clapping Adonis, who whirls and dips, claps his hands and jumps his way through a *Zembekiko*. There are other staff members, the presence of whom only now does Ian begin to notice. There are two other women and a few men too. One of the men is cleaning glasses just along the bar from the young beauty and the rest are clearing tables, wiping them over and laying fresh cloths and setting them for another evening tomorrow - well, later on today to be accurate.

Ian rises, walks hesitantly over to the bar, where he fully intends to try and talk with this vision, this Aphrodite. Just as he gets to within hearing distance, against the volume of the music, the young barman asks him, "You want a drink? What you like?"

Before he can do anything about it, the young girl stubs out her cigarette and walks away to help with the tables. His chance is gone and he asks for a tonic water.

Over the course of several months Ian and Adonis make the trip from Chippenham together over to the taverna about twice a month. Ian has to admit, privately, not to Adonis, that he would be bored senseless on occasions, not because he doesn't like the music or the food, but because he has precious little input in any of the conversations. But the boredom never comes because he instead simply studies the girl. Finally, after he's been enough times for all of the staff, including this young enchantress, to greet him by name, he musters up the courage to talk to her.

She is placing a plate of souvlaki on the table before him when he asks her, almost blurting it out for fear that he won't get it out at all if he doesn't, "What's your name?"

"Chrissy," she replies. But doesn't make as if to walk away.

"Nice name," says Ian, feeling himself flush instantly. "Do you live far from here?" He asks her.

"No, not far. London Road." She replies, even in those few words betraying a thick Greek accent.

"Really? I work on the London Road. Do you know Halton's Furniture Store? Not that you would I suppose, but I..."

"Yes. I know. I pass often. It's near to my home. My home is Gross-venor. You know it?" She pronounces Grosvenor like it's got two "ss's" in the middle. Ian finds this deliciously attractive. He can't believe that he's having a kind of conversation with this girl. He's desperate to keep it going, but he knows that she has to get on with her work.

Chrissy gives him a very wide smile, one that indicates that there might just be a chance here. But he tries to keep cool. She walks off to carry on with her work.

Hours later, when the place is emptying of the last few clients and it's approaching five o'clock on a Sunday morning, he takes a deep breath and approaches her as she busies herself behind the bar, preparing to close it up. Adonis and Savvas, the taverna owner, watch from a distance, both amused and possibly even willing him on. Adonis is pulling on his light jacket and pressing some cash into Savvas' hand.

"Umm, Chrissy," begins Ian. "Do you have much time off? I mean, I really would like to learn some more Greek, oh and, more about Greek music and musicians. I was just wondering, you know, whether perhaps..."

"I no have work Mondays. I don't work daytimes too. And Tuesday if Kyrios Savvas say so, I no come in."

"Well, I finish quite early on a Monday, maybe we could grab a coffee or something? Can I phone you?"

Over the succeeding months Chrissy's English improves and Ian's Greek doesn't. It doesn't matter because her fears that once he'd encountered the young Evanthia, no more two and a half years old when he proposes in January of 1973, that he'd be out of there like greased lightning, prove unfounded. Instead he falls head over heels for both mother and child and Chrissy can't quite put her finger on the reason, but she falls for Ian in a big way too. He is not bad looking really, and he's absolutely nothing like Stathis, but she feels a secure future within the arms of someone who'll love her unconditionally awaiting her with this man and it feels good.

At the wedding there is Greek dancing and much merriment, as Adonis and all the other Greek folk that Ian's come to know shove money into Chrissy's dress while they dance and affirm that they've accepted Ian into their sanctum of real 'like-family' friends. The young, quiet, non-luminary has come up trumps and married the girl of his dreams. From the moment they wed he tells her that she no longer needs to work in the taverna. The two of them invite Savvas and his wife over as an expression of thanks for the way he'd helped Chrissy out with the job in the first place and her cousin Lela, who she'd lived with up until the wedding, comes too.

From that moment on, Ian Anderson's circle of close friends is one hundred percent Greek and he loves it. Of course, his wife tells him the whole story long before they marry and many a time over the years as Eve is growing up Ian finds himself feeling guilty over the fact that he sometimes thanks God that Stathis fell out of that tree.

Now and again Ian and Chrissy discuss how much they ought to tell the young Eve about what had happened, but the child is so happy and content with her "parents" and her nicely balanced home life that they tell eachother, on several occasions up until they simply stop discussing it any more, that they'll leave it a while yet.

It would be a shame to rock the boat by confusing the poor child after all.

John Manuel

14. 2013.

Following the clearing of the air between Tom and Eve alongside the Kennet and Avon Canal that Sunday in August, Eve does feel better and returns to something more like her usual self when she's around Tom and the kids. She's optimistic about finding out about her real father now that she has a family name and a home village to work with. She's already decided to give up the internet search as a bad job, because if she and Fay can go to Sorona, she's sure that they can make enquiries and subsequently contact with any surviving members of her family who may still be living there.

She and Effi are into the habit of seeing eachother once a month now too, Eve usually driving over to Effi's house on a free weekday morning, but she's also finally managed to invite Effi over for Sunday lunch with the family. Effi is excited about meeting Eve's husband and children, since she has such fond memories of Eve as a child and Eve's mother as a friend from all those decades ago.

Effi drives and so her little Vauxhall Corsa is soon to be seen moving hesitantly along Tom and Eve's road at around 1.00pm on the pre-arranged September Sunday in response to Eve's invitation. Once Effi has spotted the correct house number at the end of the cul de sac, she draws up alongside the kerb in front of the house and is soon at the front door, ringing the bell.

Eve throws the door open wide and spreads her arms to the woman who she now counts as her own friend, not just her mother's.

"Great! You found us. My directions must have been OK then. Come in, come in."

"Well, actually," replies the older woman, "I have SatNav. A gift from Philippos, my youngest. He fitted it and everything. I wouldn't have a clue, but I've just about got the hang of how to put in a postcode and then follow the instructions. I must admit I do rather like the gentleman's voice." The women share kisses on both cheeks as Tom pops his head into the hallway at the far end and calls,

"Aren't you going to bring her through, sweetie? Time she met your worse half isn't it?"

The lunch progresses much as would be expected, with the older woman making it very evident that she's in seventh heaven keeping such company. She helps Eve with the clearing up while Tom fixes some filter coffee and they're soon ensconced on the easy chairs in the lounge.

Eve asks Effi, "One thing we've never established, Effi, is how you first came to England yourself."

"Oh, yes, well, it all has to do with how I first met Alex, my former husband."

"We're all ears," says Tom, placing a tray with a coffee filter and three mugs on the coffee table. A box of After Eights keeps them company. Both Zoe and Andrew, who did turn up for their Sunday lunch, have now disappeared. Zoe has gone off to meet some school friends for some serious hanging-out and Andrew's in his room, a fact made evident by the thumping of the music from his hi-fi, which is emanating from the ceiling above the grownups. He's preparing for a night out with his mates, pretending to be old enough to drink in a few of the local pubs. He knows the ones in which he can usually get away with it.

"Did you meet Alex here, or out in Greece?" Asks Eve.

"Neither. I am from Rhodes, but we have relatives through marriage in Cyprus. Back then the British were everywhere in Cyprus and we'd gone over for a wedding. Some distant cousin of my mother's I think. But we went partly for the wedding and partly for my mother to catch up with a few relatives that she hadn't seen in a long time. Of course, while we were there I went out with a few of my cousins. There were boys in the party so it was allowed - just about!

"We were in this bar when a few British soldiers came in. If I remember rightly, they were under very strict instructions as to how they ought to behave. Alex immediately stood out to me and, for some strange reason, he said the same about me. To cut a long story short, he asked my parents within two weeks for my hand. They were glad to get me off of theirs I think!"

The other two laugh with Effi at this aside. She helps herself to an After Eight, but as she slips it from the box she asks, "May I?"

"Of course," answer Tom and Eve in unison.

"Well, it was a huge risk, but I took it because it meant getting away from a fairly difficult period in Greece's history and, to so many of our friends and relatives in Greece, Britain was the place to be if you wanted a good and comfortable life. The climate was always secondary to such considerations. So Alex and I married on the base in Cyprus, with very few guests, and before long I was on a plane flying to the UK. I stayed with his parents in Widcombe for a while because I couldn't stay with him as he still had several months to go before he was being posted back to the UK.

"It was a very odd way to begin married life, I can tell you. At least though, unlike Chrissy, I could already speak some English before I came. Being from Rhodes Town, I don't know if you've been, but I grew up in Analipsi if that means anything to you," Tom and Eve shake their heads in confirmation of the fact that it doesn't, "Well, the society I grew up in was marginally more modern that what you'd have found in a remote village, like the one your mother grew up in, Eve. So I'd learned some English in school. I soon found myself having to use it. Living for those first few months with parents-in-law who spoke no Greek at all, it was learn fast or nothing.

"They were good folk though, I have to say, *doxa to Theo*. Anyway, you two don't want to hear all the details about me and Alex. I'll just say that for the first fifteen years it was a good marriage and I am very proud of the two boys we brought into the world. Alex's problem was that he couldn't keep himself for his wife only. Doing all these small building jobs and dealing at the crack of dawn with all those women in their nightgowns when he turned up to build their extensions… well, you get the picture. He wasn't a bad man, just a weak one. But I have to say that since I've been on my own at home I've nothing to complain about. I do visit Rhodes most years, often twice during the season, but I'm never going to move out there to live now. Not at my time of life and with my two sons well and truly convinced of their 'Englishness'. I couldn't live two thousand miles from my boys. It's hard enough having a couple of hundred miles between us a lot of the time.

"But, Evie," Effi reaches out and takes hold of Eve's hand, "You are very much like your dear mother. I missed her awfully when we first drifted apart. I always wanted to re-establish contact and, when you turned up at my front door last March I was, just for those few moments, so excited at being able to see her again. That was until you gave me the news, that awful news. I, …I so wish…"

Effi can't go on. All the emotion of the love and loss and the intervening years is too much for her. She starts to cry and Tom leaps to her aid with a box of tissues from a side table.

"It's OK to cry, Effi," says Eve. "I can't imagine how hard it must have been for you when I brought you that news. But knowing how hard it's been for me, …well, crying does you good I think."

After a minute or two, during which the gentle older woman gathers her emotions once again, she says, "Have you made plans about what you are going to do Evanthoula mou? Are you going to try and find your father's family?"

Eve casts an anxious look at her husband, who gives her a reassuring smile and a very slight nod of the head. That's all she needs, so she replies:

"I haven't made concrete plans yet, but I am going to make the trip. I have a good friend who's offered to come with me, so we're hoping to go very soon. Whatever happens, I'll be sure to update you Effi."

"I'd like that," Effi replies.

Later that week Eve is once again sitting in Costa Coffee, hands clasped around a Mocha, staring across the table at her friend Fay.

"Come on then, out with it girl. What are you planning? Are we going to Greece?"

"Yes, Fay, if you're sure you want to hold my hand through this, then I'd love for us to go."

"What about Tom? Is he OK with this? You know, going from what you've told me before."

"He's fine. The kids are fine. In fact I think secretly now that they're all looking forward to a 'while the cat's away' moment when we're gone!"

"Right then, my girl! Where do we start?"

Eve explains that she'll check out the hotels in Lamia again and she and Fay can then decide which one they'll stay in. They'll go for two weeks for the first visit, as one week wouldn't be nearly enough. They'll fly to Athens, probably EasyJet; then hire a car for the duration, straight from the airport. Eve will sort that out on line before they fly.

Eve Watkins has been to Greece a couple of times in the past, but only on family holidays to an island. She's never been to the mainland and certainly never had to book a hotel and a hire car independently. They'd always taken packages before, as the children were smaller and it made economic sense. Not that she is unduly anxious though, as she's well familiar with the internet and, like so many of her generation, makes regular purchases on eBay and other retail websites. She's ordered shoes, jewellery, vitamins and books and so feels quite confident that she can handle this new travel experience.

Eve tells Fay that her idea is to check into the hotel at Lamia and take a day or two to relax, maybe ask a bar or taverna owner about how to get up into the mountains to Sorona, but that's all. Once they're happy with what information they have gleaned, they'll set off one morning and drive to the village. There's bound to be at least one taverna and as many bars there surely. They can order a drink and then ask about the name Stefanos, maybe if someone looks old enough they can even ask if they remember the accident when someone of that name fell from the tree during the olive harvest. She doesn't know what her mother's maiden name was, but if they find anyone at all who knows the Stefanos family they ought to strike gold.

Effi has told her during one of their chats that her mother's mother, that is her Greek grandmother, was only about fifteen when she had Chrisanthi, which although at first a shock to Eve, she came to understand when Effi explained that this wasn't at all unusual in Greek village life at the time. She's calculated that her grandmother, if she's still alive, would be about seventy-seven. There is a chance, albeit a slim one, that Eve's grandmother on her mother's side still lives. Now wouldn't *that* be something.

In view of the way Eve's work schedule pans out, it looks unlikely that they'll be able to make the trip this year. Eve thinks that since the season is already nearing its end, flights will soon be more difficult to come by. Fay reminds her though that they're going to Athens, not to an island. Surely flights from the UK to Athens, especially if they go from Gatwick, should be no problem, even during the winter months.

Eve nevertheless resists the idea of going off-season. She worries about the weather conditions, since even the UK news has occasionally carried reports of severe weather in mainland Greece during the winter months. The whole experience anyhow would be a much more pleasant one with fine, warm, sunny weather. Yes, OK, Eve's primary reason for going is to try and discover something about her heritage, but no sense doing it when she and Fay can't get in a spot of sightseeing and sunbathing too, not to mention some al fresco dining.

Reluctantly, Fay agrees that they'll plan to go in May of 2014. In the interim, Eve will continue to see if there's anything else that Effi can remember from what Chrisanthi had told her, plus she'll carry on looking on-line, just in case anything does crop up that will be helpful. Eve's work means that to plan that far ahead makes much more sense, plus it carries the bonus that Tom and the children can see that she's not going off half-cocked and perhaps leaving them in the lurch with insufficient preparation for her absence. All in all, patience is a virtue Eve tells Fay, while inwardly thinking that it ought to be Fay saying that to her.

Mid-January 2014

Eve calls Fay on a crisp, frosty blue-sky morning. She stares out of her kitchen window at a white lawn, in the middle of which is a young apple tree on which hangs a bird feeder. Blue tits and a robin have her fixated while the phone rings at the other end. There's a click.

"Hi Fay. How you diddling?"

"Good thanks, Evie. Got me some news, have you?"

"How does May 1st to the 15th sound to you? Any plans that would mess things up if we went then?"

"Don't think so. Give me a mo'. Nope, book it baby!"

"OK, I'll book the hotel and the flights. Soon as I have a total figure for the two together I'll come back to you. Can you let me have your passport details so I can input them on the airline website then? You're sure Richard won't mind? And what about Charlotte and Bryony?" Eve is referring to Fay's husband and two girls, who are of similar ages to her two.

Fay assures Eve that she's already primed the family and, after riffling in a bureau in the sitting room and keeping Eve holding for a few minutes, obliges with the passport details.

Since they'd last discussed the trip in any detail, back in

September, Eve has found a couple of web sites that she's been trying to get to grips with. One of them is the Greek State Archives, which fortunately is available in English as well as Greek. After reading reams of text, though, she's still drawn a blank with that one. She's also found several that talk about Church records, Civil Registers and the like, but not been able to turn anything up. By and large, what she's found further confirms that the best thing is to go out there and ask people.

Someone's bound to know something, aren't they?

15. May 2014.

Eve and Fay are queuing at Passport control at Athens Eleftherios Venizelos international airport. They haven't been away together, just the two women, for many years. Fay is busy texting her husband and Eve is trying to see if anything's moving among the bodies in the queue ahead. The flight landed on time at just after eleven thirty, having taken off from Gatwick at an unearthly hour. It had been around midnight when both women had left Chippenham to make the drive to Gatwick in Eve's Mini. Apart from a very brief comfort break at which they availed themselves of two takeaway coffees (to help keep them awake) the journey had been uneventful, largely due to the lack of traffic at such hours.

During the flight both women had been too pumped up to sleep, with Fay rather diligently studying the Greek road atlas she'd managed to pick up in the UK a week ago. Slowly shuffling forward in their quest to have one of the surly uniformed officials with the sunglasses examine their passports and officially let them into the country, Fay says:

"Should be a fairly straightforward drive. We take the A6 to the outskirts of the city, then for a quick spurt we go up the E75 and then on to the A1, which looks like the same road to me anyway on the map. It's the main motorway of Greece, goes all the way to Thessalonica in the North."

Eve doesn't reply, apart from emitting an 'umm'. Her eyes remain fixed on the glass booth that they're hoping to reach before much longer, inside of which sits one of the uniformed officials.

Finally they're walking away from the car hire desk with a heavily made up Greek girl in a crisp white blouse and navy pencil skirt who speaks very good English. She walks them to their car, a compact hatch, and explains a few things about the controls. After she's told them very firmly but with the appropriate degree of bonhomie to remember to stay on the right-hand side of the road, she retreats with a "See you in two weeks, Have a good holiday!"

As the two women stow their cases in the boot, which just about takes both with no room to spare, they slam it shut and prepare to climb in. They're both going to do some of the driving and really have little idea as to how long it's going to take them to get to Lamia. Not that it should matter as it's still only around 12.30pm and the evenings are long at this time of the year. The trip is actually around two hundred and thirty kilometres and so, without stopping, should take them a little over two hours, barring any traffic problems.

Eve is feeling unexpectedly trepidatious now that she's getting close to hopefully resolving her mystery and so asks, "Fay, will you drive first? Do you mind?"

"No problem. Give me the keys." Eve drops the keys into her friend's hand and walks around to the left hand side of the vehicle.

"Umm, Eve," says Fay, "That's my side! It's left hand drive remember." Eve slaps her sides with her hands and gives a smiley sigh, before walking around the car again.

The air is warm and makes both women feel quite hot, since they'd left the UK at the crack of dawn in about eight degrees C and with consistent rain. Here it's a bright sunny day with light winds and the temperature is rather a pleasant mid-twenties C. They're soon on the road and are both surprised at how urban and manic the first few kilometres prove to be. Somehow neither woman had imagined modern day Greece to be so, well, modern. They've both only ever visited islands prior to this trip anyway.

Finally, having skirted the sprawling metropolis that is modern Athens, they head north, past Agios Stefanos toward Kapandriti and Malakasa. All the while wondering at how unexpectedly modern the Greek road system is these days. Before long the road is passing through open countryside and Eve decides to wind down her window and let some air through the car's interior. She offers her face to the wind and the gentle warmth of the sun and is once more lost in a reverie. She's watching a buzzard soaring way above them when Fay says,

"You OK, Evie? You're awfully quiet. I suppose it's all getting a bit, ...close now, that it?"

Eve turns her head inward from the breeze and looks across at her friend. "You know me well, don't you Fay. I'm glad about that. I have to admit, yes it is all getting like it's crowding my brain. I'm so, well, I dunno, confused and yet excited. I so want to know more about where I came from, but ...I don't know, I s'pose I sound contradictory, but it's a bit frightening too. Thanks Fay. Thanks for coming with me."

"As if I'd have let you do this on your own. Anyway, I don't need much excuse to come to Greece now do I?"

Eve smiles at her friend and pats Fay's thigh in a gesture that says,

"I really appreciate you". She returns to gazing out into the breeze.

After about an hour the road skirts the shores of a lake to their right. They've been gently climbing for a while and it's quite a surprise at first.

"What's that lake called?" Asks Fay, casting a glance at Eve's lap, where the map is resting, not having seen much use for a while since it's just been a case of following the one motorway for ages. Eve studies it briefly and answers, "*Iliki*" I think. Beautiful isn't it." She finds herself studying a flock of waterfowl way out on the lake's surface.

They make good time, as the road is sparsely populated with vehicles. Now that it's well into the afternoon, siesta time, there is much less private traffic about. After an hour and a half the road is skirting the coast and they are taking in stunning views of the huge island of Evia across the shimmering water to their right.

After around two hours they're driving along several kilometres of dead straight road, with huge power lines to their left and the predominantly white splodge that is the town of Lamia growing ever larger in their line of sight. Looming above the town are the mountains where lie Eve's family roots. Soon they leave the motorway and take the exit road that swings them left toward the outskirts of the town.

Fay decides to pull over while they take a look at the directions that she's printed out to help them find the hotel, which is in a downtown area.

"This is nothing like I expected at all," says Eve. This area looks like somewhere in America, all these huge drive-ins off the side of the road and the scrub-like landscape. Both women study the A4 pages that Eve has printed out to find the exact location of Hotel Xenia. There's a pink spot where Eve has marked the hotel's position with a highlighter on a Google Map of an aerial view of the town. After a few minutes during which, if the truth be told, both women steel themselves for the experience ahead, Fay says,

"OK. Let's do this. Do you want to drive now, or shall I carry on?"

"Be my guest," says Eve, "I'll try and navigate."

More by luck than judgment half an hour later they arrive outside the hotel, which is situated in a very busy street with shops everywhere and bumper-to-bumper cars and motorcycles jammed in at every conceivable angle along each kerb. They've already succeeded in getting their nerves well and truly frayed as they've tried to head in one direction whilst finding that the one-way system sent them in another.

"I can't imagine what I was thinking," says Eve. "This place is so much bigger than I'd imagined. It's huge. Where on earth are we going to park the car?"

"Look," says Fay, "When in Rome, right?" I'll bung on the flashers and double park right by the hotel entrance. You dash in and ask them what they suggest we do about the car. Since it seems to me that that's how the locals do it, then let's go native!"

"OK, let's do it."

Fay does as she's suggested and waits while Eve jumps out, narrowly avoids impaling herself on the handlebars of a motorcycle that stands between her and the pavement and pushes her way through the heavy glass door of the hotel entrance. Inside, a fairly respectable reception area greets her, with potted plants and marble all over the place. There's the entrance to a hotel bar to one side and the main desk on the other.

There's no one behind it. Eve's just about to panic when she spots a bell on the desk, which she quickly approaches and bangs her fist down on to with rather more enthusiasm than is required. The loud ping has the desired effect, as a slim middle-aged woman appears from the door to one end of the desk, looking for all the world like she's just been woken up unexpectedly, which, of course, is the case.

"*Kalispera, boro na sas voie-theeso?*" The woman asks.

"Umm, sorry," replies Eve, "But do you speak English?"

"Yes, of course," replies the woman, in a thick accent.

"Well, I have a booking for 14 nights. A twin room, in the name of Watkins." Eve wants to continue with a question about the car, but she's interrupted.

"Ah, yes. Sorry. I took you for a Greek. Welcome to Lamia Miss Watkins. Do you have cases?"

"Yes, of course, but we're wondering what we should do about the car. My friend is outside double-parked."

"No problem. We have private parking. I show you." Without awaiting Eve's response, the woman comes around the desk and makes for the hotel's entrance door. At the door she stops, turns around and says to Eve, "That is your car?" Pointing with her right hand at the hatchback where Fay is busy drumming her fingers on the steering wheel and peering in towards the hotel anxiously.

"Wait here, please," says the woman and she's gone outside. Eve watches as she approaches the car, then gesticulates animatedly with both hands as Fay lowers the window and appears to be nodding in response to some instructions that the woman is giving. She then stands erect once more while Fay turns off the hazards and seemingly drives off.

Eve waits anxiously as the woman returns to the hotel lobby and tells her to "come with me, please." Following the woman through a couple of doors they're soon in a corridor, the other end of which is flooded with light from the outside, the door at the far end being propped open. Arriving at this door with her host, Eve is relieved to see a modest parking area, with probably about nine or ten spaces, a couple of which are vacant. Within a couple of seconds the car appears from the lane at the other side of the parking lot and Fay drives in, where she's directed into one of the spare spaces by some vigorous hand signals from the woman.

Once they're all back in Reception, cases on the shiny marble floor beside the two Englishwomen, the woman once again assumes her position behind the desk and refers to the reason why she had addressed Eve in Greek in the first instance.

"You must have Greek blood Miss Watkins. You look so much like a Greek."

"Well, thank you. I do as a matter of fact. It's the reason why we're here actually. And it's not Miss, it's actually Mrs. Watkins …and Mrs. Trenchard, Fay is my best friend."

"I'm sorry, do forgive me. My name is Sevasti. This is my hotel. I hope you'll be very comfortable here."

The check-in procedure accomplished, Sevasti shows the women their room. It's comfortable, if somewhat compact. But it looks like they'll be fine. There is a small balcony overlooking the busy street below, but when the doors are closed the sound of the town going about its business is adequately muffled so as not to disturb one's sleep. Both Eve and Fay take showers and lay out their clothes, pack them into drawers and wardrobes, decide who'll sleep in which bed and then decide to make a brief excursion outside to see if they can get a few things to keep in the room, plus maybe check out where to eat later on.

Arriving at reception at around five they see Sevasti sitting behind the desk, fiddling with the mouse on her computer. She looks up and smiles.

"Are you comfortable. Is everything all right?"

"We're fine thanks," replies Eve. "Perhaps you can help us though. First, is there a supermarket nearby where we can get a few things for the room, maybe a bottle or two and perhaps a jar of coffee and some milk." There is a small refrigerator under the desk in the bedroom. "Plus, we're hoping to eat out somewhere nearby tonight, hopefully walking distance. Can you recommend anywhere?"

Sevasti obliges on both counts. Just a few hundred metres along the street is a modest supermarket that should be able to cater for any or all of their needs, plus a few blocks back toward the town centre there is a taverna which Sevasti can recommend, primarily as it's run by her cousin.

"If I may ask, and please tell me if it's none of my business," says Sevasti, just before the women make for the door into the street. Eve and Fay stop and turn back toward their host. Addressing Eve she goes on, "But I think you said that you were here because of your having Greek blood, is that so? I am wondering, what do you mean and would I be able to help you? Are you looking for family?"

""You may well be able to help, Sevasti. Tell you what, we'll go check out the supermarket and, when we get back I'll tell you what I want to do. You may well be able to help because I have no idea what to do now I'm here really."

The hotelier gives a warm smile of consent and the women head out into the street. Half an hour later, Eve and Fay push the glass door open with their shoulders as they return to the hotel, each of them with a plastic carrier bag emblazoned with the logo of a supermarket chain in both hands. Fay takes both carrier bags from Eve and heads for the lift. Eve approaches the desk and calls out for the absent Sevasti, who soon appears once more from the door at the end of the desk.

"Sevasti, perhaps we could have a talk in the bar before Fay and I go out to eat tonight. Would that be OK, say about 7.30?"

"No problem." replies Sevasti, who Eve is already beginning to quite like.

At 7.30pm prompt the two women, both feeling much more relaxed after another shower, a change into cotton trousers and light tops with cardigans over their arms, plus having already sunk a gin and tonic each on their balcony, walk into reception from the lift door and head for the door leading to the hotel's modest bar, which is empty save for the hotel proprietor and a tall Greek man, whom she introduces to the women as her husband Gianni.

Eve and Fay settle on to a couple of bar stools as Gianni goes behind the bar and asks them what they would like. Having agreed on another G&T each, Eve addresses Sevasti while Gianni fixes the drinks.

"Where do I start? That's the sixty four dollar question," Eve begins. "Well, so as not to bore you too much with all the details. My mother was Greek, although I was brought up in England. I always thought that my father was English until a year last autumn, when we lost my mother. Dad had died ten years earlier from a heart attack. Anyway, going through my mother's documents I found that my parents hadn't married until I was almost three years old. What really gave me a shock was that my parents' marriage certificate lists Mum as a widow, although she'd have only been twenty-two at the time.

"Visiting an old friend of Mum's, who's a Greek living in the UK, she told me that she knew that my mother was married to a Greek man out here in Greece and that they had me before Mum moved to the UK. So, it seems that I am one hundred percent Greek and I never knew it.

"Mum was from a village that's apparently near Lamia, Sorona. Do you know it?"

Giannis placed a drink in front of each of the Englishwomen, "On the house," he says. Then, before even his wife can say anything, he adds, holding up both hands, palms outward in response to Eve and Fay's response that it would be far too kind of him to give them their drinks for free, "Know it? I'm from Sorona. It's my home village."

16. Sorona, April 1970.

Two weeks after he'd met late in the evening with the couple, Petros and Sofia, Papa Mihalis is looking at his fob watch and drumming his fingers on the table. His is one of the few houses in the village that does have a telephone. He glances at it anxiously, looks at his watch again. The priest, unlike most of the others who have phones installed, actually does have people to telephone, people to communicate with.

He jumps as the apparatus trings into life. He quickly grabs the handset and places it to his ear. He is sweating as he listens to the voice on the other end.

"Right, good. ...Thank God. I was beginning to think that you weren't going to come through and then what would I have done? You have the money? ...Good, right, I'll be there."

He slams the phone down, rises and in an instant sweeps out through the door, almost catching his black skirt in the jamb as he slams it behind him. Apart from the rare modern convenience of a telephone, Papa Mihalis also has a car, one of only a handful in the village. He starts it up in the darkness, switches on his lights and, after a brief visit to a small house on the edge of the village where he greets a woman who, carrying a bundle clutched close to her chest, joins him in the car, is soon speeding down the twisty-turny lane toward the lights of the town many metres below.

On a quiet stretch of road, far from the streetlamps of Lamia and even further from the village he's come from above, he pulls up right in front of another vehicle, which is parked up on the verge in the darkness, lights off, waiting.

Ten minutes later, he and the woman, minus the bundle but considerably relieved that the contact turned up, are once again driving back up the mountain to the village of Sorona, his business for the evening almost concluded, but not quite.

17. May 2014.

Eve and Fay are sitting in the taverna that Sevasti had recommended. The only other clientele are Greeks, in the shape of one or two couples and a family of four. The two Englishwomen are quite excited to be somewhere far away from the usual tourist trail. The food is arriving dish by dish and they soon have a table laden with food to occupy them for the next hour or so. They have chosen to drink a Greek Rosé wine with their meal.

As Eve tucks into her swordfish steak, with tzatziki and a modest salad garnish on the side, she raises something that she hasn't up until now told Fay about.

"Fay, I wanted to tell you something else. Something that I hope you'll tell me is stupid and that I shouldn't be worrying about. But I need to tell you anyway."

Fay's face adopts a perplexed expression. "What ARE you talking about Eve?"

Eve emits a long sigh, then continues, "Well, it's Tom. In the past month or so he's been doing something that he's never, ever done before, in all our years of marriage. You know Tom. He's very predictable, usually. I can't remember a time before the past couple of months when he didn't get home from work at six o'clock sharp, or not long after."

"Yea, so?"

"Well, like I said, you'll tell me I'm being stupid, but several times a week for the past couple of months he's been ringing me to say that he'll be late. Stuff to do at the depot before he can leave, that sort of thing."

"You're being stupid. Tom, *your* Tom, playing around? No chance Eve. He's probably telling you the truth. That's all. What with all the tough times every business is having nowadays, there are probably a hundred reasons why he needs to put in a few extra hours."

"You think so?"

"Eve, I don't know why you even thought for a moment that your Tom has anything going on. It's fairly evident to everyone how much he adores you and his kids. I can't believe it, I really can't."

"But, Fay, you know. You've been with Richard for as many years as I've been with Tom. When you know someone THAT well, you also know when something isn't adding up. You get a kind of sixth sense."

"Overactive imagination more like. Look, Eve, drink your wine girl. Call him when we get back to the room. I bet he'll gush all over you. It'll even be embarrassing for me just hearing your side of the conversation!"

"I suppose you're right, Fay. But it's still odd. The depot always closes at the same time and all the staff always get out of there within minutes. I've been there a few times over the years. Nothing changes. So why would Tom be staying on. Or is he going somewhere else?"

"Why not just ask him? He'll probably say that he's got a lot of filing and paperwork to catch up with on his computer or something. Maybe trying new ways to drum up clients with other businesses or something. Ask him Eve."

"How can I ask him Fay? Won't that immediately tell him that I don't trust him? Then, if he is innocent..."

"Which he *is*."

"Well, if he is, all right, ..he is then, it will damage our trust just making him think that I've got suspicions." Eve takes a mouthful of bread and tzatziki, then sips at her wine. "I don't see how I'm going to resolve it."

"Eve. There's nothing to resolve. Your Tom isn't the type. Trust me, I know. I bet you'll agree with me. There are umpteen other people we know whose husbands leer at you when you talk to them and they can tell that their wife or significant other isn't looking. It's certainly happened to me. Especially Allan Browning. What a letch. I don't know how Maddy puts up with him. But you know what I'm saying Eve, your Tom has never ever done that to me. That tells me a lot about his character. Believe me."

'OK, Fay. Well, I'm glad I told you about it. You have put my mind at rest. But I will phone him later anyway."

"You do that. I'm going to call Rich anyway, so we can both have a natter with our dearly beloveds before we go to bed."

Both women continue eating in companionable silence for a while. Then Fay starts up the conversation again.

"Bit of a result finding out that our host's husband is from your home village, Eve. Bound to make things easier, don't you think?" They hadn't been able to pursue that avenue earlier in the evening as the bar had become unexpectedly busy. A few business people had arrived for a night or two and they wanted to hit the bar right away. These things don't change the world over, after all. But at least Giannis had told them how to find the right road when they were ready to make the trip.

"Definitely. And it will be nice to go out with the two of them on Saturday, when we'll have their undivided attention." The couple had told the women that they have family who'll tend the hotel on Saturday evening, to give them a night off. Since Eve, being of Greek stock, was obviously 'one of them' and possibly even related to Giannis, they were definitely in the process of taking Eve and Fay to their bosoms.

"So, what are we doing tomorrow? Any ideas as to how you want to proceed now? It's your show Eve, I'm just tagging along to give you moral support. You set the agenda."

"Well, since I'm now so close, my nerves are getting the better of me. I thought that I'd leave any efforts to try and talk to anyone in the village until after we've talked in depth to Giannis. But I do fancy driving up there tomorrow just to see the village for ourselves, get our bearings so to speak. Only for an hour or two. Then, if you like we can zip along the coast a bit to Stilida, which looks like it has a beach. I found it on the map. Looks like a nice place to chill out for a couple of hours."

"Can't see much wrong with that. What do you think? Get up and have breakfast as and when we like before setting off?"

"Exactly."

The following morning, at something around eleven thirty they're heading uphill out of the town and into the foothills to the north of Lamia. Eve is driving this time and Fay navigating, although following Sevasti's directions means that once they're on the right mountain road they should inevitably end up in the village of Sorona. The previous evening both had called their men and talked for twenty minutes or so before turning in. Eve was fairly OK about how Tom had been. She'd talked to Zoe too, although Andrew had been out. She still felt that Tom was withholding something though, but she decided not to burden Fay with her misgivings.

After an hour or so, during which Eve found that she had to drive very slowly on occasion, owing to the twists and turns in the lane, they'd been climbing almost continually when they round a bend on the side of the mountain and are presented with their first view of the village. This, then, for the first time in her life, is the village where she'd been born, the village where both of Eve's parents had hailed from way back in the middle of the previous century.

Sorona sits on the steep side of a mountain, probably about a hundred metres above sea level, maybe more. As the road enters the village it slopes away to one's left, and climbs steeply to the right. Almost immediately upon entering the village the narrow road forks, the left option descending immediately into a fairly large square, now seemingly used predominantly for the parking of pickup trucks and cars. Following the right fork one stays almost level and quickly finds that perched twenty feet above and to the right, its geranium and lantana-clad garden descending steeply to a head-height wall beside the road, is the "*To Steki*" kafeneion, looking much as it had in 1970, when Chrisanthi had passed it for the last time in her life as the baker Giorgos drove her away and down to Athens airport, over 200 kilometers away, as she began her epic voyage to the UK to start a new life.

Passing the *To Steki*, after just maybe fifty or so more metres the road opens into a sloping *plateia*, beyond which is a narrower street leading on through the village. To the right is a lane leading up to a *kastro* which is perched commandingly above the village some thirty or more metres further up a steep slope, up which the road snakes left and right to accomplish the climb. Eve stops the car here and they get out. They stand here for a few moments taking in the scene. Behind them to the left is the larger *plateia*, the entrance to which by vehicle is the other end, which they'd passed upon entering the village. On the right, with a mezzanine terrace of wood bordering this smaller *plateia* is a taverna, which looks like it's either new or has recently been renovated. It's called Athanasia's. Further along the lane dead ahead is the Taverna *O Meraklis,* also a survivor from the days of Chrisanthi's youth.

Bordering the farther side of the large *plateia* is an old church and beyond that the houses of the village tumble invisibly down the steeply sloping mountainside. To glimpse these dwellings one would need to walk a while through the square and down the other side.

The sound of male voices emanates from the terrace of the *To Steki* above and slightly behind the two women. Visible even from where they stand is the edge of this balustraded terrace and it's fairly evident that it's still quite crowded with the village older men, playing cards, dominoes and generally putting the world to rights over their *Ellinikos*. Eve is acutely aware that people of her own flesh and blood may well be among their number. For some reason she's suddenly overcome with anxiety, fear, apprehension, quite how she'd describe the feeling even she doesn't know.

"Can we go now?" She asks Fay, who is tempted to reply 'but we've only just got here' but realises that her close friend's feelings about all of this will be quite different from her own.

Saturday evening, May 3rd, Eve and Fay arrive at Reception to find a stranger behind the desk. It's a woman who resembles Sevasti, although slightly less slim, and so they conclude that perhaps they are sisters. Eve approaches the desk.

"Hello, we are meeting Giannis and Sevasti here now to go out to eat." She says to the woman.

"I know. Pleased to meet you, I am Stella, Sevasti's sister."

"And you speak very good English too by the sound of it." Replies Eve.

"Thank you. You must be Eve Watkins and…" looking from Eve to Fay, "You are Mrs. Trenchard, yes?"

Both women nod and smile. Stella picks up the phone on the desk. "*Sevastoula?* They are here waiting for you." She says and replaces the receiver. "They are coming now." She tells the two women.

Eve and Fay no sooner take seats in the armchairs among the potted plants, when the two Greeks who will be their company for the evening appear from the door leading through to the private parking area. Sevasti smiles warmly and Giannis says,

"Come through please ladies. We shall take our car."

They drive out of town and once more rise into the hills, but soon arrive at a village that's not Sorona. In fact Eve and Fay are quite lost. Giannis swings the car into a small parking area below a wooden stairway leading up on to a balcony, on which a few diners are already seated. When the four arrive up on the balcony they are greeted by an inviting scene. The taverna is set into the hillside, with its balcony affording a breathtaking view out from the hills and all across the town of Lamia some distance below. Further away again they can see the main road that the two women had driven along in their journey from the airport and to the left of that the last of the evening sun's rays glisten on the deep blue of the sea in the gulf that leads out into the Aegean.

As it's May there is still an hour or so of daylight left, so the lights in Lamia below are not yet on. Eve finds herself already relishing the approaching evening as she foresees herself observing the dying daylight and the magic of all the streetlights below as they gradually come on. Giannis and Sevasti are obviously well known to the staff as they are greeted warmly, introductions are made and all four are shown to the best table on the terrace, with an uninterrupted view over the grand landscape below. Giannis orders a bottle of Ouzo and the menus are brought for each to peruse. First though, the waiter who brought them says, once again in fairly good English, "Tonight we also have…" and he lists a few specials that are not to be found in the menu.

"What do you say if we order for you and we eat the way we Greeks do tonight? Yes?" Giannis is addressing both of his guests, who nod enthusiastically in unison. "And before you say anything, we are paying. I will hear no argument."

Eve protests, "But we're your customers at the hotel, we have to at least pay half of the bill tonight!"

"I won't hear of it!" replies Giannis, "We have just discovered a fellow countrywoman, so tonight we celebrate you finding your true origins!" At this he raises his glass of Ouzo and with a familiar gesture invites all three of his companions to clink theirs with his. They all comply.

Once the meal is under way and all have begun to tuck into the myriad dishes that have been placed in the centre of the table, in fact, so many dishes have been forthcoming that another table has been placed alongside the first, Giannis asks Eve,

"So, then, Evanthoula, it seems that you and I are both from the same village. That explains, of course, why you are so beautiful." He says this with a huge grin that demonstrates that he isn't flirting, not right in front of his wife, but rather bestowing a compliment.

"Yes. I can't quite believe that as soon as we arrive here we bump into someone like you. How lucky is that?"

"Well, it's probably not quite so strange as you'd think. After all, there are most likely more people who stem from Sorona living in Lamia than actually live up in the village nowadays. But tell, us, when were you born, if I may ask a woman such a question?"

"I was born in April 1970. My father, who was called Stathis Stefanos, died falling from an olive tree while my mother was expecting me. It would have been around November 1969, during the olive harvest I was told. I have no memories at all though of either the village or anything in Greece. I was taken to the UK when I was a baby."

"Well, that is interesting, Eve."

"Why?" Eve asks.

"Simply because I was born in September of the year before. I would have been six months old when you came along. Strangely enough, you and I lived very near to each other for the first few months of our lives."

John Manuel

18.

As the evening wears on Eve does indeed marvel at the way the scene changes as the sunlight fades to black and the lights of Lamia come on, creating a magical panorama beneath them. From the terrace they can hear the occasional owl and see bats swooping in the night sky as the company converses, with no embarrassing silences at all. The two Greeks are making it very evident that they are delighted that by sheer chance Eve chose to book herself and Fay into their hotel. They really show, indeed by word as well as body language, that the two women are as welcome as if they'd been family, which Giannis assures Eve that she almost is anyway.

Giannis tells Eve that he doesn't remember much before his second birthday, but growing up in the village he did know Stathis' mother, his father having died shortly after Stathis had his fatal accident. Eve doesn't know her mother's maiden name yet, and so Giannis isn't sure regarding which family she was from, owing to the fact that, unbeknown to him as a child, no one ever referred to the young widow, Chrisanthi, who'd been shipped off to the UK before

Giannis was much past one year old. By the time his memories begin to take shape, he is able to give Eve lots of names, but neither of them knows quite what connection, if any, these may have to Eve's mother. Eve has borrowed a ballpoint from the waiter and been writing every name that Giannis can come up with down on a serviette.

So far she has written down the name of the priest that was still serving the village until Giannis reached his early teenage years. Papa Mihalis was huge of girth and the young Giannis was always scared of him, owing to his size and the huge grey beard that spilled down his front. He always smelt of alcohol and strong tobacco too, which didn't help things. She's also written down the name of the baker, a man called Giorgos who had a daughter Voula. The baker had died in 1982 and only then did his daughter accept someone's hand in marriage, a man who, as it happens, was another Giannis, who had a brother called Dimitri. Their family name was Katsandadis. Giannis and Sevasti's surname is Loukara, so Eve has written that down too. The kafeneion is called To Steki, as it was back in Gianni's childhood years too. Now though, it's run by Kyriakos, the son of Minas and Panayiota, who'd been running it in the sixties and seventies. Kyriakos is around sixty now, thinks Giannis. He of course has a wife, but she's not from Sorona anyway.

There is taverna *O Meraklis*, just off from the square, that was there in Gianni's childhood years. Athanasia's, the one that Eve and Fay had seen during their very brief visit the other day, wasn't there back then. It's only been open about five years on the premises that used to be the bakery. There is no bakery in the village any more. There is only one tiny general store apart from *To Steki* and the two tavernas.

Giannis can remember lots of names of people who are for sure no longer there, since they'd be long gone by now. In fact, he tells Eve that the village is only partially populated these days, now that the youth don't want to stay around and, even if they did want to, they couldn't, since there is no work, unless they want to toil and labour to scratch a living from the land. These days tourism rules as king and so many of the younger generation have gone off to Halkidiki or the islands. The 'flower' of Sorona is now scattered all across the Aegean Sea.

As the hour approaches midnight and the table is littered with the debris of a delicious meal, the four of them sit around fingering the stems of their glasses of Metaxa brandy.

"I can't recall having eaten better than that for years," declares Fay. Eve quickly agrees.

"Glad you enjoyed it. So you like eating the Greek way then?" Asks Sevasti.

"Well, if that's the way Greeks always eat, and I've enjoyed it so much, there's further evidence of my Greek blood!" declares Eve with a smile. Both she and Fay have very rosy cheeks from the brandy. The meal had been served, as is always the case among Greek families, as dishes in the centre of the table, with each diner starting out with an empty plate before them. Everyone helps themselves from whichever dish in the middle takes their fancy. It's what is commonly called *mezedes*, which literally translates as 'appetizers' or tidbits. It's actually a Turkish word in its shorter form, *meze*, but there are very few Greeks who'd acknowledge that. They've eaten some excellent fish done over charcoal, some octopus, squid in breadcrumbs, lamb kleftiko and any number of smaller dishes including tzatziki, hummus, Greek salad and pitta bread sprinkled with paprika. There were Kalamata olives and a couple of karafes of the house Retsina. All four have loosened their waistbands and are feeling very mellow. Giannis has something more to say before he suggests that they ought to head back.

"So, when are you going to go back to the village and ask around? Tomorrow maybe?"

"Well," replies Eve, "there's not much point leaving it longer than necessary now. I have to admit to being scared in some ways, excited in others. It's almost like I've come this far and it scares me that I might find out the truth. Can you understand that?" She addresses this last question to all three of her fellow diners.

"Of course. It must be very momentous for you. But if you like, I could come with you. How would that be? That way I could at least introduce you to some people that may be able to help you find out about your real father."

Eve and Fay exchange glances and nod to eachother.

"That would be marvellous. I don't know how to thank you, Giannis." says Eve.

"You don't need to thank me. It will be an honour to help you re-establish your Hellenic roots, my sister."

Eve feels herself losing it a little. Sevasti, spotting Eve's rapidly filling eyes, interjects, "Why don't you go and settle up Gianni. I'll get these ladies back down to the car."

Next day, it's Sunday May 4th, at around eleven thirty in the morning, Eve, Fay and Giannis set out in the hire car. Eve has insisted that they take their car this time and so Giannis accepts graciously. He climbs into the back behind the two women. As the time approaches twelve fifteen, they pull up in the *plateia* below the *To Steki* and Eve switches off the engine. She inhales and exhales deeply and says, "Well, let's do this."

They climb out and Giannis suggests that they first go up to the Kafeneion and speak to Kyriakos. He will know anyone and everyone after all.

As they climb the steep steps to the kafeneion's terrace, Eve and Fay are once more greeted by a hubbub of male voices. There are no females sitting at the tables at all. It's a clutch of men, predominantly from age fifty upward. There is the sound of backgammon pieces being slapped down on to the board and playing cards being flipped. A large flat-screened TV that no one's watching burns in the corner, some sporting event or other failing to attract the attention of the clientele beaming from the screen. Most of them disapprove of such contraptions invading their sacrosanct *parea* space anyway.

Threading their way among the tables, acknowledging various greetings from the seated men, they arrive at the kitchen area where Kyriakos and his wife are beavering away making coffees and fixing other drinks.

Kyriakos, a tall, distinguished, looking man with greying temples framing a still abundant head of wavy hair spots Giannis and lifts both hands in evidence of his delight.

"Aach! Theh mou! Kalos to! Geia sou Gianni mou, ti kaneis?" Exclaims the proprietor. His wife, a chubby woman with a dour face attempts a smile and returns to a row of tall glasses in which she's mixing the ingredients for a series of iced coffees. She places one of them under the electric spinner and whizzes up a foamy mass at the bottom.

"Ti exoume etho? Dio koritsia? Exeis kerdisei to Lotto pedi mou?" asks Kyriakos. Roughly translated, that's "What have we here? Two girls? Have you won the lottery?"

The men kiss on both cheeks and exchange vigorous hugs and slaps on the back. Eve finds herself wishing that the culture in

Chippenham was as warm.

After a little more conversation in Greek, Giannis explains to the women that Kyriakos doesn't speak English. "Just as well I came, now I come to think of it. I hadn't thought about the language problems you might have encountered," he says to the women. "Right, what do you want to ask him first?"

Eve is momentarily fazed, before gathering her thoughts, not to mention her feelings, and replying,

"Ask him if he remembers the accident when my father died."

The two men converse some more, Giannis evidently asking his friend to recall events from over forty years ago, when he was a boy, maybe in his teens. Eve thinks she hears her mother's name mentioned, but she can't be sure. Giannis then turns to Eve,

"Yes, of course. It was tragic. The whole village was in shock for weeks afterward. His wife especially was distraught. She left the village within a year and no one ever saw her here again. That would have been your mother, Chrisanthi, yes?"

"Yes, yes," replies Eve. "Ask him if he knew my mother's family. What were their names?"

Once more Giannis and his friend talk. He breaks off to tell them, "Kyriakos would like to offer you both a drink. Won't you sit down?"

The two women comply and ask for iced coffees. It's time they tried them out, they conclude.

"How would you like them?" asks Giannis.

"We don't have any idea," replies Fay. "Tell him to make them in the way he thinks we'd like them, right Eve?"

"Fine by me." says Eve. The men continue to talk, after Kyriakos has barked a command at his wife across the kitchen. She nods without turning her back and sets about preparing two frappes with milk and sugar. Most Greeks take them black, but not the foreigners. As Giannis once again turns to the women, his wife trots over and places the two drinks in front of them, along with two glasses of water.

"Right, Kyriakos says that Stathis' wife was called Chrisanthi..."

"That was my mother!" cries Eve, unable to restrain her reaction.

"Yes, I told him this. He says that her father is now long gone, but she has two brothers, one of whom still lives in the village with his wife. Stathis' parents are also both dead now. He had no siblings that Kyriakos can remember..."

"My mother had two brothers? I have uncles! I can't believe it. Can I meet them?"

Giannis talks again to his friend. After a moment, he tells Eve, "You can meet your uncle Gianni, same name as me as it happens. Your other uncle now lives in Canada, so that may take a little longer."

Eve is now quite overcome. Her mother had siblings. She had two brothers and one is right here, right now, in the village. She goes over this in her brain several times, as if trying to help the information to sink in, to register. Despite this startling, life-changing discovery, she again feels the trembles of nerves coming over her body. Can she deal with this now, right at this moment, today? Or does she need some more time to prepare herself. But then, she's here in the village. Surely she must now see this through. Fay understands the doubts that her friend is turning over in her mind. She speaks up.

"Eve, Eve. Why don't we just take a few moments to let this sink in? What say we take a short walk around the village, just to breathe a while, take in the environment. You're forty-four now, a few more moments won't make much difference. Do you think that might help?"

"Yes, good idea." Both women take deep sips from the straws in their frappes and Fay tells Gianni, "We're going to just go outside for a while. Eve needs some air. Can you wait here for us?"

"No problem. Kyriakos and I have a lot of catching up to do anyway. Off you go and - relax, OK?"

The two close friends rise and make their way outside and down the stone steps toward the square below. Across the square from the bar is the old Byzantine church, looking very picturesque in the bright midday sun. They slowly stroll arm in arm across the square. There are few people about. There are steps down beside the church that lead into a warren of tiny whitewashed streets tumbling down the slope below the church. The women continue on down these steps and are soon walking slowly among the modest village houses. One or two old women in black, wearing headscarves greet them in a thick accent that makes it difficult for them even to understand the greeting for "good afternoon," but they nod and smile anyway. Here and there they pass a tiny walled courtyard, where they spot an outdoor sink and draining board. Occasionally in these a woman is seen working at some green vegetables over a bowl in the shade of a lemon tree. If she spots them she nods or waves a hand with a sharp knife gripped between the fingers. Before fifteen minutes have passed they reach the furthest edge of the village and, in order to skirt their way around and follow their noses back to the kafeneion, they turn right and follow a lane that appears to be the edge of the village. In this lane the houses are slightly better spaced, not so on top of one another.

They notice that a lot of the houses have padlocks and chains on the modest wrought iron gates leading into their small courtyards. The ones that do have these locks show an accumulation of dried leaves on the stone floor of the yard and often the glass in the electricity meter's box is shattered, allowing the elements to reach the meter within. There are cats everywhere, most of them dozing in the early afternoon sunshine. Occasionally a dog can be heard barking somewhere a little further away. Occasionally the tranquility is broken by the sound of a motorcycle engine being started up and driven away, invisible to the two women.

After they have climbed a steep street for quite a while, perhaps a hundred metres or so, they again need to bear right to avoid walking out of the village and into the countryside beyond. There is a house set just a little way away from the end of the street. It is surrounded by its own ground, which is given over to a hard-floored yard with a washing line stretched along its length, plus quite a few fairly mature citrus trees and vines, plus bougainvillea all contribute to the impression that the garden is tended and the house occupied.

As they make as if to walk past there is a sound that tells them that someone is in the garden. As they reach the part that borders the back of the house, which due to the steepness of the land is higher than the front, there comes into view a lean-to, inside of which is a workbench. On the bench is some machinery and working on it deep in concentration is a well-built, still fit-looking man of something near sixty years of age. They are drawn to look at him for a moment, whereupon he senses their presence and returns the gaze. At first he appears to be hostile, but then, no doubt disarmed by the fact that these two strangers are both very easy on the eye, his face cracks a generous smile, one that reaches right into his deep brown eyes.

Eve can't take her eyes off of him because he looks so familiar. Fay already senses the same and decides to step away. After what seems like an age while he appears to be sizing them up, he calls out, in

English,

"Are you lost?"

"No! Yes! Well, not lost exactly..." calls Eve. He puts down his tools, wipes a pair of greasy hands on a piece of rag and walks over to the fence between them. He is now standing not three feet from Eve, she on the lane and he in his garden, an aluminium fence atop a white wall separating them.

He approaches the fence so that he can extend an arm across it to shake Eve's hand.

"Giannis Katsandadis, pleased to meet you. And you are?"

Eve can't help herself. She simply replies, "I am your niece."

19.

Giannis Katsandadis can't quite believe what he's just heard. This stranger, this woman who, granted, does look like his mother, oddly enough, says she's his niece. The other woman is definitely not Greek, but this one, well, 'You know' he thinks, now looking at her more intently, 'she's very much like mama. I hadn't seen it at first, but now....' He says:

"My niece? What is your name?"

"My name is Evanthia and my mother was Chrisanthi Stefanos. I believe that you are her brother, if I'm not making a huge fool of myself. But if you're not then you must be related in some way, because you bear a striking resemblance to my mother."

The man's face goes ashen. He stares hard at Eve and for a moment neither knows what to do or say. Then his face softens again and he moves to the side, toward a gate in the fence, saying as he goes, "I believe you may be right. You must come in, please."

Opening the gate wide, he beckons to both women to enter his garden. As Eve comes alongside him, he touches her sleeve and she turns to face him squarely. Once again there is a moment of uncertainty, before he grasps her and pulls her to him, encasing her in his arms. Within seconds his shoulders heave, as he cannot stop himself from sobbing. She soon joins in. They both cling to eachother for a full two or three minutes, during which time Fay isn't sure what to do with herself, she feels so superfluous. She tries to busy herself by casting her eyes around the lush garden. A ginger cat arrives and rubs itself against her leg, so she is grateful for the opportunity to crouch down and pet it.

After what seems like ages, Giannis releases Eve and holds her by the shoulders at arm's length.

"You must be the baby my sister took with her when she left Sorona for good all those years ago. You are so like Chrissy. You are also very like my mother, Sofia."

"Your mother? She is still living? My grandmother?" It's all getting a little too much for Eve. Her eyes are even more clouded with tears.

"Oh yes. She's in the village. She is seventy-eight now, not too steady on her legs, but her mind is razor sharp. She never really got over my sister leaving, even though both my parents told me that it was for the best, since she wasn't ever going to find any happiness here. But why are we still standing out here!! You have time, yes? You must come in and meet my wife, Voula. And please introduce me to your friend."

"Oh, yes. Sorry, this is Fay. She's my best friend and has been for twenty years. She agreed to come with me on this trip, to see if we could find out about my family."

Fay shakes the man's hand, says "Delighted to meet you." Both women follow Giannis along the path to the patio and then into the house via the kitchen, where Giannis calls out,

"Voula! Voula! Come quickly, I have someone you will want to meet." This time he speaks in Greek, so the visitors don't understand what he says, but they have a pretty good idea anyway. A few moments later, after they hear the sound of feet padding down some stairs, a stout woman with a full head of shoulder-length dark hair and a face that still could be called pretty, even though she's beginning to make the transition from middle age to senior citizen, enters the room.

Giannis says some more to her in Greek, but the excited tone of his voice tells Eve and Fay that he's explaining who Eve is and how amazing that she should just turn up out of the blue like this.

After he's done the explaining, he asks Eve and Fay, "What would you like? Some tea, coffee, something a little stronger perhaps? I have Metaxa and some Scotch whisky. Whatever you wish..."

Eve and Fay exchange glances and Eve says, "Perhaps a Metaxa would be a good idea right now, thank you." Giannis asks his wife to oblige and he shows them through an arch into a quite modern salon area, with some comfortable-looking sofas and a minimalist oak wood coffee table. There are a few potted ferns and table lamps to complete the contemporary feel of the living space.

Once all three are seated and Voula is making clinking sounds in the kitchen, Giannis asks,

"So, Evanthia, I really can't understand how you got here. Perhaps you'd better give me the story, from the beginning."

"I don't know if you have long enough," replies Eve.

"Oh I do, I do. I don't work much these days and, anyway, my long-lost niece has just arrived outside my house so I have as long as it takes. Voula doesn't speak much English, so I shall have to explain things to her as we go along, do you mind?"

"Not at all, but where to begin. There's so much ...and yet so little."

Eve composes herself and decides to start with the story of her mother's death and the finding of the marriage certificate. At the news of Chrisanthi's passing Giannis has to stop her to confirm that his sister has actually died. This he finds hard to take and his face betrays a deep sadness. By now his wife has placed a tray on the table, on which are three glasses of Greek brandy, one cup of herb tea (for Voula) and a glass dish of what looks to the Englishwomen like marmalade. There are two small teaspoons perched on the edge and two smaller glass dishes beside it. There is another plate, a china tea plate, on which are three or four circular biscuit-type things that are shaped in a closed circle, the colour of bread. There is also a small metal holder full of paper serviettes folded into triangles.

As he tries to digest the fact that his dear older sister is no longer living, Giannis takes a large gulp of Metaxa. "It's going to be very hard to tell my mother this." He says. "We'll have to be very sensitive. I don't know what this will do to her, poor thing."

Eve hasn't got very far yet and realises that this is the first time she's had to tell anyone about the death of her mother who is actually a relative, her own brother no less. She realises that she could have perhaps put it more tactfully. She asks her uncle,

"Do you know if my mother kept in touch with her mother, your mother, and your father, after going to the UK?"

"Oh yes. For the first few years there were letters. They dried up eventually, but my mother still has every one. They are all in Greek, of course, but I'm sure we'll be able to read them to you, Maybe make copies for you if you would like that."

"But of course, I would."

"Anyway. Perhaps you ought to go on."

And she does. She relates how she visited her mother's Greek friend, who told Eve about Sorona and the sketchy details that she knows about how Eve's birth father died. She tells Gianni a little about her English father, Ian too. She tries to reassure Gianni that her mother had found a kind of happiness with her life in England. There was, however, always a slight undercurrent of sadness, born of the fact that she never ever came back. What the reasons were for this Eve doesn't really understand. She tells Gianni that she just had something deep within her that made her embark on this journey of discovery. She knew that she had to understand who she really was, where she really came from. Her husband Tom has family and that's OK, that's nice but, Eve felt, feels, that she doesn't have anyone of her own now. This gave her all the more reason to find out if there was anyone still here who would remember her mother, who would be real blood relatives for Eve to hopefully connect with in some way. She hadn't dreamt for one second that she would find someone like an uncle, a grandmother!

The afternoon wears on with Giannis telling the women that his wife was the daughter of the village baker, who sadly died in 1982. This man, Giorgos, had been a close friend of Eve's father and had actually been the person who'd driven Chrissy to the airport on the day when she finally left the village for good, in the autumn of 1970. Stopping now and again for some interpretation of language, Giannis and Voula tell Eve what they remember of her father. How he'd gone away when a slightly younger man, served in the military, worked at sea, before he came back to the village and married Chrisanthi. Giannis explains to Eve and Fay that it was nothing unusual for girls in their mid-teens to be married off in those days. It was often a decision that they had no part in, having been decided upon by the families concerned. Of course both Giannis and Voula had been much younger than Stathis, but they knew him as an outgoing, happy kind of man whose death put the whole village in shock for a long time.

Giannis also tells Eve that she has another uncle, his slightly younger brother Dimitri, who now lives in Canada, but will no doubt want to be put in touch. Dimitri has a wife and four children in Toronto. Of course Dimitri's kids are grown up now and totally Canadian, even to the extent that they hardly know any Greek, something of which Giannis evidently disapproves.

Suddenly Eve looks at her watch and cries, "Oh my God, Fay!! Look at the time!! Giannis will be frantic!! We have to go!!!"

Eve's uncle looks puzzled, "Giannis?" he asks.

"Yes, sorry, but our hosts, the people who own the hotel we're staying in in Lamia, they're called Giannis and Sevasti. It was Giannis who brought us up here today and we left him in the café in the square, hours ago."

"Aha! That will be Giannis Pelekanos, of course I know him. He is at the Kafeneion you say, with Kyriakos no doubt?"

"Yes, yes, that's right." Answers a distraught Eve.

"Don't worry, I'll call them now. Relax, relax." Giannis Katsandadis pulls a mobile phone from his shirt pocket and taps its face a few times. He holds it to his ear and says something in Greek. A brief conversation ensues, then he laughs heartily. He closes the connection and says to the women, "All is fine. The two men hardly noticed that you were missing, they've been talking so much themselves. I'll walk you back up. But first, let us write down some contact details."

He bids his wife find some paper and a pen and they busily scribble down e-mail addresses, phone numbers and postal address details. Giannis writes his own details on a separate sheet, tears it off and hands it to Eve.

They bid goodbye to Voula, who replies with *"na eisaste kala, tha ta poume xana,"* and set out to make the short walk up through the tiny streets back to the kafeneion. Giannis walks alongside Eve, Fay follows behind for two reasons. One, she doesn't want to intrude on this momentous reunion and two, the streets aren't wide enough for three to walk abreast anyway.

As they walk, Giannis takes Eve's hand in his own and says, "Evanthoula *mou*, I think it best that I tell my mother about this before you meet her. That way she can get over the initial shock of knowing that dear Chrissy is no longer alive before she sets eyes on her granddaughter for the first time. She will be terribly sad, yet immensely happy to see you. I think I shall call you at the hotel, I have the number, and we shall arrange for a celebratory family meal together, which will have to be at my place. But you and I will stroll up to mother's house too, because you will find you can learn much more about your family, the family you have never known, from the wall inside that house."

"The wall? What does that mean Giannis?"

"Dear Evanthoula, wait and see! I'll soon show you."

They reach the kafeneion, where the other Giannis and Kyriakos are still engaged in an animated conversation over a couple of *Ellinikos* on the terrace overlooking the village *plateia*. Giannis catches sight of the two women with Eve's uncle and waves cheerfully. When the three walkers have climbed the steps to the balcony, the two Giannis embrace and kiss on both cheeks, something that Fay especially finds adorable about the Greeks. Grown men do things to show their filial affection and friendship here that British men can't bring themselves to do. The tactileness of the Greeks has grown on Fay.

Once final greetings have been exchanged and the party is ready to return to Lamia, Eve's uncle Giannis reminds her that he will call the hotel in a day or so, if she can exercise a little patience until then. Arrangements need to be made. There must be a celebration after all. She's told him that she and Fay have until next Thursday week before they are booked to fly back to the UK, so a couple of days ought not to cause any problems.

Just before Eve climbs back into the car for the return journey down the mountain to the town, her newly discovered uncle, who's walked down with them to the car, takes her once more into his embrace and squeezes her tightly.

"It's been an eventful day, Evanthoula *mou. Ta leme syntoma.*"

Later that same evening, Eve and Fay have now been out to eat, just the two of them this time, and they visited the same taverna that they'd gone to on their first night in Lamia, the one recommended by Sevasti. This time the proprietor greeted them as if he'd known them for years and they enjoyed an excellent meal, followed by a free dessert of homemade orange cake pie with ice cream which the women enjoyed immensely, all the more so because it was free, as was the generous glass of Metaxa which had followed it. They've now returned to the hotel and are sitting on their modest balcony, the pulse of Lamia life throbbing a few feet below them in the shape of the ever moving road traffic and pedestrians stalking the pavements, traffic lights and shop signs beginning to flash and glow brighter in the gathering gloom as the evening wears on. Eve is calling Tom to tell him some of the day's momentous events.

Her husband answers his mobile, says "Hello wonderful. How is it going?"

Eve can hardly wait to explain about the chance meeting with her uncle and how they're soon going to be meeting her maternal grandmother as well. She tells him that she also has another uncle in Canada and how much the hotel's owners Giannis and Sevasti have helped them. She's hyped up and rattles on for some minutes without a pause. When she finally begins to run out of steam, Tom interrupts,

"Sounds like an awful lot's gone on in a short time. You sure you're handling all this OK, Evie? Pace yourself, girl, this is a huge bombshell you've just had land in your lap. I hope Fay's proving a good support, though I've no doubt she is, bless her."

"She's exactly what she needs to be, love, there but not there if you know what I mean. It must be hard for her," Eve glances across the table at her friend, who's texted her husband and is now reading a book on her Kindle. She looks up briefly, smiles, returns to her whodunnit. "She's right beside me, holding my hand, yet keeping out of the way when it's the best thing to do. She probably doesn't realise it, but I couldn't do this without her."

"I know, love, I know. Only sorry now that I couldn't come with you myself, but you know how it is with work."

"It's OK. You've got plenty of time to meet my new family. We'll be able to come out here another time soon, just us two, 'cause the kids probably won't be interested in coming."

"You never know. Are you going to ask, by the way, how your children are?"

"Oh Tom, don't be cruel. It's only been a few days and if I know our two they haven't even noticed I'm not there."

"Oh they have all right. Zoe's already irritated at the lack of our resident cook in the kitchen. Andy's not so bothered though, he's got shares in MacDonald's anyway. They send kisses and raspberries."

After a few more banalities they sign off, Eve tapping the "end" button on her phone's screen and placing it down on the patio table before her. She takes a sip of the herb tea that steams in the cup beside it. They both have a cup in fact. They bought some Chamomile from the supermarket along the road and decided that it would be a good idea before turning in for the night.

"So," pipes up Fay, "How are your suspicions now, Evie? Laid to rest I hope?"

"Oh, I don't know, Fay," answers Eve, "He's never really given me any reason to doubt him in all the years we've been together."

"Well, there you are then."

"Yes, but, that's the thing. Since he's never been secretive before, why is he being so now?"

"Secretive? Eve, listen to yourself. Didn't you tell me that he'd explained why he was coming home late from time to time? How is that being secretive? Smacks a bit of paranoia my girl."

"He didn't say 'I love you' when we signed off just now. He always says it. Oh Fay, why can't I get it out of my head that there is something? I don't know, I can't put my finger on it. It's just that I've known Tom for so long now that I know when there's something he's not letting on about."

"Probably just his anxieties about all this, Eve. Get your mind on to something else, please."

For the next couple of days Eve can hardly keep herself in check, waiting to hear from her uncle in the village about when they can go up again, wondering about Tom and why he'd been staying on at the office, purportedly anyway, for the last few weeks before she came away. It's all Fay can do to stop losing her temper with her close friend. She just keeps telling herself that she doesn't know how she'd deal with such a situation if the roles were reversed. To top it all, Eve is also harping on about why her mother seemed to have shut her

Greek family out of her life as the years went by in the UK. Wouldn't it have been the normal thing to keep in touch with her siblings, her parents, old friends she'd grown up with? Why hadn't they had holidays out here while Eve was growing up? Surely that would have been the normal thing to do, wouldn't it? The breakdown in communication also explains why her mother didn't really talk much about her Greek past to Eve as she was growing up.

On the morning of Tuesday May 6th, Sevasti approaches Eve and Fay over their breakfast in the hotel's modest dining room.

"Good morning ladies, Eve, your uncle is on the phone. Would you like to take it on reception?"

Eve rises and walks through to the desk, where the phone receiver is resting off the hook awaiting her hand. She picks it up, excited inside over what her uncle is going to say.

"*Kali mera*, Uncle Gianni, so glad to hear from you."

"Ah, so you are beginning to remember your Greek. Bravo my child. How have you been, a little anxious I would guess?"

"Well, yes, I am rather wound up and so keen to meet my grandmother. Have you told her about me?"

"Of course. She was very sad to hear that her Chrissy was no longer alive, having always held out the hope that one day she would see her again. Since my father died some years ago, she's kept herself going thinking about Chrisanthi and what she might be doing, whether she is happy. Now she knows that her dear daughter did have a good life, but will never see her again on this earth. It's hard for a mother, as I'm sure you would know."

"Poor thing, the poor dear thing. Does she want to see me?"

"Oh yes, for sure. If it's all right with you, you could come up on Friday evening and spend the weekend at our house, with Voula and I. On Saturday morning we can walk up to mum's house, when you shall meet her. You can spend a few hours with her then, leave her to sleep during the afternoon, then she'll join us for a family and friends celebratory dinner at the village taverna that evening. I have arranged for a Bouzouki player and guitar player to entertain us, so it may turn into a long night. I hope that you'll cope with that. You may have to learn some dance steps, my child."

"It all sounds amazing. I can't wait."

"Well, I shall drive down to Lamia and collect you at around seven on Friday evening. Be ready in the hotel reception, is that all right with you?"

"Perfect. I'll look forward to seeing you then."

Having replaced the receiver, Eve walks back, almost skipping, into the dining room, where Fay is chewing on some marmalade toast.

"All sorted then, Evie? What's the plan?" Eve explains the outline plans for the coming weekend. Fay grasps her hand and squeezes it. "Well, my girl, seems like this trip has turned out to be far more successful than you could have dreamed of right enough. So, do I assume that from now until then we are to behave like regular tourists?"

"I'd say you've got that about right. And, since you've done all this for me and you've had to hang around while I get all the attention. You set the agenda for the next few days, Fay. Whatever you want to do, we'll do it."

And so they do. Fay wants to dedicate Wednesday to a drive down to Athens for a lightning visit to the Acropolis and the Monasteraki and Plaka areas. She's done her research. Today, Tuesday, she's keen to drive over to the beach at Stilida for some serious sunbathing and a swim or two. Thursday she suggests they do a walking tour of the town of Lamia, since they have yet to really see the sights here. Eve is grateful to have a schedule mapped out which will help her deal with having to wait until Friday evening for her real initiation back into her mother's family.

They follow Fay's plan more or less. By the time it's around midday on Thursday, they are sitting in a pavement café in downtown Lamia, sipping frappé coffee through their straws and enjoying the warm sunshine as they watch the world go by. Fay decides to put her thoughts about the coming weekend to Eve.

"Evie, about tomorrow, when Gianni's coming to collect you to take you up to the village for the weekend."

"Not me, Fay, ...us. Of course you're included."

"But, well, do you think you'd mind if I stayed behind? I really don't think you're going to need me around this time and it'll be a pretty hard thing for me to be there in the shadows all the time. I know your family will be kind and try to amuse me, but it'll be out of duty and will detract from their main concern, which will be to get to know you better."

"But Fay, you mustn't think..."

"Eve, listen. It's OK. I rather think that this is a pretty big deal for your Greek family too, not just for you. It's over forty years since they said goodbye to your mother and now here you are, all grown up and with a family of your own, walking back into their lives, looking like your mother and making them think that she's never aged. It'll be weird for them I'm sure. But they're all going to want a piece of you and I'll... well to be honest, I don't think I'll enjoy it much. I'd be much better off here, I can certainly amuse myself in a Greek town for a couple of days while you can then concentrate on the important things without having to worry about me sitting in a corner feeling left out. Makes sense, don't you agree?"

"But Fay, I..."

"Eve, think about it. Go on, give yourself a minute to think about it. It's your moment. It's your milestone, your watershed, your life! It isn't mine. I came here to help you in your search. Well, look, your search is over. I'll be here when you get back on Sunday night, or Monday morning, whichever it turns out to be. Then we can spend the last few days chilling before we fly home. Go on, say you agree that it's for the best."

Eve's facial expression slowly changes from one of 'imploring anxiously' to resignation. Her friend has been, is being a brick, but now it may be that Fay's right. This bit she should do on her own. It's not Fay's life-changing event, it's her own. Why put Fay through a weekend of awkwardness when she doesn't need to. She sips a little of her iced coffee.

"Well, if you really think you'll be OK here…"

"Eve! I'm almost forty-four, I'm a big girl now too you know. I'll be absolutely fine. I'll relax and walk, maybe nip over to the beach for a while, since you won't be taking the car up to Sorona. Are we agreed then, hmm?"

Eve reaches over and squeezes her good friend's hand and nods. She's almost tearful about this but doesn't want to let on. She turns her face away to compose herself, pretends to be watching some people walking across the road, dodging motor scooters and cars.

"OK, Fay. Agreed."

20.

At the top end of the village of Sorona, there's an old single storey house with a rectangular courtyard out front. The gate is situated in the centre of the shoulder-high rendered wall that encloses the courtyard. It's an old wrought-iron affair, painted blue many years ago but now more rust-coloured than the blue it once was. When someone opens it, it drags a little on the concrete floor and there's an arc of rust-coloured lines on the ground to give away the course that the old gate takes each time it admits someone, or allows someone out. It is closed and locked with a bent piece of wire that hangs in a loop from the top corner of the gate when it's open.

From the gate (and consequently the wall also) to the front wall of the house is probably about fifteen feet. The courtyard is roughly rectangular and runs the full width of the front of the house itself. There is an old metal front door, with a three-quarter depth frosted glass section which is perpetually opened from inside, but protected on the outside by a fitted mosquito screen, which has seen better days. It hasn't done a very good job of preventing the irritating insects from entering or leaving for a decade or two by now. The door is roughly the same colour as the gate.

To the left of the front door, fixed to the wall at around eye height, is an old aluminium meter box, within which is the electricity meter, which on close inspection reveals one of those little horizontal disks with a black section marked on its edge that one can see moving as the disk revolves, thus revealing that there are in fact appliances within that are using current. On either side of the door, a little further out than the meter box are two windows, one either side, thus giving the front of the property a fairly symmetrical façade. Each window has wooden shutters, both as we observe them today, Saturday May 10th, 2014, propped open with those little metal clasps that anyone who's visited Greece will be familiar with. They stop the shutters banging back and forth if there is a wind blowing, which, up here in a house toward the top of a village that's perched on a mountainside, is usually the case.

The window sills are a foot deep, front to back, and on the one to the left sits a little metal censer, blackened with use, which the occupant believes will invoke the blessing of the almighty on this humble home and keep the evil eye at bay. It's debatable whether this has had any success for the occupant within. The whitewashed walls are of rendered cement, as is the perimeter wall around the courtyard, but the white has long since faded to a dirty grey, with many a patch and peeling area. There are two mature trees growing out of circular holes (edged with those red terracotta bricks that have six holes going right through them) in the courtyard floor. Each tree is still laden with lemons, not even half of which have been picked since they ripened some months ago. There is a wire washing line stretched at an angle from the house wall to a metal post set into the wall in one corner, a few wooden pegs hanging expectantly from it. There is also a "Belfast" sink, set into a cement worktop at one end of the courtyard, in which sits a plastic bowl. Beside this work-area is a once brightly coloured, though now faded and cracked, bucket with a mop handle protruding out from it and resting against the house wall in the corner. Placed with their backs to the wall there are two old metal tube-frame chairs with faded red plastic seats and backs, the kind that have those little holes in them in a kind of grid pattern, positioned right beside the front door and there is a small square wooden table between them, on which sits an ashtray and a plastic bowl filled with some green vegetables or other. Beside the bowl is a once-sharp kitchen knife with a wooden handle.

This, then, is the abode of Kyria Sofia Katsandadis, seventy-eight-year-old grandmother of Evanthia and mother of the now deceased Chrisanthi. She is seated in the chair nearest the front door, which at this precise moment is wide open, revealing a dark aperture into which, if one were to peer from the front gate, not much detail could be discerned owing to the bright morning sunlight without.

The old woman is slight of stature, still slim, but with gnarled hands and a deeply creased face, born of not only decades of intense sunlight but also of grief over her losses. Somewhere in that face there still lurk the remnants of a once stunningly pretty young girl, but you'd have to look hard nowadays. She is dressed head to toe in black and, irrespective of the time of year, her head is never to be seen without the face being framed by a headscarf, also black, tied beneath her delicate chin and jaw line. She works rhythmically on the vegetables in the bowl, having once again picked up the knife and taken it in her bony right hand. Behind the bowl is a smaller white ceramic dish, into which the woman, whom we know now as Sofia, born 1936, is placing the vegetables that she's finished dressing in preparation for cooking. She hears still, but not as sharply as she did years ago. Thus the two figures that are walking up the steep lane that levels out as it passes her front gate can approach to within a few metres before she lifts her head to see them.

Giannis and Eve have talked non-stop since he picked her up from the hotel yesterday evening and drove her up to the village. Now - after a hearty breakfast during which Giannis and Voula were bemused to find that Eve didn't fancy chunks of bread, cheese, ham and olives, but rather some chopped fruit and boiled oats, which they did fortunately have a modest supply of in a packet somewhere in the back of a cupboard - he and Eve are on their way to have Eve meet her maternal grandmother.

To say that Eve is nervous would be the understatement of the decade. It's around eleven o'clock and the sun is shining in a cobalt sky, heating the day to the point where Eve already feels too hot and it's still only May.

*

Meanwhile, down in Lamia, Fay is feeling bright and enthusiastic about the next couple of days, during which she plans to walk and walk, then walk some more as she explores every nook and cranny of this working Greek town, which she's discovered since doing some Googling last evening is almost the same size as Chippenham population-wise. That's where the similarity ends though, since Lamia is much more urban, with most of the population seemingly living in apartment blocks, all of which are built to give every abode at least a small balcony on which to enjoy the outdoors. Fay steps out in knee-length shorts and strappy top allowing her shoulders to feel the warmth of the sun, when she's on the right side of the street that is. In the shade though she's still plenty warm enough, although it amuses her to see Greeks going this way and that wearing jackets and jumpers and the vast majority in blue jeans and boots too.

Having walked wherever the mood would take her for over an hour, she decides that it's time to find a café and take her first coffee of the day. She's already seen various monuments, the main shopping area of the town and the huge hill with what looks like a castle on top that dominates the scene when one looks above the rooftops. She makes a mental note to find her way up there after she's perhaps eaten a snack for lunch. Turning a corner near yet another mobile phone shop, she finds herself in one of the main squares of the downtown area and to her delight there's a large café right there in the square, with inviting yellow umbrellas and comfy-looking molded plastic chairs. There is also a kiosk across from the café area where people are buying newspapers, cigarettes and bottles of water. She doesn't know the name of the square, but she likes it, as there is a constant flow of traffic around the central pedestrian area and the waiters are dodging it to reach the tables from the building.

She's soon nestled into a chair at a small table on her own and a good-looking young man soon arrives and bends over her to ask her what she would like. Evidently spotting from her blonde hair that she's probably not a local, he says,

"*Oriste*. Welcome madame. You would like a menu?"

"Oh, no, not yet anyway. But I'd love a frappé please."

After he's extracted from Fay how she'd like the coffee, he risks life and limb crossing the road as she settles in to study her surroundings. He's back in a few minutes and places a long cool frappé before her, along with a glass of clear water. He also places a small dish on which she finds a biscuit, individually wrapped in cellophane. He places a small bill in a Perspex clip on the table too, says "*oriste*" again and is gone to serve his other clients.

Fay thoroughly enjoys the next half an hour or so, spent simply watching people going about their daily routine, She sees no one at all that she'd consider a tourist and this pleases her. It's nice to be somewhere where most foreigners don't come. She feels more 'authentic', which is the only word she can conjure up to describe her feelings at this precise moment. In fact, carrying on a little self-analysis, she concludes that she's hardly felt happier for a very long time. She's entirely free to do exactly as she pleases for the next thirty-six hours at least. It's a feeling of luxurious indulgence.

Suddenly, two people catch Fay's eye. At first she just notices that they're walking past among the throng of locals, but she soon realises that something is different about the man. It's a couple, a man with a woman, but the man …well, surely this can't be. In fact it must be a hell of a coincidence, but he looks the spitting image of Eve's husband, Tom. But Tom is in the UK holding the fort while Eve is out here discovering her roots, right? Right. So this guy, however much he may resemble Tom Watkins, simply can't be him.

Or could it be? Surely not. Fay slides a little further down into her seat as the realisation hits her that, were the man to look her way, he'd be sure to spot her. But then, since it's not really Tom why should it matter.

You know how we all so often see people that look like someone we know and for a moment it phases us when we perhaps lock eyes and there isn't any hint of recognition. Or perhaps we hear the person speak and it's an entirely different voice. That's the kind of moment I must be having. I don't know why I'm worrying that he might look this way, yet

I can't help myself. Often when this kind of thing happens, the person turns their head and suddenly the resemblance vanishes. Yet this man's turned his head every which way and it still looks like Tom.

But it CAN'T BE. Am I losing it? I know, it may be crazy, but why not? There's nothing to lose and it'll probably lay this uneasy feeling to rest in an instant.

Fay pulls out her mobile phone and starts tapping. She's texting Eve's husband to see if this man's phone buzzes. She types something simple.

"Great day again today. Eve's up in the village and I'm a free spirit."
That'll do. Now I'll send another, "Sorry Tom! Meant that to go to Richard! Dunno wot got into me, Fay."
Ok, now…

The couple take their seats at a table mercifully at the far end from Fay's. Unless he turns his head right around like an owl he won't now see her as easily. Fay watches him intensely. He's shown his lady friend to her seat with a hand placed firmly on the small of her back while he moved the chair for her. As they sit, he holds up a hand as if to say, hold on.

He pulls his mobile phone out from his shirt pocket and is quite obviously reading it. He looks up at his companion, then again back down at the phone, as if he's had two text messages. Now he throws his head back (*palpable relief?* thinks Fay) and replaces the phone in his pocket.

Oh my God. What AM I going to do? This surely can't be happening. What's he doing here? Now? And with a woman? She looks Greek from here, but if I had to be super analytical I'd say that maybe she isn't because her clothes, although tasteful, don't match what most Greek women about town are wearing. The both of them are under-dressed for Greeks, as I am of course. How can this be? And why here of all places? Surely if Tom IS carrying on, he'd have gone somewhere else.

But to come to the same place his wife is staying?

But, of course, he's planning to have it out with Eve while they're here. That must be it. He's going to confront her and tell her what he's got planned and at the same time destroy all the happiness she's just found. How can he DO THAT? But then, men, aren't they all the same in some ways? "Oh, I just fell in love. What was I to do about it?" How often do we hear all that rubbish? Oh God, oh God. Why did I have to sit here of all places? Why did they have to turn up here of all places? What am I going to do? I'll have to tell Eve. But should I? Perhaps there is some perfectly rational explanation somewhere. God knows where though.

Fay returns to watching the couple. She can't drag her eyes away now. It's a fascination that she wouldn't be able to break even if Tom were to come over and confront her.

Maybe that's it. Maybe that's what I should do. I should march over there and say 'Hi Tom, this your new girlfriend, then?' Who am I kidding? I was never that brave. Perhaps I should just quietly pay up and leave. After all, what if Tom HAS been carrying on and is about to break it off. Maybe he wants to come clean with Eve and ask, no beg her to forgive him.

No, that can't be it. If he was breaking it off then he wouldn't want to come over here and do it in Lamia of all places. He must be planning a confrontation.

Oh no, why did I have to see this?

Maybe, no, maybe, you stupid woman Fay, maybe you've got it all wrong anyway. Perhaps that man really is a double of Tom and the phone was just a coincidence. Yes, that's more like it Fay. Give yourself some time to think. Don't go jumping in the deep end when there's no water in the pool anyway.

Having reasoned up until this point, Fay attracts the waiter's attention and hands him a few coins. He thanks her, bids her a good holiday and she walks briskly away, in exactly the right direction so as to prevent the man seeing her. No sense tempting providence.

She is soon lost among the streets of Lamia, alone with her contradictory thoughts. One moment she's convinced that there's nothing to it, the next she's decided that Eve's life is entering complete deconstruct mode and she's helpless to do anything about it.

At least she's here for Eve if it comes to that.

*

A few metres before they arrive at the gate, Giannis stops, restrains Eve by the forearm and says,

"You OK, Evanthoula? Are you ready? She knows we're coming about now."

"Ready as I'll ever be. I am rather scared, though I know there's no reason to be. C'mon, let's do this."

Giannis smiles and they walk on. Reaching the gate he pushes it open as far as it will go and gestures for Eve to enter the courtyard. The old woman has now heard them and is looking their way. She smiles and, with considerable effort, rises to her feet, bringing her up to her full height of five foot two. She was taller in her youth.

Eve walks hesitantly toward this old woman, who to her at first looks simply like any other old Greek village woman that she'd have seen in a moody photograph on a tour operator's web-site. She paints the picture of the traditional old Greek ya-ya that tourists love to gawp at, perhaps ask if they can have their photograph taken with her. Eve's mother had been sixty-one when she died almost two years ago, so she never reached this much greater age. She fell two decades short, in fact.

As Eve takes the few more steps necessary to reach the woman, who now is stretching her arms out toward her, she gets a better look at the face and instantly sees within it, beneath the wrinkles and creases, the face of her mother. In that instant the tears begin flowing.

Sofia, on the other hand is looking at a woman who's about two decades older than Chrissy had been the last time she'd set eyes on her only daughter, yet she too sees Chrissy in this apparent stranger's gaze. She too is overcome by the moment. The two women, strangers and yet connected in some very deep inherent way, grasp eachother and soon the older one has Eve's head in her hands, her palms covering Eve's ears as she gazes upward, deep into Eve's eyes and mutters,

"Panayia mou, Kristos kai panayia mou. Chrisanthoula, Chrisanthoula mou, girises? Alithina girises?"

Giannis, who is standing alongside the women, whispers to Eve, "She's saying 'Holy Virgin and Christ! Is it you returned Chrisanthoula, is it you really returned?'"

Eve is slightly alarmed. Can this woman be thinking that she is really her mother resurrected? Although of course, since this woman hasn't seen Chrissy for so many years, she'd be finding it hard to understand that her daughter is dead, wouldn't she?

With Gianni's help as interpreter, the old woman, after bidding Eve be seated for a few moments at the outdoor table, says, "It's all right my child. I know you are my granddaughter and not my beautiful Chrisanthoula. But you are so much like your mother I just had to say what I said. I am sorry if I frightened you. I know I look very old, in fact I AM very old, but I still think clearly, don't worry. But I'm sure you also understand that it's hard for me. I lost my dear Petros many years ago now. He'd have so loved to see this day. So you see, I lost my daughter when she was so young, so young. Then I lost my dear husband. Thank God and Christ that I have my sons. Even though my Dimitris is all that distance away in Canada, he is a good boy. Giannis sometimes lets me talk to him on that thing, that miraculous little screen thing that he has at his house."

Giannis interjects here with a word or two of his own: "She means Skype, Evie. Once a month or so I set up a call with my brother and bring mother to the house so she can talk with them. That's his wife and children too. They usually come over to his house especially, when they can."

After a few more moments, the old woman rises, steadies herself with a hand on the table and then reaches for Eve's arm, intent on leading her granddaughter arm-in-arm into the house. Once again with discreet interpretive whispers from Gianni, she says,

"Come, come inside. I must make you a drink. You will sit with me a while child. I will show you your heritage." Eve remembers what her uncle had said about his mother's wall. As they enter the gloom of the house's interior, Eve doesn't really see the dark wood furniture, white lace doilies everywhere, she doesn't notice that the bedroom is in fact a bed to the right on a raised area through an arch and under which are wooden cupboard doors for storage. She doesn't really see that the floor within is simply cement that's been worn smooth by decades of feet treading upon it. What she does see the moment her eyes adjust is that the back wall which faces her as she enters this humble residence is completely covered in photographs, the vast majority of which are old sepia or black and whites, set in frames of all shapes and sizes, some with smaller prints tucked into their frames partially obscuring the photo that's behind the glass. Some photos are in colour, but it's quite evident that the colour has been applied in that way that it was done fifty years and more ago, by brushing colour over a black and white print. There are a few more recent ones that actually were taken with colour film, but these are very few in number.

Eve is at once fascinated and awed. Her host leads her by the hand to a wooden chair quite near the wall, just beside a huge heavy wooden sideboard; a piece of furniture that gives the impression that it's been put there to prevent the photos being hung right down to floor level. Sofia pats Eve's hand and walks away and around through the arch and then through a door at the far left end of the main room, a door that Eve hadn't even seen when she'd walked in. Giannis comes and stands just beside his niece. As the sounds of cups on saucers is heard from within the next room, Eve looks up at a smiling Gianni and says,

"Now I get what you meant about the wall! My family's history is on this wall, right?"

"Right. See that man there?" Giannis points to a photo that's portrait-shaped and approximately A4 sized. It's set in a thick dark wood frame, almost black. It's a photographer's portrait of a man's head and shoulders. He gazes out at the observer giving nothing away about his mood, as his face bears no hint of any expression. He does, however, from the fact that his shoulders are visible, wear a uniform, which to Eve looks naval. He is handsome with a firm jaw line and strong neck. His has a thick mane of black hair, parted on the side and swept back, probably with some hair cream holding it in place. It's very short at the sides and back though. His nose is a strong Greek nose which, although quite long, doesn't detract at all from the dashing good looks that his face used to entrance young women with; including the twelve-year old Chrisanthi as he'd been digging her grandmother's grave back in 1963.

Eve responds with a nod, catching her breath, since she's certain what Giannis is going to say.

"Yes, Evie, that is your father, Stathis Stefanos."

Eve can't take her eyes off of the photo. She's so crammed with raging emotions that she quite forgets where she is and who she is with. All of her conscious life at that moment is in her gaze at the face of her real father, the man she never knew as a result of a freak accident in an olive grove.

After several minutes in which Giannis understands the need to allow Eve to sort out her emotions, Giannis taps her shoulder and points at the small side table that's been placed before her. There is a glass of fruit juice and some boiled sweets individually wrapped in a glass dish. There are cubes of Feta cheese and some village bread, a side plate with a steel knife with a bone handle resting on it. There is also a small plate of *Koulourakia*.

Eve says "*efharisto*" to Sofia and the old woman smiles, then replies, "*parakalo*". She has already noticed how Eve had been staring at the photo of Stathis and so Sofia points to another of the larger frames, in which is an oval cutout through the decorated mounting card, through which a happy couple in their wedding clothes can be seen gazing out at the observer. As was the fashion in those days though, they once again don't show even the hint of a smile. The body language does, though, indicate that the man is very protective of his bride, his fingers are visible around her waist, on the opposite side from where he stands close to her. He wears a dark pinstripe suit with large lapels and she a very traditional white wedding dress and she has a veil that's pushed back over her head to give a full view of her face. Eve gazes almost in agony at the young face of her mother, the blushing bride alongside her bridegroom, Stathis. The couple have their 'front' hands clasped together firmly.

How much happiness they had dreamed of. How long their lives together were going to be. What optimism had prevailed on that fleeting day way back in May of the year 1967.

Sofia tells her grandchild, "I still have your mother's wedding dress. Would you like to see it?"

And so the day wears on and Eve never once loses her interest and fascination in all that she is told, or in all that she hears by way of explanation about the innumerable photographs on her grandmother's wall. By the time four o'clock rolls around, her grandmother says,

"*Aach*, Evanthoula *mou*. I am tired. I cannot miss your party this evening, so you'll have to excuse me because I must take a nap."

A few moments later Eve and Giannis are taking their leave of the old woman who, Eve tells Giannis as they set out on foot, she thinks is "quite wonderful."

That evening Eve finds herself totally overdosed on love, kindness, kisses, hugs and new relatives and friends. Most of the village arrives at taverna O Meraklis for the shindig. Eve is introduced to so many cousins, uncles, aunts and more besides, that she totally loses count. She even meets some relatives of her father, although her paternal grandparents are long since dead. By the time that eleven o'clock comes around the musicians are in full swing, the tables are laden with the remnants of a splendid Greek village meal and the glasses are chinking at a rate of knots. It seems as though several decades of gloom have been lifted from the village of Sorona and they want Eve to understand that she is the reason. Plates are smashed, paper serviettes are tossed into the air as men dance the *Zembehiko*, whirling and dipping, whooping and high-kicking their way around the floor in the middle of a circle of people on their haunches and all clapping the beat.

Eve is dragged around the floor so often that she actually picks up one or two of the more basic dance steps. As soon as anyone notices that she's got it there are whistles and cheers and cries of "True Greek!" and "She's a natural! It's in her blood!" and more besides.

Old Sofia has been present and now she's gone as the hour passes midnight. Giannis has driven her the few hundred metres up the hill to her house in his car and she's gone to bed happy, after telling her son how proud she is of her granddaughter and how she never wants to lose touch ever again, as long as she lives on God's earth.

At something close to five in the morning the last of the revellers is staggering out of the taverna and Voula, Eve and Giannis are walking the few metres home to their house. Eve doesn't awake until three o'clock in the afternoon on Sunday, when it takes her a full five minutes to work out where she is and what's happening in her life. She has a humdinger of a headache and so staggers to the kitchen for water, where she finds Voula busy preparing the evening meal. Giannis is out in his lean-to tinkering with a machine, which is his favourite pastime.

Eve takes her glass of water and walks out to sit on the terrace for a while. The afternoon sunshine warms her face as she gazes at the magnificent view down the hillside to some other hills beyond and a partial view of Lamia in the distance. She tries to take stock of all that's happening to her. Her own husband and children, so dear to her, seem to be of another planet right now. She can't rightly imagine her usual life in the UK. At this moment it seems that her whole being is here, in this village, among these impossibly welcoming people. She's only known them a few days, most of them a few hours, yet she feels as though she's loved them forever. At this precise moment she feels like this is where she belongs, where she ought to be. She has real flesh and blood here. OK, so she can't speak the language ...yet. She is however, at least here and now, determined that she'll rectify that situation as soon as she can.

I am Greek, after all. It's my heritage and I should be able to speak the language of my family. I don't know how hard it may be to learn, but I'm going to give it a try. I feel so guilty about this, but I really don't want to leave Sorona. I don't want to go back to my life in Chippenham. Where is Chippenham from here? May as well not exist. Am I wicked to think that? For almost forty-four years I've been a regular English girl and yet now, how can I go back to that as though all of this hasn't happened? I can hardly believe that I've only been away from home about ten days, yet it feels like my life back there no longer exists.

I'm probably being very childish really, I know. In the real world we have to accept our responsibilities. But I've really no idea how I'm going to go back to manipulating peoples' limbs for a living and fixing Sunday lunch, washing my son's rugby kit and helping Zoe with her homework. Tom, my Tom. Am I betraying you by thinking this way? Probably. But the fact is, I can never again be the Eve I was before I came here - fact.

And there are still unanswered questions. Why could Mum never bring herself to come back? Why DID she eventually cut off contact with her family out here, who so obviously loved her? What really happened here before she was packed off to Britain? Whatever it was, she didn't want to talk about it and that's why I never learned much about her past.

Ah well, in a few days I shall have to fly back to my normal life. The kids will wonder what all the fuss was about and they'll be expecting their mother to be the same old mother they've always known, available at their beck and call. Tom will walk in at six every evening and we'll all sit down to our dinner at seven. How long will I be able to keep all of this here - these people - to the fore in my mind? Maybe Tom WAS right after all. Should have let sleeping dogs lie. Now I've been here and done this and found my past it's going to be impossible to go on like that. No it isn't, stupid. Get a grip Eve! Grow up girl.

If I were to really think about staying here, how would I live? Where would I live? I don't even know what the winter is like here, perhaps that would give me a good reality check. Everything's great when the sun's shining...

Eve is suddenly conscious that she has company. Her uncle and aunt have joined her, cold drinks in their hands. Voula says something and Giannis interprets for Eve.

"Voula says that she thinks that all of this will have changed you."

"That is an understatement." Replies Eve. "The thing is, I don't really know where to go from here. I only have just over three more days and then Fay and I will fly back to the UK, a different universe really."

"Is it good for you if I drive you back to the hotel tomorrow morning? That way we can have a quiet meal in tonight, just the three of us. I'll see if we can Skype with my brother Dimitri in Canada, it'll be Sunday lunchtime there. Would you like that?"

"This may sound strange, but can we take a rain check on that? I really would like to see and talk to him and his family some time, but I think I'm OD'd on new family right now. My brain hurts! I'm not sure either if my heart can take it. My figurative heart that is."

"No problem Evanthoula *mou*. We'll eat here as Voula is preparing a meal anyway though, yes?"

Eve looks at her uncle. She meets his gaze and wonders at how she could only have known this lovely man for just a few days. Perhaps all this is just a weird dream. Maybe she'll wake up and none of it will have happened. She's sitting on a private terrace on a hillside in Greece, bougainvillea waving softly above her head in the breeze, enjoying warm sunshine and the company of long lost family, her family. Somewhere across the valley she hears the sound of bells, probably goats, maybe sheep. She gazes upward at the blue dome above and catches sight of a buzzard soaring, high up on the thermals.

No, this IS real. This IS now. But what will tomorrow be?

21.

It's around eleven o'clock on Monday morning May 12th. Fay is reading her Kindle on the balcony of the room when Eve knocks on the door. Of course she doesn't have the key, since Fay stayed behind when she'd gone to Sorona. Fay rises, puts the device down on the table and enters the room, walks past the beds and opens the door. Eve smiles at her friend and they share a hug.

"Bang on time, as your text said," remarks Fay as she turns and walks back into the room. Following Fay in, Eve drops her shoulder bag on to the bed and flops down beside it.

"You look exhausted. Been burning the candle I suspect." Says Fay.

"Too true, Fay. Do you know what time I got into bed on Saturday night? Well, Sunday morning actually."

"I can't even imagine? Three, four maybe?"

"Some time after five."

"Wow, must have been a good night. You'll have to give me all the details. I'm dying to know how it all went."

"Yes, I will, but there's a lot of it. But you know what the highlights were? I saw my father's photograph for the first time and my dear old grandmother is a sweetie, she really is. Fay, the whole village - or at least it seemed like it to me - turned out for the party on Saturday night. It was like I was a world famous celebrity or something, they all made me so welcome. I even met some of my real father's relatives. Over and over people kept telling me that I'd come home. I'm completely and utterly wasted both emotionally and physically. I shall have so much to tell Tom when I call him tonight."

Fay doesn't say anything in answer to this. She almost does, but instead gives the very slightest hint of an unenthusiastic smile and looks away. Eve picks up on this instantly.

"What's the matter Fay? What is it? Has Tom spoken to you? Are the children all right? Have I missed something?"

"No, no. Everything's fine Eve; just fine. You want to know what I did while you were getting the 'This is Your Life' treatment?"

"Of course, but first, let's get down to the café along the road shall we? I feel a frappé moment coming on."

"Sounds like a plan," replies Fay, to a degree recovering her presence of mind. A few moments later the two women are walking arm in arm along the bustly Monday morning street, gazing into the occasional shop window, then arriving at the café, where they take seats at a table close to the edge of the kerb, so that they can drink not only of the iced coffee that they're going to order, but of the soul of this town. They want to ring out every last drop of the atmosphere, get it to register in their minds and hearts for when they arrive back in England late on Thursday night.

After ordering their drinks, Fay asks, "So, have you made arrangements for keeping in touch?"

"Yes, we have. I promised Gianni that I'd Skype him and Voula once I'd given myself a chance to get back into my real life for a few days. You know, I think I'm going to need to empty the washing machine, get something out of the freezer, sew a couple of buttons on, maybe manipulate a few legs and arms before I can convince myself that I've got a regular life, 'cos it's sort of been on hold for a couple of weeks. You know what I mean?"

"I think so. It's just like a nice laid-back holiday for me, isn't it? I mean I haven't been putting myself through such a great big emotional mill as you. Anyway, want to know what I did with myself?"

"I'm all ears, fire away." And she is. Eve realises that she does actually want to have her mind distracted for a while; it's all been so intense this past few days.

Fay begins by telling Eve that she'd eaten out alone on the Friday evening, got chatted up by the waiter, Adonis, who was at least ten years younger than she was and soon Eve is throwing her head back with laughter. She then tells Eve of her decision to walk the town on Saturday, taking as long as she wanted to cover every inch of the place that she could manage in the time available. She tells Eve about a few coffees taken in this square here or that corner café there, of the meal she ate that evening, but doesn't go near the experience of seeing the couple, who she still can't shake out of her mind as actually having been Eve's husband Tom with another woman. If it was Tom and he had a plan to leave Eve, then surely he had also planned to phone his wife sooner or later. 'Today is Monday,' Fay thinks to herself, 'so he must be going to ring Eve pretty soon if it really was him.' She also tries to convince herself anyway that they'll fly home on Thursday and Tom will be waiting at home for Eve and that will be that.

She tells Eve that she couldn't resist going back to the same taverna last night as she'd eaten in on Friday, to see if the young Adonis would continue wooing her, which, of course, he had. He'd told her that his cousin along the coast has a boat, a yacht, and why didn't they go off for a sailing trip, just the two of them and the ocean. Once they were out at sea they'd be able to make love and slouch around the boat naked for days if they wished. Fay couldn't believe the forwardness of the boy and Eve just has to take out a tissue from her bag and dry her eyes from the tears of laughter. The story helps both women, Fay to get her mind off the Tom look-alike problem and Eve to calm her churning emotions over all the things that she's just experienced up in Sorona.

Fay finishes her account of how she'd spent the weekend and they both sip at their straws in comfortable silence for a few moments. Eve now remembers how Fay had reacted when she'd mentioned calling Tom tonight back in the room earlier.

"Fay, you haven't heard from Tom or the kids have you?"

"Of course not, Evie, why would I have?"

"I don't know, but I couldn't help noticing back in the room, when I mentioned calling Tom, that you had an odd look on your face. I don't know, but it was like there was something, something on your mind."

Fay's mind is racing. What does she do now? Ought she to tell Eve? She wavers to and fro between the Hobson's choice of options before coming up with an idea.

"Oh, well, yes, sorry. Forgot to tell you. You know how we sometimes say we feel like someone's walked over our grave? Can't for the life of me understand why we say that, but I saw someone on Saturday and it gave me a start for a moment."

"You *saw* someone? Like, who?"

"Well, there I was sipping at a frappé in a café in one of the squares when a man sat down at the table nearby and just for a moment he looked a lot like Tom. Gave me a start that was all. Nothing more to it really."

"Nothing to it. How much like Tom, Fay?" Eve knows her friend well enough to realise that this still isn't the whole story. That's the trouble when you've known someone since your schooldays, they can't easily lie to you. Of course, in Eve's experience of Fay as a friend, this has never until now been an issue.

"Oh, well, enough to shock me for a moment, that's all. Once he'd been there a while I realised it wasn't him and that was that. But you know, Eve, you must have had it happen to you. You see a person who bears a strong resemblance to someone you know and just for an instant your mind convinces you that it is that person. When they're out of context it can phase you for a while, that's all."

Eve decides not to press her friend. She's not really convinced with the explanation though. Trouble is, Fay senses this too.

"Let's grab some lunch." Eve says, throwing a few coins on the table and rising up determinedly.

Now it's Fay's turn to be uncomfortable. She knows that her explanation hasn't convinced her friend and it worries her. She doesn't want this to hurt their relationship. She's never lied to Eve in all the years they've known eachother. It doesn't sit well with her. Before long, as they stroll the streets on the lookout for somewhere that takes their fancy in which to take a light lunch, she's beginning to feel deeply unhappy.

If she doesn't tell Eve the whole story, then Eve will continue to grow ever colder, since she knows that there is something. If she tells her, she runs the risk of Eve being completely devastated by the possible scenarios that this throws up.

They eventually decide on a small sandwich bar that looks like it'll fit the bill. They go in, sit down and order a couple of smoked salmon baguettes and two tonic waters to drink. Fay decides that she has no choice but to come clean.

"Eve, you and I have been friends for a very long time, right?"

"Oh dear, Fay. Sounds like you're going to confess to some terrible deed." Eve is worried that her friend will do just that. She's attempting to put a touch of humour in here, but not succeeding.

"Well, no, of course not. I've done nothing to hurt our relationship Eve and never would. You know that."

"You're scaring me though, Fay. This is a preamble to something I'm not going to like, isn't it?"

"Well, I really am not sure, Eve, but, well, you know that man I saw." Eve simply nods, an expectant look on her face as she stares intently at Fay. "Well, he was with a woman, Eve. I did have rather a long time to study the two of them and - well - I'm probably way out of the ballpark, but I couldn't believe that it wasn't Tom, the man looked so much like him."

"Yea, but, Fay, surely. It would be impossible, wouldn't it?"

"Of course. That's what I kept telling myself. But they looked to be quite close and it made me feel uncomfortable so I hatched a plan."

"A plan? What sort of plan? If you talked to them then you already know if it was Tom. It wasn't, Fay, was it? Tell me it wasn't Tom. How could it have been?" Eve is getting a little more wound up now.

"I sent Tom a text. I pretended it was for Richard, so I then sent a second one, apologising to Tom for having sent it to him by mistake. I thought that if it really was him then I'd see him pick up his phone, not once, but twice." Rather ominously, Fay stops there.

"And he did, didn't he." Eve says this with a flat tone, a tone of resignation as she begins to feel that her husband really could be doing something behind her back. Suddenly all those late nights at the office come flooding back into her mind. Could her Tom, whom she always thought she could read like a book, be having an affair?

Fay nods, hesitantly. It's almost as if she herself is ashamed of what she'd seen, like by having seen it and related it to Eve she bears some of the guilt, if there is any guilt to be borne that is. Then she rallies herself with platitudes, "But Eve. It could just as easily have been a coincidence. I mean, look how many people are constantly on their phones these days. Tom? Out here? Like you said, why would he be? If he is having an ...I mean, if he is doing something secretively, then why here when he would run the risk of us seeing him?"

"There would be only one explanation. That he wants to confront me out here, away from the kids, and tell me what he's up to. Finish it with us."

"Oh Eve. Listen to how far-fetched that sounds. Tom loves you Eve. He loves YOU. You can see it in his face every time he looks at you."

"Things haven't been right lately though, Fay. I did tell you about my fears didn't I."

Fay struggles to reply, but can only manage "Eve! I ...I, this isn't happening."

Both women had lost their appetite. They paid the bill anyway, walked briskly back to the hotel and are now once more sitting on the balcony. Both are silent, each struggling with her own thoughts. Fay is feigning reading her Kindle, but her mind's going over and over that café scene. Was there anything she'd missed that could tell her emphatically that it wasn't Tom at that table? Eve is simply staring at the street below. She is watching people going about their lives in complete oblivion to what she's going through just above their heads.

Look at them all. They've all got their routine. There's a couple with two toddlers coming out of a shop. There's a youth on his bike, humping the pavement, throwing his bike stand down with his foot and striding into the greengrocer's, probably on an errand for his mother. Look at all those car drivers. They're all going home tonight to their regular little lives. The traffic lights carry on going from red to green, then back again, entirely unconcerned about what I'm going through.

"Where's my phone?" asks Eve quite suddenly. It's around five and she gets up, goes inside, then comes back out again clutching the phone. She taps its glass front as Fay watches from the corner of her eye.

The phone at the other end is ringing and Eve is waiting for it to be answered.

Tom's voice echoes in his wife's ear, "Hi darling. This is a strange time to call me. Everything OK? Or are you just so keen to give me all the gen that you just couldn't wait?"

"Where are you Tom?"

"Where am I? Why Eve? Where do you think I am?"

"Tom, just tell me. Where are you?" She can hear her husband's discomfort through the momentary silence that follows.

"Eve, what's up, love? You're not making any sense. You call me at, at, at three o'clock in the afternoon to ask me where I am? Have you been on the bottle?" She hears a half-hearted laugh, like he's trying to placate her and hoping to put her off the scent. It didn't fail to meet her notice though, that he'd taken a moment to sort out what the time is in the UK.

"Tom, I only want you to answer me, tell me you're at your desk at the depot. You are, right?"

"Evie, what is it? Are you worried about one of the kids? Has Zoe or Andrew texted you with an odd message or something? You want me to check on them right?"

Eve is getting agitated. "Tom, why don't you just say where you are?"

"Because, darling, I'm wondering what's got into you. This isn't like you. You were supposed to call me after seven tonight, when you're sitting on your balcony having a quiet drink with Fay. Now you call me at an odd time and seem to be hung up on where I am, when you know where I must be. What's the matter, do you not trust me all of a sudden?"

Now he's cornered her, or so she feels. Does she want him to think that for some reason she doesn't trust him? But then, if he's acting in a way that he's never acted before, ought she not to respond with a 'yes'?

"Look, Tom. Indulge me, all right? Just say yes or no. Are you in the office in Melksham? That's not too difficult, is it?"

She hears a heavy sigh. Eve knows Tom well enough to know that he's searching for a way to answer truthfully without giving something away. He makes as if to answer, she hears the breath against his phone, but as yet no words come out. Is that traffic noise she can hear behind him, now that he's gone silent for a moment? Did a woman's voice just ask him in a subdued whisper what was going on? Is Eve imagining such things, or perhaps not?

Tom sighs again, Eve hearing the rush of his breath. He answers, "OK, Evie. I was hoping to spring this on you in my own way. I'm not at work. I'm in Lamia. I'm a few blocks away in another hotel."

'I KNEW IT!' thinks Eve. Her mind suddenly bursting with anger, fear, rage, confusion and several other emotions all at once. She tries to control herself as she asks her husband, as calmly as she can,

"Just answer me one more question. Are you with anybody?"

"Yes, Eve I am, and we were planning…" Eve shuts off the call and slams the phone down on the top of the balcony's table, which fortunately isn't glass, but white uPVC. Fay looks at her with alarm.

"What Eve? What's happened? What did he tell you?"

Eve is unable to answer her friend. Instead she throws her arms around her own shoulders, drops her head and begins to cry. No, she doesn't just cry, she wails. She wails with such force that people on the pavement below look up to see where this sound is coming from. Then she throws her head back as far as she can and screams. Fay is at a loss as to what to do. Eve gets up, staggers through the net curtains into the room and throws herself on to her bed, convulsing all the while with her sobs. She is so pent up that she can't talk. She can only let her grief out with noises, noises borne of a great affliction within the soul. Eve Watkins has gone from floating on air to drowning in anxiety and grief in just a few short hours and she cannot begin to understand why.

She remembers having thought to herself some time ago now, when she'd first learned of her mother's past and of her father's not being her actual birth father, when Tom had suggested that she may be better off if she let sleeping dogs lie, she remembers feeling like her life was deconstructing before her. Now she feels like a wrecking ball has crashed through the walls in the house of her whole existence, her very soul. Suddenly her life at home as she knew it is gone and it's too early to know if she has a life out here in Greece. Nothing seems to have any certainty about it any more. A husband whom she'd doted on, whom she'd thought was going to be beside her for life is sitting in a hotel not a stone's throw away with another woman. How could he be so cool about it?

Eve's mobile vibrates and again begins to chime on the patio table. She ignores it. Fay, who's beside Eve on her bed, trying to comfort her in some way, looks out through the nets at the table. She looks first at the phone, then down at Eve, who's now curled into a ball and still convulsing, says,

"Evie. Your phone…" Realising that Eve isn't going to move, Fay goes out to get the phone. Picking it up she sees that it reads "Tom" as it pleads for attention. Tom's own face is dimmed behind the word. "Evie, it's Tom," says Fay. Holding the phone out toward her friend. Eve doesn't move, apart that is from her convulsions. The phone goes on ringing, demanding a response, Eve continues to keep her head buried under her arms on the bed.

'Ought I to answer it?' Fay asks herself, as it persists in ringing. 'What would I say? Something he said must have confirmed our worst suspicions. I don't want to talk to him. But maybe I should.' While Fay continues to deliberate, the ringing stops. Then, a few seconds later there's a buzz as the phone leaves a reminder of a missed call for Eve.

The phone on the bedside cabinet rings. Fay picks it up. It's Sevasti, concerned over the noises she's heard. She asks if everything's all right. Fay says that Eve's had some bad news, that's all. They'll be down to explain later. She thanks the Greek woman for her concern.

Fay sits back down beside Eve as Eve's phone rings yet again. She places the phone on the bed in front of the curled up body of her friend, Eve sees it through her arms, moves her leg and with one deft flick, kicks it on to the marble floor, where it skids across and under the vanity unit against the other wall. The ringing again goes on for a while, rattling around the room in its brashness before it stops, bringing an awful silence, but for the whimpers that Eve is now emitting. Fay strokes her friend's hair and says, "Evie, maybe it's not what it seems, hmm? Maybe there's some other explanation. Come on love, sit up, why don't I put the kettle on and we'll have a coffee or something? She glances over at the tray on the dressing table, where a small travel kettle and two cup and saucer sets sit expectantly. There is a small dish containing a selection of tea bags and coffee in sachets. There are sugar cubes and those small round foil containers of condensed milk.

Eve gradually stops convulsing and her whimpers subside to a regular sniffing as she reaches the final stages of crying heavily, her nose having filled in the process. Fay thrusts a tissue into the palm of Eve's closest hand. Eve slowly brings that hand to her face to swab the tears and blows her nose loudly into it too.

"Evie, Evie love. Say something. Tell me I'm right, hmm? There may be some rational explanation."

Eve suddenly sits up. She gives her friend a very slight smile, a sad smile of resignation that says 'I know you're trying to help, but nothing will.' She stands up and begins to undress. When she's thrown all of her clothes and underwear on to the bed haphazardly, she marches into the bathroom and Fay hears the shower coming on full pelt. She decides that in order to occupy herself anyway she'll make that coffee, or maybe chamomile tea. They have a small jar of honey, so she decides that she'll spoon some in too.

By the time she's made the tea and carried it out on to the balcony, Eve is still in the shower. Fay goes into the bathroom, since Eve didn't even close, leave alone lock the door. Eve is standing in the shower, piping hot steamy water flowing right into her upturned face. She hasn't bothered with the curtain and Fay's lower legs and feet begin to get soaked. Eve's arms are rigid against her sides, she stands like a statue. Fay decides to intervene and reaches for the shower lever and turns off the flow. Over a couple of rails on the opposite wall there are two large white bath towels, so Fay pulls one from the rail and gently taps her friend's body, drying it from the water droplets that cover Eve from head to toe. When she's satisfied that she's made Eve dry enough, she throws the robe from the back of the door over her dear friend's shoulders and leads her out of the shower tray and into the bedroom. Eve doesn't resist as Fay takes her out on to the balcony, pulls out the chair and gently presses her shoulders to make her sit down. Fay pours the tea from the small white teapot and spoons some honey into each cup. Placing one cup and saucer close to Eve's elbow, she smiles and says,

"Drink this love. It'll help."

"Help?" It's the first word Eve has muttered since slamming the phone down after cutting Tom off. "Help? What …how can it help Fay? What you saw was Tom wasn't it. He just told me."

"Told you? He told you he's in Lamia?"

"Yes, cool as a cucumber, Fay. He told me he's right now just around the corner in a hotel with another woman. How can a cup of bloody tea help me, Fay?" Eve stares out from the balcony into space. All the hubbub of the busy street is zoned out of her mind. All she sees is her mental picture of her husband of nineteen years, in the arms of this woman whose appearance she can only imagine as yet.

Fay goes to say something, thinks better of it. Eve continues staring at nothing in particular. Fay slowly stirs her chamomile tea and honey with a small teaspoon, places it on the saucer and lifts the cup to her lips and sips the hot, sweet liquid, then opens her mouth to speak again, and again says nothing.

Where do they go from here? Fay's out of suggestions.
Eve is half out of her mind.

22.

It's still the twelfth of May, that same Monday evening. It's now around 7.30pm and Fay has managed to persuade Eve to get dressed and come down to the bar. Maybe they can talk with Sevasti and her husband. Whilst Giannis is behind the bar fixing both women a gin and tonic, Sevasti is busy out at reception, behind the desk, doing stuff on the computer, the screen's glow reflecting in her face in the subdued lighting of the lobby.

A tall man, evidently not a Greek from his swept-back mane of fine, mousy hair, walks into the hotel from the street. He's wearing a smart polo shirt and chinos. He looks about forty-five to Sevasti, who prides herself on how accurate she can be when guessing someone's age. His demeanor is hesitant, he looks across at Sevasti and approaches her, but not with any degree of confidence.

As yet Sevasti hasn't heard what caused Eve's outburst. The women haven't been downstairs more than a quarter of an hour and are even now only making small talk with Gianni in the bar. She has no idea who this man is, and so assumes that he is either going to ask directions or perhaps enquire about a room. She looks up at him with her regular welcoming smile and speaks.

"Good evening, sir. What can I do for you?"

"Ah, right, good. You speak English. Am I that obvious?"

Sevasti smiles some more, trying to put the man at his ease, "In this trade, sir, you become quite good at guessing someone's nationality. You'd be amazed at the little things that make it easy to differentiate an English person from a German, or a Scandinavian, for example.

"But, anyway, do you require a room?"

"Umm, no. I was rather hoping that you might be able to tell me if Mrs. Eve Watkins and Mrs. Fay Trenchard are in, perhaps?"

"They are sir. You are a relative? Are they expecting you?"

"Well, no, probably not. It's a little delicate. Would it be possible to tell them Tom is here? I'm Mrs. Watkins' husband. I kind of sprang a bit of a surprise on her earlier. I need to see her to explain a few things." Tom stops, realising that he doesn't want to tell this woman any more details, largely so as not to burden her with a stranger's problems anyway, beside the fact that it's not her business. Then he adds, "You're sure they haven't gone out?"

"No, they're still in the hotel. If you'd like to take a seat over there Mr. Watkins, I'll tell your wife that you're here." Sevasti extends a hand in the direction of the sofas near the potted palms. As Tom retreats to the seating area, Sevasti picks up the phone on the desk. "Gianni?" She says in Greek, "Would you tell Eve that her husband is in Reception? Thanks."

Eve is finally feeling a little calmer. Not any happier, no, but at least as she sips her gin and tonic through a straw and stirs the ice and slice of lemon around in the glass, she finds that she can begin to think more clearly. Fay is keeping quiet, apart from expressions of concern and the occasional squeeze of her friend's shoulder or hand. Eve's phone is still on the floor in the room under the dressing table. It's as if by retrieving it she'll find that she has to confront Tom and she's not sure whether she is ready yet. Will she be able to listen as he calmly explains what he's doing with someone else? At this precise moment, probably not.

The phone behind the bar tinkles briefly and Giannis picks it up. "*Malista*," he says and replaces it. Looking at Eve, he says, "Eve, it seems that your husband is here. He is waiting in Reception."

Neither Fay nor Giannis is quite ready for Eve's reaction. Slamming her drink down on the bar, she flies off her bar stool and marches straight out of the bar into the lobby. The glass that she's slammed down is only saved from cracking to pieces by its substantially thick bottom. Large splashes of the clear liquid have, however, been liberally sprinkled all over the surface of the bar.

Tom is startled as Eve marches into the lobby, a look of sheer thunder and rage on her face and, as she approaches his seat, he rises to greet her. He has been rehearsing what to say, how to explain to Eve what he's been doing, but he's not going to get much of a chance. It's like Eve has lost all sense of self control. She's flipped, as some would say. She's unable to stop herself. It's like she has no say in the matter, her mind and mouth have taken on a life of their own. She screams,

"WHAT THE HELL ARE YOU DOING HERE? DID YOU THINK YOU COULD JUST MARCH IN AND PAT ME ON THE HEAD? S'ALL RIGHT EVIE, I'M OFF WITH MY TART BUT YOU WON'T MIND WILL YOU? AFTER ALL, YOU'VE GOT YOUR PRECIOUS LITTLE GREEK FAMILY NOW ANYWAY, RIGHT?? RIGHT TOM??'

By now she's jabbing him in the chest with the forefinger of her right hand. Tom tries to respond, "Evie, Look…"

'EVIE!? DON'T YOU CALL ME EVIE! THAT'S RESERVED FOR PEOPLE WHO LOVE ME. YOU DON'T KNOW THE MEANING OF THE WORD, DO YOU TOM WATKINS? BUGGER OFF OUT OF MY LIFE - GO ON!!"

By now she's pushing him with both palms, arms at full stretch. She's slamming her palms repeatedly on to his chest. Tom's being forced backwards and he has to negotiate his way around the sofa and toward the glass door into the street. He's wondering where they can actually have this conversation. He's acutely embarrassed to be having it here, but not too sure he'd like it to continue in the street either. He catches a glimpse out of the corner of his very wide eye the hotel's Receptionist standing with both hands at her mouth, a look of horror painted all over her face. He stumbles over one of the huge terracotta pots and almost flattens the six-foot-high palm growing out of it. He recovers his balance as the tirade continues.

"I HATE YOU. I HATE YOU. I HATE YOU, YOU, YOU… YOU BASTARD! GET OUT, OUT!! GET OUT!!" She's still in a fury and he's beginning to wonder quite what he can do. By now he's pushing the glass door open into the street with his back. His female companion, who's been waiting out in the street a few yards away throws her hands up in disbelief at what she sees. Out from the hotel, going backwards, comes Tom and a crazy woman is now trying to pull his hair out with one hand whilst thumping him on the shoulders and chest with the other. She's quite deranged. Eve pulls at the fabric of Tom's polo shirt, then pushes hard, making him struggle to keep his balance. He's never seen Eve like this and is quite unable to get her to quieten down so that he can talk to her rationally. The other woman moves toward the couple, hands outstretched, although quite in vain. She's just totally fazed by what's going on in front of her. Eve hasn't noticed her at all.

Tom falls backwards over a moped, sending it tumbling over on to the bonnet of a parked car. He's almost on the floor when Eve lands a punch on his jaw. She's screaming incoherently and gives him one more really hard shove so that he stumbles almost on all fours into the road from between the parked vehicles along the kerb.

…Straight into the path of a truck with the word 'PAGOS" [Ice] emblazoned on its side. The driver blows his horn but cannot stop in time. Tom is thrown up on to the short stubby bonnet of the truck, crashes bodily into the windscreen and lands on the other side flat on his face on the tarmac in the middle of the road.

For the merest instant, it's as though everything stops, everything stands still. The woman who was waiting for Tom outside is in shock, her mouth open but no sound coming out. She's unable to assimilate this scene at all. Just emerging from the hotel's doors are Giannis, Sevasti and Fay. People in the darkening street gather to stare, the truck driver leaps from his cab shouting that he wasn't to blame, the man just appeared in front of him, no one's listening to him anyway and the British don't understand a word of it.

In Lamia there is a quite modern and well-equipped hospital. This proves to be a great asset and a lifesaver in Tom's case. He had broken a few ribs and there were fears that a lung may have been punctured, but these proved unfounded. He did take quite a substantial blow to the head though when he hit the truck and the road and this is what still concerns the doctors. It's early morning, Tuesday May 13th. Last night now seems like a nightmare, a blur of some kind of wild moment that Eve doesn't recall too well. She's been tranquilised and Fay sits in the seat beside her in a hospital corridor, just at the entrance to the ward where Tom is now sleeping. He was brought in by ambulance last night, Giannis having had the presence of mind to call the emergency service the moment he saw Tom getting hit by the truck.

Giannis and Sevasti couldn't come to the hospital together, since they have other guests at the hotel, but Giannis did come in the ambulance, explaining to the medics that the victim and his assailant were from the UK and that it had all been a misunderstanding. He chose to say that they'd been horsing around, playing some kind of mad game and it had all got out of hand. This had eventually satisfied the attending police officers who eventually left them alone to be cared for by the hospital staff. The truck hadn't suffered any damage, apart from a bent windscreen wiper and so the driver, having been interviewed by the police and told that they may be in touch again should it be necessary, went on his way shaken, but otherwise OK.

No one paid any attention to the moped that Tom had knocked over and the bonnet of the car that it had landed on was already pretty battered and scratched anyway. The moped's owner had returned a couple of hours later, found his moped on its side ('again!' he thought), lifted it up and driven home none the wiser. The car's owner lives around the block from the hotel and hasn't as yet shown up. When he does he won't even notice the extra couple of scratches and the new small indentation on his car's bonnet.

Here, in the corridor of the hospital ward, Fay and Eve sit quietly. Fay smoothes Eve's hair, tucking strands behind her friends' ear lovingly. Occasionally a staff member emerges from a door, walks a few metres and disappears through another. The girl at the ward's reception desk sits there in her green scrubs, looking at a computer screen and chewing the top of a ballpoint pen.

"Evie," says Fay, "Shall I go and find us some coffee? Do you want anything to eat?"

Eve shakes her head, her blackened eyes, from a flush of tears and last night's make-up, stare across the corridor at the opposite wall, which is painted a drab beige colour. There are marks at around chair-height from innumerable collisions with beds and gurneys that have been wheeled to and fro over the years.

"You sure, sweetie? Hmm?"

Eve shakes her head again, then nods, then responds, "Coffee, Fay. No food. Just coffee."

Fay nods, rises, picks up her clutch bag and begins to walk off in the direction of the lift lobby. As she takes her first step, Eve speaks up again. "Fay!" Fay turns, looks down at Eve and waits, "Thank you. Thank you for everything. Where would I be without you Fay?"

"Shut up you tart." Answers Fay, trying to inject a little humour, but it's the affectionate kind that finds it mark, since it does elicit the very smallest of smiles from the corners of Eve's mouth.

Fifteen minutes later, when Fay returns, she finds her friend sitting exactly as she'd left her. She hands Eve a cardboard cup with a plastic lid, containing hot steaming coffee, which Eve accepts and cradles in both hands. She's carried the coffees one on top of the other and also has a salad baguette in the other hand. She opens the paper bag, in which the baguette is wrapped and peels the paper back to expose the end of the roll. Sitting back down beside Eve she looks at Eve, raises the sandwich in acknowledgement and says "Do you mind if I..? You know, ...rather hungry myself."

Eve looks momentarily at Fay and says, "Go ahead."

After Fay had chewed a few mouthfuls of her food and sipped a few times at the coffee, she asks Eve,

"Evie, speak to me. How are you feeling? I know you love Tom, that's why you're here, right? Don't beat yourself up about this, Evie. It must have been so hard to control your emotions in the circumstances. We're all only human after all. Do you feel ready to talk to Tom now maybe?"

Eve lets out a long sigh. She slouches back to the extent that she's able in the plastic corridor chair. She looks at Fay,

"I suppose I'll have to at some time. Oh I don't know, Fay. With all that's happened in the past couple of weeks, I'm swimming in a pool of emotions that's so deep it's …it's like I can't touch bottom and I can't swim. Any moment now I'll go under for the last time. I should have let him talk, Fay. Not that I can ever forgive him, but I should have heard him out I suppose. If you'd seen the look on his face when I was attacking him, Fay. I've never seen that look on Tom's face before. I've never done what I did last night before, come to that.

"However bad he's made things in my life, I only made it worse last night. I know that."

"It's always easy with hindsight though. Well, not 'easy' per se, of course, but you know what I mean. If we always took the time we ought to, to think about things before we act, the whole world would be a very different place I suppose."

"Have you phoned Richard? What did you tell him?"

"I have, yes. But I only told him that we'd be home on Thursday as planned. I said that we'd had a couple of surprises, but he didn't press me, so I told him he'd get the whole experience blow-by-blow when I get home. The girls are fine, not missing me all that much I suspect."

A door opens a few metres along the corridor and a woman in a white lab coat emerges. She approaches Eve and Fay. She's evidently a doctor and can speak pretty good English.

"Mrs. Watkins, your husband is awake. He's still very tired and drowsy, and he doesn't really remember much about what happened to put him in here. But if you'd like to go in and see him for a while, please do. Don't stay too long though."

As Eve gets up, the doctor adds, "I don't think he's sustained any permanent damage. But we are going to keep him here for observation for a while longer yet. We need to be sure that there is no more serious injury than concussion. His ribs will be painful for probably six weeks or more, but it's not going to require surgery, simply that he take care not to overdo things." She smiles, stands in thought for a moment, as though there were something else, then walks away and through a pair of double doors further along the corridor.

Eve is still riveted to the spot. Fay says,

"Are you going to go in?"

"Should I?"

Fay's expression is all the answer she needs. Just before she turns to walk in the direction of the room in which Tom is laying, a woman appears around the corner at the lift lobby end of the corridor. She's quite Greek, looking, though dressed perhaps a little more colourfully than would a Greek woman, though nevertheless tastefully. Eve spots her immediately and locks eyes with her. This alerts Fay, who turns around to see what Eve is looking at and spots the woman she saw sitting in the café with Tom on Saturday. Eve registers Fay's look of recognition from the corner of her eye. The woman, who's about Eve's age, seems unsure about how to proceed, as indeed is Eve. Fay too wonders what she can do, if anything, but realises that it's probably not down to her to intervene. She nevertheless worries that Eve will blow again.

Eve feels her emotions once again rising. She's never clapped eyes on this woman before, yet instinctively feels that she's the one that Tom was with in the hotel room when they'd talked on the phone. Here, standing before her, was the reason for her whole life crashing down around her. She's on a razor's edge trying not to cause another scene like the one at the hotel. Mentally she's gouging this woman's eyes out, but she's wrestling with herself. The woman smiles slightly and begins hesitantly to walk toward her. This really rattles Eve, who now thinks that the woman is brazen, audacious in the extreme. To Eve the woman ought to be beating a hasty retreat, but here she is closing the distance between them.

Her mind not fully in control, she marches toward the woman, slaps her hard across the cheek and continues out to the lift lobby, where she doesn't wait for a lift, but rather bounds two at a time down the stairs.

The woman, eyes watering from the sting on her cheek, says to Eve's back as she runs away, all the while rubbing her cheek with a hand,

"Please! We need to talk! Eve, please!!"

Fay is now standing not three feet from this woman and doesn't know what she ought to do. Deciding after a millisecond that she ought to be with her friend, she mutters a few words to the woman as she too makes for the lift lobby to catch up with Eve,

"Can't you see what you've done?" and she too is gone. The woman turns and takes a few steps after Fay and Eve, calls out again, "But you must *listen!*" But it makes no difference, neither Fay nor Eve have heard the words.

The woman flops down on to a seat exactly where Eve and Fay had been sitting moments before. She starts to cry and pulls a white handkerchief from her clutch bag. Dabbing her eyes and blowing her nose, she mutters in a soft whisper, to no one but herself. "Why, my sister? Why?"

John Manuel

23. Sorona, 1970

The decades from the 1930's until the early 1970's in Greece were harsh for the majority of the populace, especially those in poor rural areas. Apart from the internal political upheavals and the world war, which was followed in Greece by a bloody civil war that turned former friends and neighbours into deadly enemies (the seeds of this war were sown back in 1942, when the Greek government went into exile and thus lost all hope of controlling the situation on the ground at home) there was a clutch of opposing political factions, many of them left wing, which did little in a practical sense to help the lot of the poor subsistence farmer. Of course, throughout the country, most of the population were farmers, scraping a living from the land as best they could.

There were orphanages all across the country where it was a common occurrence for the staff to find a bundle on the front doorstep in the morning, a bundle which turned out to be a baby, whose parents felt that they just couldn't afford to feed and clothe it themselves. Some others would go to an orphanage, plead with the staff to look after their child and leave with the hope, however remote, that they would be able to return at some future time and reclaim their own.

At some time during the 1930's an idea was hatched to alleviate the overcrowding of the orphanages. Perhaps, at the outset, the idea was a noble one, for it would produce much needed income for the institution to enable it to continue to function. These orphanages thus began selling babies to families from other countries for a fee. False papers were generated, money changed hands and childless couples, primarily from the United States, would go home one or two thousand dollars poorer, but with a child that they believed to have been legally adopted to bring up as their own.

The problem was, the people involved in this scheme began to see it as a way to also enhance their own lifestyles. What started out as possibly a practical solution to a tragic problem soon changed into a racket, a racket that involved the trafficking of infants. Parents who'd left a child with an orphanage and went back, perhaps two years later to hopefully collect their son or daughter, were handed a false death certificate and sent away broken hearted. All the while their unwitting child was growing up as an American. There can be no doubt that many of the adoptive parents had paid out their cash in good faith. After all, they desperately wanted a child to bring up and they had what appeared on the surface to be the correct paperwork to prove that they had adopted legally.

Other ideas soon struck those who were running the operation. Thus when young Greek women gave birth, many were told that their child had been stillborn by people with a lust for profit that precluded their sense of compassion and decency. Young women were sent home after nine months of joyous anticipation, with a piece of paper, a false piece of paper, telling them that their bundle of joy was no more, having allegedly died at birth. Compounding the heinous nature of the crime, adoptive parents were handed the line that the child's mother had died in childbirth, thus leaving the child available for adoption. So many young Greek mothers wept, whilst at the same time their children were crossing the Atlantic Ocean, still very much alive.

In just one decade, the 1950's, one estimate says that around two thousand Greek children were adopted by American families without the permission of their natural parents. The American couples were, of course, duped. They were, by and large, also victims, since they believed as a rule that they were doing a great good in taking on these orphans and giving them a chance at a better life. The fact remains, though, that thousands of people who were brought up as Americans are actually natural Greeks with families back in Greece who know nothing of their existence.

It was only during the decade of the 1970's that this practice was finally brought to a halt, a few years after Chrisanthi was born in a mountainside village a few kilometers north of the town of Lamia.

In the chill darkness the Priest's car winds its way back up the twisty-turny road from the town below to the sleepy village above. In April, in this part of Greece still experiences chilly nights and families sit around their log fires at home, as close to the flames and to eachother as they can get to keep from letting the cold seep right into their bones. The Priest pulls up in front of the house where earlier in the evening he'd picked up the woman with the bundle. She gets out, to the sound of an earnest whisper from within the vehicle,

"Remember!! Not a word!!"

She throws a hand back in his direction, as if to say, 'Don't worry about me. I can keep my mouth shut.' The wad of Drachma notes she's shoving into the fold of her garment that covers her breasts will see to it anyway. She is soon through her creaky front door and lost to the darkness.

The car continues on to a place where it can make a u-turn, whereupon, after making the manouevre, it creeps back into the village and stops outside the Priest's own rather grand residence. Locking the car, the ample silhouette of the driver is seen silently ghosting uphill through the bereft streets of the village until it arrives at a gate into a courtyard, a rectangular courtyard, across which it steals surreptitiously and a tap is heard on the metal of the door of the cottage within. The door is opened and the Priest disappears inside.

Petros and Sofia Katsandadis gaze anxiously at the Papas, their faces glowing spasmodically in the flickering light of both their candles and the logs burning on their hearth. They say nothing, waiting for the visitor to do something they're expecting.

Pulling an envelope from within his cassock, he plunges a hand inside and draws out another wad of Drachmas. Counting out the expected amount, he places it on the wooden dining table between himself and the expectant couple.

"As agreed." he says. He smiles halfheartedly and adds, "You realise how important this is. I mean, that no one speaks of this again. If anyone other than you two and the midwife gets wind of this, we'll all be for the high jump. You understand, right?"

There is just the hint of a threat in that final word. In truth he's more worried about his job as village Priest, together with his prospects of a pension from the church, than he is for the reputation of this humble family. He goes on, "As I said before. Everyone wins. Your daughter still has one child and she now has the chance to get away from here and maybe find a better life for the both of them. You are relieved of the burden and no one need be the wiser. I shall bid you goodnight."

Without ceremony, he shakes both of their hands in a formal fashion, then turns and exits into the blackness outside.

Petros Katsandadis turns to his wife and draws her to him. She is crying. Neither of them touches the money on the table, they can't bring themselves to do so at this moment. It's like blood money. The cash of betrayal is how they perceive it. Even so, pragmatism will take over in the chill light of the morning, as yet still several hours away.

In another house not far away on the edge of the village, their widowed daughter Chrisanthi sleeps, awaiting the next time her remaining child cries to be fed, when she'll rise, expose a breast and answer its need. She is beside herself with grief, convinced, as she is, that she will never see her remaining baby's twin again.

She is, of course, quite correct in that assumption.

Two days later, as Chrisanthi's parents begin plans to send their daughter away to Britain, Chrisanthi nurses the infant Evanthia at her breast in her parents home, unconscious of the fact that at this very instant, her other child is being carried aboard a ship in the port of Patra, to begin its voyage to the United States of America.

Forty-four years will have passed before the two sisters, separated at birth, meet again.

Papa Mihalis trained as a priest in the Greek Orthodox Church with another young man who has remained a close friend up until now. Whilst Papa Mihalis ended up serving the mountainside community of Sorona, where his own family has roots, his friend wound up in Patra, serving not only a large part of the town but also as patron of a local orphanage. Sitting with the administrator of the said establishment, he'd been told on a few occasions about the money that was to be made 'helping' foreigners, primarily Americans, to adopt. The contacts are established through lawyers in America, who act as go-betweens, mediating for the would-be parents and the officials of the orphanages who appear to have babies that desperately need homes, of which there just aren't enough in Greece itself.

The priest from Patra telephones his old friend Mihalis regularly, to begin with it was to make use of the telephone anyway, but as time passed he's begun slowly introducing little snippets of information about the baby business. He didn't at first want his friend exhibiting scruples that might just get him into hot water.

He needn't have worried. Before long Mihalis had come to know the whole story and begun wishing himself that he could profit in some way. When Stathis died in such tragic circumstances and then his young widow turned out to be expecting, he began to think that something might come of the situation. Of course, he is present in the house when she gives birth, just in case anything happens that might require his services. Owing to the tragic circumstances, the family had decided to keep most of the villagers at bay, with the exception, that is, of the village midwife, who officiates at the birth as a matter of course. Even though the young Chrisanthi's belly had evidently been very large before the actual birth, no one had foreseen that she was going to produce not one, but two babies. Within minutes of both infants having arrived in the outside world, a fact which produces feelings of surprise but also of dismay over the consequences of a nineteen-year-old widow having to find some way of providing for them, the Papas springs his idea on the family. After all, he's had a few months in which to speculate on how he may be able to profit from this situation.

"No one outside this room knows that the girl has produced twins. Your sons are at their friend's house to keep them out of the way. Only you two [he addresses Chrisanthi's parents] and Kyria Eleni [the midwife] and, of course, myself, know.

"I believe that I may be able to help you alleviate this situation, indeed perhaps provide you with the wherewithall to send Chrissy away to the UK, as I know that this has been in your minds ever since Stathis died so tragically. It seems that God in his goodness has seen fit to enable you and your daughter to salvage something out of this most tragic of circumstances."

He doesn't bother mentioning that he also stands to profit quite nicely from this deal, should the parents agree to what he's going to propose.

And so he begins to explain what course is open to them if all present will swear to secrecy. The following day he is on the telephone to his friend in Patra, explaining how he has just come across some 'merchandise'. The process begins at that very moment and ends with the Priest's return to the house after he and the midwide have delivered the 'goods' to their contact by the roadside outside of Lamia.

John Manuel

24.

Ioanna Loukara is American. At least, that's what she thought for the first couple of decades of her life. She has an 'official' birthdate of April 30th 1970 and was raised by a loving couple, Mr. and Mrs. Steven and Jessica Vaughan of Baltimore, who married in 1967 and found soon thereafter that they couldn't have children.

When their lawyer told them that there were children in Greece that desperately needed loving parents and that for a fee of two thousand dollars he could arrange all the paperwork and bring them a bouncing, healthy baby to raise as their own, they were beside themselves with joy.

As she grew up, from the earliest age at which they thought she'd grasp it, her parents always made the truth clear to their daughter. She'd been adopted and her parents apparently had died when she was a baby. She'd been born in Greece, but more than that they didn't really explain. Steven and Jessica loved their daughter unconditionally and retained her Greek name out of respect for her deceased parents. They weren't to know that the orphanage that had arranged the deal had chosen that name out of thin air in order to expedite the false paperwork with minimum delay.

Chrissy and her parents had decided not to name the girl they were to lose, for it would make the loss just a tiny bit easier to bear. When it came time for the midwife to take the child, they'd simply pointed to the cot and she'd chosen on the spot which one to take. That was when Chrisanthi was named, and not a moment before.

When Ioanna was in her twenties and studying to be a lawyer herself, a friend and fellow student of hers stumbled across a TV show quite by accident. Her friend was Greek and used to get news of Greek TV programmes from her family over in Athens. A show had aired on national TV over there that had exposed the decades-long scandal of illegal adoptions and it had apparently caused a sensation in Greece. This had got Ioanna to thinking about her own origins and thus she'd begun in her spare time doing research to see if she could discover anything about her natural family. She didn't place it very highly on her list of things to do, but whenever she had a little time, she'd write to various government organisations in Greece and see what response she received. Her adoptive parents always supported her in this.

It wasn't until well past the year 2000 that she found an organisation called *Association for the Search for Children Adopted Without the Consent of Their Natural Parents* operating in Greece, but now too in contact with a sympathetic website formed by some New York Americans searching for their true pasts.

By the time 2013 had come around, Ioanna had all but given up. That is, until she'd come into contact on-line with a Mr. Tom Watkins from the UK, who, unbeknown to his wife Eve, had embarked on some research of his own. Grabbing quite a few links from what little work his wife had already done on her computer, he'd started out with the intention of getting to the heart of the matter before Eve did, so that he could present her with a dossier that would hopefully help her come to terms with the fact that she was never going to really get to the bottom of it all. Thus their family life would revert to the 'normal' that Tom knew and loved from before Eve had discovered her mother's marriage certificate.

Much to his own surprise, Tom had been somewhat more successful than Eve. He put this down to the fact that Eve had kind of given up on the Internet once she'd found out from her mother's old friend from Batheaston that she was from the Lamia region in central Greece. She even had the name of the village, Sorona. This left Tom to carry on alone and it wasn't long before information came to light from the Greek organisation that a priest from a village near Lamia had actually been apprehended not long after arranging for a twin baby girl to be spirited away soon after birth and sent to an orphanage in Patra that was one of the main protagonists of the baby-selling trade. Apparently, the information on-line was that the two brothers of Chrisanthi had reported that they'd heard more than one baby crying in the first couple of days after the birth. They'd been told to keep quiet and threatened by none other than the priest himself. But they'd told their employer anyway. That was enough to spark an investigation, eventually. It seems that the employer had kept it under wraps for a few years for reasons no longer clear now.

At this point, Tom had quite a lot to go on. He knew the age of the person he was looking for and he knew that it was a female. Ioanna, meantime, had dug up proof that the paperwork for her adoption was falsified and the lawyer that had dealt with it in New York, not her parents' lawyer, but the next one in the chain with whom he'd been dealing, had been tried for conspiracy. He'd

John Manuel

provided information that a baby he'd supplied, which ended up with a couple from Baltimore, was indeed brought to the Patra orphanage by a priest who'd collected it from Sorona, near Lamia. Bingo!

The last few weeks before Eve's trip out to Greece had seen Tom making last minute arrangements with Ioanna to surprise Eve right there in Lamia.

What a great day it was going to be, when Tom, Eve's loving husband, could top off all of Eve's joy at finding her real roots by introducing her to the long-lost non-identical twin sister she never knew she had.

And he'd do it right there, in Lamia. He'd fly out on a different flight, meet Ioanna in Athens and they'd travel together to Lamia and plan their surprise.

What a surprise.

25.

Ioanna sits down in the hospital corridor and weeps.

"Why, my sister? Why?" she murmers as she dabs her eyes with a handkerchief. She sees two feet arriving in front of her. Looking slowly upward she sees a nurse standing there.

"Mrs Watkins?"

"Umm, no, I am her sister."

"Ah. So sorry. Is Mrs. Watkins here? Nearby perhaps?"

'Umm, well, I think she's outside. She just left, just this minute."

"Mr. Watkins is asking for her. Could you find her, please?"

How does Ioanna explain that this won't be as straightforward as the nurse thinks. How does she reply that she herself may be in danger of being assaulted if she goes after Eve. Either way, she has the presence of mind to reply,

"Yes, sure. I'll go now. But may I see my brother-in-law first, please? Just for a moment."

"Of course," replies the nurse and invites Ioanna with a hand gesture to follow her.

They enter a room that's buzzing with electronic equipment. The doctors are taking no chances with Tom's head injury and a couple of electrodes appear to be monitoring his brain activity, others his heart. Various beeps form an audible accompaniment to the conversation.

"Ioanna? Well, we didn't quite foresee this, did we?" Tom attempts a smile of irony. Ioanna smiles back and takes Tom's hand.

Tom continues, "Ioanna, I have an idea. Can you take my mobile phone out from the cabinet please?"

Out in the hospital grounds Eve is sitting on a kerb, Fay is standing with her. Fay opens up the conversation, the first words they've spoken since Eve slapped Ioanna's face and stormed out.

"Evie, look, sooner or later there's going to have to be some talking you know. It may as well be sooner than later. I've no idea what the hell is going on, but I still like to think that something may be salvageable from all of this. What do you think?"

Several kilometers away on the floor of the womens' hotel room, under the dressing table, Eve's mobile phone buzzes, the dial lights up and the words "1 message received" appear.

Unfortunately, there's no one there to pick it up and read what it says, which is as follows:

"Evie, the woman is your sister. You are one of twins. THAT was the surprise we had for you. I love only you, Tom xxx".

Ioanna, after sending the message as per Tom's instructions, replaces his phone in the cabinet beside his bed, kisses her brother-in-law on the forehead and walks out. She makes her way along the corridor to the lift lobby and takes the lift to the ground floor.

Once there she makes for the coffee shop, but there is no sign of the women there. She goes outside and looks around. Gazing across the parking area she catches sight of the two women. Her heart instantly jumps into her mouth.

I sooo hope she's read that message. If she has then surely she'll react much differently this time. I can't be judgmental. I know how this must all look to her. Plus I already see much of myself in her. I also am fiery tempered. I go off half-cocked all the time and then regret it afterward. But I didn't fly halfway around the planet to give up on this now.

Well, here goes. Funny how leaden one's legs can feel sometimes. Come on baby, you can do this.

Ioanna walks slowly yet deliberately across the parking area. A four by four cruises the area looking for a space big enough to park in and momentarily blocks her view of Fay and Eve. It passes and they are still there. Eve is looking at her now, though. It doesn't look like the gaze of someone who's looking at her long-lost sister. Ioanna swallows hard and attempts a smile.

Fay looks apprehensive, her arms already striking a pose as if to restrain Eve if she goes wild and lunges at her perceived adversary. Eve stands up, dusts the bottom of her trousers with her hands. Her face adopts a deep frown.

"Have you read it? The text? Have you *read* it, Eve?" calls Ioanna. At that instant she knows the answer to that question. What to do now. What to say. The first thing that comes into her head is "I am your sister! EVE, I AM YOUR SISTER!"

Eve replies, now already getting wound up again. "What in hell do you MEAN? I don't have a sister and if you mean that we're both women - as though that ought to make it any BETTER, THEN GIVE IT UP! IT WON'T WORK."

Fay gets a lightbulb moment. Places her hands on Eve's shoulders, says, "EVE! LISTEN TO HER! I *KNEW* there was something about her the first time I clapped eyes on her. She looks a helluva lot like you Eve. Wait, keep cool, listen, please, Eve, PLEASE."

Eve is like a lion poised to pounce, yet she doesn't move. Finally something seems to be penetrating. She remains as if on 'pounce' alert, yet waits. Somewhere in the recesses of her brain a chord strikes. This woman IS about my age. She DOES look Greek - and she does look a bit like me. She waits. Ioanna approaches to within a few feet, she's evidently frightened.

"Eve, you are so lucky to have Tom, he loves you so much. He loves you so much that he found me for you. He *found* me Eve. I am Ioanna, I was born April 1970 in Sorona. My mother was Chrisanthi Stefanos. Oh Eve… you and I, we are twins. I've waited all my life to find out where I came from. So have you, I know." Ioanna pauses, waits for Eve to react. Eve does, she says,

"Go on." She speaks those words flatly, seemingly devoid of emotion. She adds nothing more. So Ioanna does go on,

"Eve, Tom told me that he had to finish off making the arrangements whilst he was at work. He knows you weren't buying his story about why he was coming home late, but he didn't want to spoil the surprise."

'American accent,' thinks Eve. "You're American. How can we be sisters?" Eve knows that her resistance is crumbling. But now she wants to be convinced, so as to be really sure that this isn't all a fabrication.

"Eve, you are British. Does that make you any less Greek than I?

Yes, I was brought up in the States, but I always knew I was adopted. They told me my parents were both dead. It was Tom who told me that my mother - our mother - had lived on until 2012. Oh, Eve, if only you'd have seen me when I realised that I would never be able to meet her. You were the lucky one, you had her for all those years." Ioanna now can't go on. Her throat has constricted too much and she must cry. She cannot speak. Here she is in a hospital car park trying to convince her natural sister of who she is. She's still not sure if she's succeeding. She does know, though, that what she's told Eve could only have come from someone who's genuine.

Fay says, "Evie? Evie, Say something. Surely this explains everything. If only I hadn't spotted them in that stupid café, none of this would have happened." She looks at Ioanna, "I believe you, I do. You and Eve are peas in a pod now I see the both of you together." She turns back to Eve, "Evie. This must be true, must be right. This is your SISTER! For goodness sake. It's all *my fault!*"

Eve slowly drops the stance of aggression, says "Can this really be so? Can I have a sister, a real..." No more words come out, she lunges toward Ioanna, but this time with arms outstretched, they encompass her sister's body and Ioanna responds in kind. They lock themselves together as if their lives depend on it.

Fay decides to leave them to it after several minutes have passed and neither look disposed to release her grip on the other. She goes back to the hospital entrance, enters and takes the lift. Exiting the lift, she walks along the ward corridor and through the door into the room where she knows that Tom is lying. His head turns as she enters. He looks very anxious.

"What's happening, Fay?" he asks.

"It's OK, Tom. Everything is A-OK."

It's later in the afternoon at the hotel. Ioanna sits with Eve on the balcony. Eve has retrieved her phone from under the dressing table and read and re-read that text message. They've been talking non-stop ever since that moment in the hospital car park.

"I'll call the kids, Ioanna." She's already told her sister that she has two teenage children, both of whom Ioanna is anxious to meet. It ought to be break time at school as in the UK it's still the middle of the day.

Eve calls Andrew. He answers with his usual wit. "Hey Mum. I take it by now we're all happy families eh? Is she cool, 'aunt' Ioanna? Or rather, is she *hot?!* Pretty amazing surprise for you, yea? Did it go with a bang?"

Eve responds, "For once in your life be serious Andy. Yes, she's cool," she catches Ioanna's eye when she says this and both of them roll their eyes upward, "and it all went with slightly more than a bang. We'll explain when we get home. But listen, Andy, are you cool with it if we change the flights? Will you two manage without killing eachother?"

"I'll let you in on a secret Mum, Zoe's over at Trisha's and Trisha's mum said she can hang out there for a while. So I'm cool. Got a few girls in and plenty of beer. You know, looking after the place as if it were my own. No damage done that can't be fixed."

"Andy, if you do have a few girls in it'll be a first. You're going to be OK if we hang on here a few days, then, evidently." Eve knows her son. He does have a good responsible head. Gets it from his father.

"Sure Mum. Look, don't worry OK. Mr. MacDonald keeps me well fed."

Eve tells her son how much she and his Dad love him and they sign off. She calls her daughter and they too have a brief but reassuring chat, Zoe saying that it was fine with Trish's parents for her to stay at Trisha's as long as is necessary.

"So, better get ourselves off to the hospital, get that dopey man of mine back here, right?" Eve says to Fay, who's stretched out on her bed reading her Kindle. They've already spoken to Sevasti about Tom and Ioanna moving to the same hotel and checked them out of the other one, where they were booked into neighbouring rooms. This time, though, Fay and Ioanna have agreed to take one room while Tom comes in to this one with his wife.

The doctors have agreed for Tom to be discharged, but recommended that he not fly for a few more days, which suits everyone fine, especially now that Eve has run it past the kids, Fay likewise with her girls. Anyway, Fay's husband Richard is there to keep her house together.

All that remains is for Eve and Ioanna to return to Sorona together. One thing that they want to ask Gianni, their uncle, is why he didn't tell Eve that he'd reported hearing two babies crying all those years ago. Plus, they so want to go and see their grandmother, Sofia, who'll be completely amazed to see that she has now recovered not one, but both of her granddaughters.

Eve has spoken to her uncle Gianni now and it's Friday evening May 16th, the day after the date when they were originally going to fly home. Eve and Fay of course still have the car they hired, Tom having returned his to a local office. Eve had phoned the desk at the airport to extend their period of hire without problem. The four of them are driving up to Sorona at 7.00pm and they're going to go straight to Gianni's house first. Giannis as yet doesn't know about Ioanna. The sisters think it best to explain it all face to face.

They arrive at Gianni's house at around 7.45pm and all pile out of the car to be met at the gate, the exact gate where Eve and Fay had accidentally stumbled across her uncle, just twelve days ago. Giannis is there to meet them and stares bemused at Ioanna. Looking at her, yet addressing Eve, he asks,

"And who may this be Evanthoula *mou?* She looks Greek, like you."

"I think I should tell you when we are all sitting down," replies his niece. "I'd say a large Metaxa to hand will probably be of some assistance too." She smiles at her uncle as she says this, and - following Tom and Giannis being introduced - the Greek leads the way to the kitchen door, where Voula waits to greet her guests.

Eve begins, "Uncle Gianni, what do you remember about the night when I was born?"

"Before I answer you, Evie, may I ask why your husband has bruises on the side of his face and his face shows pain sometimes when he moves? Tom, have you had an accident? Was it a road accident?"

Tom answers, "Not exactly. Well, yes, I suppose you could call it a road accident. I was knocked over by a truck near the hotel, but it's only a couple of cracked ribs, which hurt now and again. Plus I hit my head, as you can see, of course. No big deal now though. But thanks for asking."

"*Aach*, we Greeks are crazy on the road. This doesn't surprise me really." He now turns to face Eve again, betraying nothing if he has realised who Ioanna actually is. "I was eighteen and Dimitri seventeen. We were told to go and visit uncle Giorgo, the baker, who was Voula's father of course, once it was clear that Chrissy was going to give birth. Everyone wanted us out of the way, so we obliged.

"So, we saw nothing of the birth. But the next day we did go home and Chrissy was shut away in my parents' bedroom. They wouldn't let us through the curtain." Seeing his guests exhibit a slight register of surprise at his use of the word 'curtain' Giannis pauses to explain. "In those days the only thing separating the bedroom area from the living area was a curtain across beneath an arch in the ceiling. Behind the curtain were the beds. During daytime the curtain was usually open, but when we got home it was tightly closed and our father made it quite clear that we weren't to try and see behind it. "Chrissy needs rest,' he said, and we obeyed.

"After eating breakfast we went off to our work. We worked at that time for a farmer in the next village, doing anything and everything, including tending sheep and goats, ploughing fields, feeding poultry, you name it."

"So," Eve asks, "did you hear me crying?"

Giannis knows exactly why Eve is asking this question. Looking straight at Ioanna, but addressing Eve, he answers: "Evanthoula, both my brother and I thought we heard more than one baby crying. Not just crying, cooing, you know, making those little noises that babies make. But we were told that we were imagining things. Chrissy was soon back in her own house, with the midwife and our own mother in regular attendance, but I've never been shaken from the belief that perhaps there had been another child and we were not meant to know.

"Very soon afterwards, one night while we were taking a drink in *To Steki*, we saw the Papas skulking around in a way that didn't seem normal. Then we saw him drive out of the village. He had to pass the kafeneion to leave the village, we were sure he had the midwife in the car with him. It was dark, but there were streetlamps by then and you know how you get momentary glimpses inside a vehicle when they pass them.

"To be honest, Eve, with all that went on and the fact that no one ever spoke about you having a brother or a sister, the whole matter was soon swept under the carpet and eventually forgotten. I do know, though, that following a late night visit from the Papas, that same night that we'd seen him leave the village with the midwife, I think, our parents had come into a sum of money, enough to make arrangements for Chrisanthi to be shipped off to England to start a new life.

"What did we know? Dimitri and I weren't a party to any secrets that may or may not have been held. Eventually it all faded into a blur and we just accepted that we had a niece, but that we were unlikely ever to see her again anyway. It didn't matter what speculation we may have come up with, nothing would have made any difference."

"But, uncle Giannis, why didn't you tell me this last week when I was here?" asks Eve.

"What point was there, Eve? What would it have achieved? I had no proof of anything anyway and, to be honest, we were all so amazed to have you back that we didn't need anything more to bring a huge amount of joy back to the family and the village."

"You had no suspicions, you didn't tell anyone?"

"We were under no illusions from Papa Mihalis, that were we to breathe a word of hearing anything in the hours following the birth to anyone, the consequences would be dire. Quite what those consequences may have been I don't know. But you have to remember that the village Priest held, still holds in many places, a huge amount of power and influence, far more than is healthy really.

"I know that we shouldn't have, but we told Mano, our employer, once about what we thought we'd heard. He told us not to be stupid, but several years - yes years - later he went to see a friend who was a policeman and talked to him about the priest's alleged schemes, and before long Papa Mihalis was replaced. End of story. I never knew what became of him. I only know of rumours about him being involved in some scheme which wasn't all together moral and it had to do with orphanages. It was all very sketchy. Then the story broke in the media. Babies had been sold in their thousands using false documents to foreign couples. The government promised a full investigation, lots was going to be done, but little actually was.

"Where did that leave us? Our sister had been gone already for some years and her letters had become fewer and shorter. We had absolutely nothing to go on. So what was the point? We had our lives to get on with. Was I in the wrong? Judge me if you want to Evanthoula, I am at your mercy."

Eve knows that she cannot pass judgment on her uncle. He was an innocent in the whole affair and, like the few others in the family and village who knew anyway, had put the whole thing behind him decades ago. She's struggling to try and understand how a young nineteen-year-old widow, already desperately grieving over having lost her husband and provider, would feel having given birth to twins, only to have one of them snatched from her breast, with no hope of ever seeing the child again.

26. Chrisanthi, Sorona 1970.

I feel completely emptied, only physically that is. Emotionally I am complete. I don't have a gram of strength left, or so I feel, yet I have the energy to feed these two. If someone had tried to explain to me how it would feel to produce a child, two children, and then have them suckle at the breast I'd never had understood. I do now. These two perfect little humans are all I have left of my dear Stathis. Dear, dear Stathis. This one, I'm sure she was the first to come out, she's got a scrunched up little face and a mop of black hair, yet I can see you in her my love. I can see you in both of them.

Why did I have to arrive at the olive grove when I did? If I'd just got myself together and left the house ten minutes earlier I'd have arrived before you climbed that tree. Or, if you'd been already up there, you'd have seen me coming and jumped down. You'd have placed your hand on my belly and we'd have told everyone at last what we'd been keeping secret. There was such a bump there that I'd reached the point where we couldn't hide it any more. But we'd had to be sure that nothing was going to go wrong. On that day, that awful day, we were ready to tell. It was meant to be such a happy day. I remember every step of that walk out to the groves, the buzzards wheeling high above in that perfect blue sky, the sparrows chattering on the fences.

And I am still, in my mind's eye, down there on my knees begging you not to go, not to die. I can smell the pungent goat droppings mingled with the olives you were harvesting. My knees still feel the dampness soaking through my skirts as I knelt there on that cold ground clinging on to you, watching you draw your last few breaths. Your strangely angled body stretched like our Lord over that awful bough, like you'd been sacrificed. I am cursed to always have that moment burned into my brain until I draw my last breath. Now all I have left of you is these two miracles. That was the day when we were finally going to put an end to all the superstitious counsel from the village women, the back talk in the plateia, the gossip about us being cursed by 'the eye'. This was to have been the day when all saw that we were fruitful, we were going to be a family. The Panagia had smiled on us at last.

I can't go through with this. I can't do it. How can I choose? I won't do it. I don't care what it takes. I'll walk to the city and I'll slave in a kitchen to bring you two up. I'll do whatever I have to do, only I can't be parted from you, either of you. You belong together, you belong with your mother.

Who am I kidding? How can I work and also look after the two of you at the same time? Now, now, don't bite, that hurts. That's better, that's much better. And you, you little tyke, you're a guzzler. See I can already tell that your personalities are subtly different.

Surely mama and papa will understand. They are parents after all. They won't make me do it, they won't. I've lost your father my darlings, I can't now lose one of you too. It will break my heart into pieces, into tiny little pieces.

The door opens and without invitation in walks the Papas, with Eleni the midwife and Chrissy's parents, Petros and Sofia. They stand in a line as Chrissy rearranges her clothes and places the babies into their modest wooden cot, then tucks them in. The Priest speaks first.

"It's time my child. Have you chosen?"

Chosen? He asks? Have I chosen? Like I was giving away one of two loaves of bread that I've baked? Chosen? How can I ever choose? I cannot. I will not. They can't make me do this, surely.

"Please, Papa Mihali, can't we forget this idea? I'm sure there must be some way…"

"My child. It's too late for that now. We can't keep you shut off from the village any longer, there are only so many excuses we can make for your not having appeared with your child. Choose the one you will keep and we shall take the other. You needn't worry, child, it will have a good upbringing, probably better than the one you're going to keep. All the arrangements have been made. It's all been agreed."

He doesn't mention the cash he's going to pocket into the bargain.

Chrissy stands up and moves in front of the wooden cot in which her children lie. She assumes a position with her back to it, hands straight down by her sides, palms facing back toward the cot. She's the mother bird and her protective instinct is taking control. The Priest looks at Petros, nods in Chrisanthi's direction. Her father walks forward, slides a hand around his daughter's shoulders. Chrisanthi stares at her mother, who is rooted to the spot, evident doubt written all over her face, yet she does nothing, says nothing, She only dabs her eyes with a handkerchief.

Petros says, "Chrisanthoula *mou*, it's for the best. This way you will have a chance, your child will have a chance at a better life. Surely you see that my child."

"No, NO!! Don't make me do it, pleeeeeeeease papa!!"

Her father looks imploringly at the Priest, who simply nods, whereupon Petros guides, with some degree of pressure owing to Chrissy's resistance, his daughter away from the cot. The Priest looks at the midwife, she gets the message from his eyes and approaches the cot, where she puts her hands in and draws out one of the babies. Neither infant makes a sound. The midwife places the child into a wicker basket and is gone from the room in seconds, followed by the Priest and Chrissy's father. Her mother Sofia remains for a moment at the door, from where she looks at her daughter, who has now collapsed on to a wooden chair and is sobbing uncontrollably. Sofia makes as if to move forward to offer her daughter some comfort, but thinks again, then exits, quietly closing the door behind her.

In a strange quirk of fate, this scene is played out more than forty years before Giannis, Chrissy's younger brother, explains to his guests what he knows about events at the time of Eve's birth. It is played out in the very same room where Giannis, Voula, Eve, Tom, Ioanna and Fay are sitting.

At around 8.00pm on Friday May 16th 2014, forty-four years and one month in fact after Chrisanthi had one of her newborns taken from her, these same two children are once again in the very same room in which they'd been so heartlessly separated. This house, having been the home built for Chrisanthi and Stathis, had remained empty for some years, until 1982 when, following the death of her father, Voula had accepted Giannis' proposal of marriage and the families unanimously agreed that they should move into this house. Voula had a bakery to her name it was true, but here was a house going begging and it made perfect sense for them to make it once more into a home.

Situated as it is, right out on the edge of the village, looking out over sweeping valleys below, it is the kind of house where, were someone within to be wailing out of desperation and grief over having lost one of her children forever, no one would have heard.

John Manuel

27.

"And now, my dear Evanthoula, are you going to introduce your sister to her long lost uncle?" Says Giannis.

'Of course' thinks Eve, 'it was pretty obvious really I suppose.'

"Tom found her, uncle Gianni. I have my dear wonderful husband to thank for this, but yes, you're right, this is my sister. I'm sorry, but it still feels odd saying that. Odd, but wonderful at the same time. Ioanna, meet your mother's brother, your uncle Giannis. Gianni, meet your other niece, Ioanna."

Ioanna stands, as does her uncle, they close up together and share kisses on both cheeks and a huge bear hug. After a couple of minutes of this, Giannis suggests that his second newly discovered niece in as many weeks sit back down while he does likewise.

"I can honestly say that my legs are feeling quite weak," Giannis says, to a ripple of chuckles in response. "Did you expect anything like this Ioanna? How are you feeling about things now?"

"I don't know where to start. I'd been searching on and off for years, when through an internet group that I'd registered with I got the message that a Mr. Tom Watkins thought that I may just be the long lost sister of his wife. Once we had compared the details and seen where I'd been brought to America from as a baby, it all fell into place. As soon as I saw Eve I knew. She didn't though, because she was somewhat distracted at the time, weren't you Eve?" She looks over at Eve with a warm smile.

"I'm so embarrassed about all of this. But you have to admit to how it all looked to me at the time. I'm only grateful that things didn't turn out worse for Tom. I've never behaved like that in my life. I was so livid. I think he's just about forgiven me, have you darling?"

Tom reaches over, squeezes his wife's hand and smiles with a nod.

"I can see that there is much more to this than I'm currently aware of!" declares Giannis.

The evening wears on with explanations and memories flying around the room. The conversation carries on over a sumptuous meal that Voula has prepared and that they all partake of on the terrace, watching the sun drop below the horizon in the process. Eventually, Eve remembers something she wants to ask her uncle.

"Uncle Gianni," she asks, her fingers twirling the stem of a brandy balloon on the table before her, among the debris of a successful feast, "You said that my grandmother still has our mother's letters. I feel that I would like to see them now. I want to know why she never came back; why she eventually gave up corresponding with her parents and family here."

Giannis rises, and, just before entering the house, replies, "Your grandmother gave me the letters after you'd visited last week. I have them here at the house. I have also photocopied them all in readiness, in case I either saw you before you left for home, or I had to mail them."

He goes inside and a couple of minutes later emerges with a bulging brown envelope in his hands. Sitting back down at the table, he draws a folded sheaf from it and hands it to Eve. It's a letter, dated November 1970. It's in handwritten Greek. Eve looks at it and frowns, says,

"I only wish I could read it."

"Give it to me Evie," says her sister. Eve hands the letter to Ioanna, who looks at it and begins reading out, in English, "Dear Papa and Mama, I have arrived safely. I have started work too. Cousin Lela is very kind and between us and one or two friends we can baby-sit Evanthi…"

"You read Greek?" exclaims Eve to her sister.

Ioanna replies, an apologetic note in her voice, "Sorry, but it hasn't come up yet. Didn't you notice my surname? My adoptive parents are Vaughans, but my husband's name, of course, is Loukara. He's Greek, raised in Athens. But we met in New York, where he practices. He's also a lawyer, studied and qualified Stateside. I decided that since I was pretty sure of my Greek heritage and since my husband was fluent in what could have been my mother-tongue, that I'd better get on and learn it." Seeing Eve's gobsmacked expression, Ioanna explains further.

"I know. There is so much ground we have yet to cover Evie. It'll take time won't it. I sort of gave up practicing when we had the first of the children. You have two nephews and a niece back in Baltimore. You'll have to come visit with them some time." She takes Eve's hand and squeezes it. Both of them realise that there is forty-four years of history to catch up on here.

"I think then in that case that we can read the letters another time. We really ought to get you up to our grandmother's house. What do you think Gianni?"

"Evie, I should tell you that your grandmother isn't well. She was so overcome with the whole experience of meeting you that she became ill. She is seventy-eight, remember. She's had a few heart problems for some years. Don't let it bother you too much. She's so happy to have seen you and has no regrets over that. It's simply that her old body is not coping too well any more, even though her mind is a sharp as a knife. Let me talk to her in the morning. After all she doesn't know at this precise moment that I know I had two nieces, not one. As she sees things, she carries a terrible secret. I'll have to sit with her tomorrow and see whether I can break the news in a way that she can cope with. Of course, there is no doubt that she'll want desperately to see Ioanna and hear all about her history. Have you explained to Ioanna about the wall?"

Eve replies, "Yes, I have. She so wants to see it."

"Right, OK. Well, you all had better be getting back down to Lamia, get yourselves a good night's sleep. We'll see if tomorrow we can arrange for Ioanna to meet her grandmother. OK? I'll call you at the hotel around midday."

As Giannis bids his visitors goodbye and he stands with his arm around Voula's shoulders and watches them drive off down through the village and on their way back down the mountain to Lamia, he frowns and says to his wife, "I only hope Mama can deal with this. She'd so want to see her lost granddaughter before she dies."

He doesn't, in his heart of hearts though, think she has the strength.

Next morning, Saturday the seventeenth of May, Giannis is sitting at his mother's bedside, spooning soup into her mouth. It's all she can or wants to eat at the moment. She looks decidedly more frail than she'd looked just a week ago, when she'd been reunited with the grandchild she'd last seen as a babe a few months old forty-four years ago.

There is a small plate of village bread on the tray beside the bed, but she doesn't want it. Giannis looks for a way to start telling his mother about this latest bombshell.

"Mama? Tell me about the birth of my sister's child. Tell me about when Evanthia was born. Is there anything that still bothers you about what happened then? What do you remember?"

She may only be skin and bone, but quick as a flash, his mother Sofia replies,

"You mean what exactly, Gianni? You never could pull the wool over my eyes. Why do you ask this now?"

"Oh, …well, I saw her again last night… She asked after you again of course. In fact, her husband has flown out here to surprise her and they've delayed their flight back to the UK. She wants to see you again before she leaves to introduce you to him; to someone else too actually."

"Mysteries now, eh my son?"

"Come on Mama. It's all so long ago and you know that I know something went on when Chrissy gave birth to Evanthoula. Dimitri and I weren't supposed to know but we had suspicions, you must know that."

"Oh I do, my son. I do." She sighs, lays back down on her pillow and gestures for her son to put the spoon down. She doesn't want more soup. He decides to be patient. He knows his mother as well as she knows her son. She's mulling something over. After probably two full minutes, during which time occasionally her lips have moved, as if she were saying something to herself, she turns her head in his direction and begins.

"Oh, well. I suppose that now, after all this time it won't make any difference. If I'm brutally honest, I would prefer to go to my grave knowing that I had told you everything. Your father's been gone long enough and Dimitri is so far away in Canada. I only have you to look out for me and so it is only right that you know all there is to know. You will decide what to tell your brother and whatever you decide will be the right thing to do.

"Your sister had twins, Gianni. She didn't have just the one child. She had two, two beautiful baby girls. The only ones who knew were your father and I, the midwife and the Papas, Mihalis."

Giannis is proud of the way he keeps his cool and doesn't let on just yet that he knows this. Rather he raises his eyebrows as if to feign surprise. She doesn't really notice anyway. She's now bent on confessing what to her is her part in a mortal sin. She wants absolution because she knows she's not much longer for this world.

Sofia is struggling with her emotions, but continues. "When they were born the Papas told us he had an idea, something which he would try and do out of his concern for us and for how Chrissy was going to manage with two babies and no husband. He made it sound as though he'd be going to great lengths to help us out, as we were his sheep after all. It would require his making some expensive telephone calls and possibly travelling to Patra, but he would do it for our sakes if we agreed. He told us that we could put one of the babies up for adoption. There were genuine American couples looking for babies to adopt and, even though it would all be above board and legal, we'd receive a fee for doing it.

"It was the money, Gianni. We did it for the money. What the Papas promised us would enable us to send Chrissy to her cousin in England, Cousin Lela, who had written to say that there was work there if anyone wanted it." Sofia was getting agitated and had to stop, take some deep gulps of air.

"Water, son. Would you bring me some water please?"

"Of course, Mama." Giannis leaves her bedside and returns moments later with a plastic bottle of mineral water and a glass. Cracking the plastic lid of the bottle and opening it, he pours some into the glass and offers it to his mother's lips, lifting her head gently with his other hand.

After she's taken a few tiny sips, she waves a feeble hand as if to say, sit down, I'm going to say more. Giannis sits and waits.

"The Papas said that Chrissy could decide which of the babies to give up. He would arrange for it to be spirited away, with the help of Eleni, the midwife, so that no one in the village would need to know. They'd all known that Chrissy was pregnant, but no one would be any the wiser when they saw her with one child. It seemed an ideal solution to the problem of how Chrissy was going to survive. You do see that, don't you son?"

Giannis nods.

"Only, …when it came time to do it, I couldn't bear it. We went to the house …we'd sent Chrissy home by then, since Eleni would look in on her and she wouldn't answer the door to anyone else. It was only for what amounted to hours really anyway. We went to the house, your father, the Papas, Eleni and me, to take away the child that Chrissy had chosen to give up.

"I ask you, Gianni. How could we have even thought that the poor girl would be able to make such a decision? All we thought about was the money. Even though your father and I only wanted it to help Chrissy get to England, it still came down to the money anyway. I was heartbroken seeing your sister standing there, pleading with the Papa not to take one of her children. We'd made promises by then. He told us he'd stuck his neck out to get things done on our behalf. There was no going back.

"Yet, Gianni, mou, I wanted to go back. I didn't want to see it through. We'd survive somehow, I was telling myself. But I was a coward, son. I let them do it. The midwife simply put her hands in the cot and took out a child. It could just as easily have been the other one she took, yet it was what it was. She left the room right away, Chrissy collapsed in grief and I left with your father. I couldn't stay. There was nothing I could do or say, Gianni.

"Do you understand it when I say that I've lived that moment over and over again every single day of my life since then? There is a girl out there, a woman today, who is my grandchild and I will never see her and never be able to ask her forgiveness for what we did. She could be anywhere in the world for all I know. But I've lived every moment of her imaginary life. I've wondered what her school friends were like, what her adoptive parents were like. Were they really good people or the parents from hell? I would never know what kind of life we'd condemned that poor helpless child to. Did she pursue a career? Did she marry? Do I have great-grandchildren who'll never know me?

"Gianni, my child. I cannot bear it any longer. I've reached the point where to go to sleep and not wake up, well that will be sweet relief for a troubled soul. I am tired Gianni *mou*. Can you forgive me, my son?" She is almost whispering these last few words as her breathing has become shallow, although she is mentally very distressed. Her heart is struggling to keep up with the stress she's now placing upon it and the oxygen isn't getting to her body cells well enough.

Giannis is crying freely. He stands, takes his mother's face in his hands and kisses her forehead tenderly. "Mama, there was and never will be a better mother than you. You aren't perfect. God knows none of us are. And we all make decisions in life that we live to regret. But you should not be ashamed of anything you have done mother, nothing at all."

Sofia, through the tears, manages a smile for her son. He goes on. "Mama, if you had the opportunity to ask forgiveness of that young child, right now, today, would you take it?"

"What do you mean, Gianni? What on earth can you mean? Of course I would, but then…"

"We have found her, Mama. We have found your other grandchild. We have found Evanthia's sister and she is in Lamia right now, eager to meet you. I am not lying and I am not joking. She wants to come and meet you. Shall I bring her to you, Mama?

"Shall I?"

28.

On Sunday May 19th, 2014 the sky is a deep, deep optimistic blue over the mountains above Lamia. Perched high up on the south-facing slope, were someone to be scanning this area with the naked eye from the city below, they would discern the white patch on the slopes that is the village of Sorona. The more eagle-eyed would even be able to make out the darker patches on the occasionally barren mountainside that betray the presence of the olive groves, which are owned by the families from the village.

Someone is indeed straining to make out the location of the village, it is Ioanna Loukara, as she stares out of the car window from the back seat, as she sits beside her sister's friend Fay. As the car changes direction with the convoluted route taken by the road, she occasionally succeeds in making out the village, whilst at other times she sees only hillsides and goats, scrubland and sky, rocks, electricity poles and old road signs.

In the front seats are Eve and Tom, with Eve driving, Tom content for his wife to do so since she now knows this route better than he. As the hour approaches eleven, they drive into the village and park up beneath the steps leading up into the *To Steki* kafeneion, where the two reunited sisters' uncle Giannis awaits, seated at a table with an *Elliniko*, talking to his friend of many years, Kyriakos, son of Minas and Panayiota, who'd run the bar back in the time of Stathis, Chrisanthi and Giorgos the baker, indeed the time too of Papa Mihalis.

Once the visitors have joined Gianni at the table, they arise and set out on foot to make the five-minute climb to the house of Sofia Katsandadis, Eve and Ioanna's grandmother, Gianni's mother.

Giannis talks to his guests as they walk. "You must be prepared for her physical condition I'm afraid. The events of the past couple of weeks have taken a great deal out of her. It's as though she'd been hanging on through the past few years only for this moment and, now that she has finally seen her daughter's child, she can go to her rest.

"Of course, to have learned that her other granddaughter had been found brought her great joy, but also revived old pain. She related to me in great detail what happened when they took you away Ioanna. It was the first time that I, in over forty years, had ever heard my mother's version of events too."

They walk on, making the occasional piece of small talk, mainly regarding how hot the visitors feel, walking uphill in full sun on a Greek May morning.

As they approach the old iron gate into the courtyard of the house, Giannis feels the need to add something. "Before we go in. I must tell you Ioanna, your grandmother feels a deep sense of shame over what happened on the day when you were taken away." The little group of walkers stands in a knot at the gate. Giannis goes on, "You see, she felt a great guilt over what they were doing to their daughter. She somehow feels that she ought to have prevented it from happening. Imagine how dear Chrissy felt. She'd lost her husband, now she was going to lose one of her daughters too, even though it had been explained that it was for the best. Whether that was really the case is of course debatable now, but it's all water under the bridge. The last thing she said to me yesterday was, 'Son, can you forgive me?' She didn't even realise at that point that she'd be able to ask you Eve and you Ioanna, face to face, that same question today. I'd never understood until yesterday how Mama carried a great weight of guilt for all these years. It's what finally wore her out. She even told me that she's ready to go to her rest, since it's a burden she can no longer carry. Does this help you understand how she's feeling?"

Eve and Ioanna simply nod, since both have linked arms and already have wet cheeks.

Giannis knocks gently on the metal front door and pushes it open, gripping the lever handle. It hasn't been locked in sixty or more years. They all file inside, into the half-light within. The bed is empty, sending a bolt of alarm through Giannis. His mother is in the chair beside the small table that he'd brought and placed beside the bed, so that he could place her soup or drinks on it.

"Mama! What are you doing up? You're naughty. Now let me help you..." he stops mid-sentence. Something is wrong. It must be the angle of his mother's head. Giannis lets out a groan as he rushes to his mother's side, falls on to his knees and grabs her hand, thrusting his face up close to hers, which already bears the pallor of death. Her hand is cold. She is not breathing. Yet on her face there is the unmistakable hint of a smile. Years have fallen away from her wrinkled skin and she looks much younger now, content even.

Giannis stays where he is and sobs. Everyone gasps in unison and no one can keep from letting the tears flow. They all hug eachother and it seems no one knows what to do first. Just as he composes himself enough so that he can get up and think about what they should do, he sees that in her hand, still clutched between her thumb and fingers, is a scrap of paper. On the small table there is a pencil, evidently the only writing implement that Sofia could find.

Gently Giannis draws the piece of paper out from his mother's rigid, cold grip and looks at it. Written in a shaky hand that is unmistakably his mother's, are these words in Greek:

"See to it that they get what would have been Chrisanthoula's..."

Sofia had sensed that she didn't have long. To right the wrong in some way at least, she'd made a last will and testament, thus trying to ensure that her lost daughter's share of the estate should go to the two granddaughters. It may only be a handwritten scrap, in pencil, but it is enough for Gianni.

Five days later, Giannis has driven down to the hotel in Lamia for a final goodbye. Tom, Eve and Fay are flying home later this evening and Ioanna too is heading back to the United States. Sofia's funeral had taken place up in the village, much as had her mother's in 1963, when the young twelve-year-old Chrisanthi had discovered what lust was while watching the muscular Stathis taking his share in shovelling the earth into the grave.

"Girls," says Giannis to his two nieces, "You realise that I am now your tenant and you are my landladies!" He smiles and they smile back. The house in which he lives, indeed has lived since he married Voula, the house in which he has raised his children and seen them fly the nest, is still legally the property of the beneficiaries of Chrisanthi Stefanos and thus of her two daughters Eve and Ioanna.

Eve turns to her sister,

"What do you think Anna? Do we raise the rent? Evict him?" They both giggle and Giannis laughs heartily. Turning to her uncle, Eve asks, "What exactly does our share entail uncle Gianni? You said you'd sort it out and tell us."

"Oh, about two hundred olive trees and a couple of properties in the village. I'll e-mail both of you once I've seen the lawyer and we've tried to get it all on paper, which won't be easy. But it will be a pleasure!"

On the morning of the day of the funeral, which had taken place during the afternoon of Tuesday the 21st, Giannis had taken Eve and Ioanna, at their request, out to the olive grove where their father had met his death. There they had seen the poignant sight of a host of trees, all crafted by the process of harvesting into that familiar flat shape, with the central boughs chain-sawed out of them, with the exception of one. There is a large tree quite near to one side of the grove, which is densely packed with un-pruned boughs, branches and foliage. Giannis had explained that, ever since the day that Stathis had fallen, no one had had the heart to touch that tree again. It had thus been left to grow and grow as a kind of memorial to Stathis, their father. Both women had stood in silent contemplation, as if in some way connecting with their lost father, right on the spot where he had landed, his body broken and his life ebbing away. They'd thanked their uncle profusely for having given them a truly important and moving moment to keep in their hearts.

Goodbyes having been said, both to uncle Gianni and to Sevasti and Gianni from the hotel, the car sets out for Athens airport with three women and one man inside. Ioanna is to take the same flight as the others to London, but from there she will catch a connecting flight to Washington, where her husband Mike will be waiting to greet her.

On-board the EasyJet flight, since they have four hours to kill, Eve and Ioanna sit beside eachother, with Tom to Eve's left, while Fay sits on the other side of the aisle, level with her friends. She's OK, she has her Kindle. Eve and Ioanna, though, are slowly going through their mother's letters home. Ioanna has difficulty sometimes with the handwriting, but she gets the gist of every letter. What becomes abundantly clear is how with the passing of the years, Chrisanthi's anger at her parents could not be suppressed. She felt aggrieved at what she had been compelled to do. She had such awful memories of those last few months at Sorona that she vowed never to go back. As the time passed and she found a measure of happiness and contentment with Ian, it became clear that she found it more and more difficult to grant forgiveness to her parents. Thus she'd finally stopped writing and thrown in her lot with her husband's family, effectively becoming British, forsaking her Greek origins.

Small wonder, then, that poor Sofia had lived with a terrible sense of guilt for so long.

29. Chippenham, Wiltshire, September 2014

Eve is talking to her tablet, propped open on the kitchen worktop, Skype is open and her sister's face fills the screen.

"So, Anna *mou*, do you think you'll be able to cope with my two animals?"

"I'm sure we'll manage. It'll be so good to meet them in the flesh finally."

"Well, you don't have long to wait now, love. We'll see you tomorrow!! I'm soooo excited!"

"OK Evie. Mike and I will be at the arrivals gate plenty early, don't you worry."

'You sure you'll get the four of us and our luggage in the car?"

"Wait 'til you see Mike's auto, my girl. You know what they say about men and why they like big cars."

Both women laugh, Eve blows her sister a kiss and they sign off. At that moment seventeen-year-old Andrew charges into the kitchen. He's got a baseball cap on wonkily and he's towing a suitcase by the handle. Eve asks,

"Your sister ready is she? We need to be out of here in ten

minutes if we're ever to make Heathrow on time. ZOE!! TOM!! What ARE you two doing up there?!"

"No good asking me. Since when did fifteen-year-old girls do anything that a bloke can actually fathom? That goes for dads too." He grabs a packet of crisps from the kitchen top and breezes down the hall with his case toward the front door, to the sound of his mother shouting,

"Hey!! those are meant for the drive up to the airport. You KNOW we said we won't have time to stop on the way! Oh, I don't know, what can I do against this constant onslaught, eh?"

Five minutes later, the rest of the family bustle down the hallway, then out through the front door, Tom takes one last look down the hallway from the open door, before pulling it closed behind him. A little light blinks on a small box on the wall near the front door. Through the frosted glass can be seen the brake lights of Tom's car as he pulls off the drive and sets off on the journey that will take the Watkins family to the USA for the first time in their lives.

It won't be the last, though.

The Author explains.

Where did the idea come from for the plot of Eve of Deconstruction?
I was actually trawling the web looking at stories about what happened in Ireland to all those poor pregnant girls, treated as criminals by the church, though often as not they were the victims, not the perpetrators. I think it was sparked off by having seen the movie Philomena, as well as a TV documentary a little while back about this whole affair. I came across an American news story on-line that revealed what had been going on in Greece apparently from as long ago as the 1930's until the 1970's. It got me thinking.

So, how much of your description of what went on in Chrisanthia's case is based on fact?
The basic fact of what was done to procure babies for Americans to adopt is true. It won't take the reader long to discover this by looking, for example, at The New York Times website, under *"Tales of Stolen Babies."* I must confess to having been shocked and amazed not only that this went on in Greece, but that it went on for so long. The organisation that Ioanna comes across in the United States, the Association for the Search for Children Adopted Without the Consent of Their Natural Parents is real.

What about the locations? Is the village of Sorona real, for example?
Well, of course, Lamia is a real Greek city and there are villages up in the hills to the North of it. Sorona, however, is entirely

fictional and its layout is based loosely on the village of Asklipio here in Rhodes, not more than four kilometres from where I live, in fact. The kafeneion and taverna in the village do sort of sit in Asklipio more or less where I describe them as being in Sorona, as does the main plateia, or square.

You refer to orphanages being involved in the baby adoption scheme, is this substantiated?

Sadly it is. But it should be said that those that were involved are now being run in entirely different and much more humane ways. There is no reason to distrust or avoid such establishments nowadays as far as I can discern.

Are any of the characters based on real people?

Well, a couple of names, maybe. The characters though are conglomerations of people in my life and that of my wife, who as you know had a Greek mother, living in the UK. She came to England, however, in very different circumstances than those under which the young Chrisanthi did.

And, since this is now your third novel, are we to expect another, since you've said on previous occasions that you were doubtful about continuing to write fiction?

How long is a piece of string? It's been the same on each occasion really. I've not planned another book because unless I can come up with a plot that would engage me as a reader, it won't be worth trying to create it for others to read as a writer. With "Eve," as with "Sunshine", I was just struck with this basic idea that I felt would work up into an interesting tale that would hopefully engage the reader. What amazes me is the fact that, once one begins to write, the story almost writes itself. I find myself having writing sessions where hours can go by because I've got into the head of the character and I'm coming out with all the emotions and thought processes that the character would have too.

Kiotari, Rhodes, January 2015.

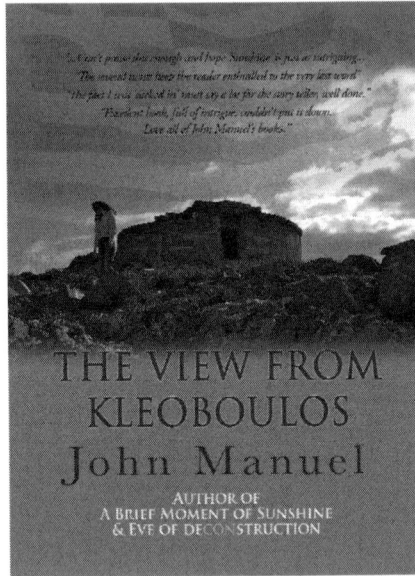

John Manuel's first novel, **The View From Kleoboulos**, was first published in 2013. It has been described as "Thomas Hardy for the 21st Century".

Reviewers' comments have included:
"The several twists keep the reader enthralled to the very last word."

"An excellent first novel that kept me gripped from beginning to end."

"Excellent book, full of intrigue, couldn't put it down."

Available from Amazon in paperback or Kindle format and as an e-book direct from lulu.com

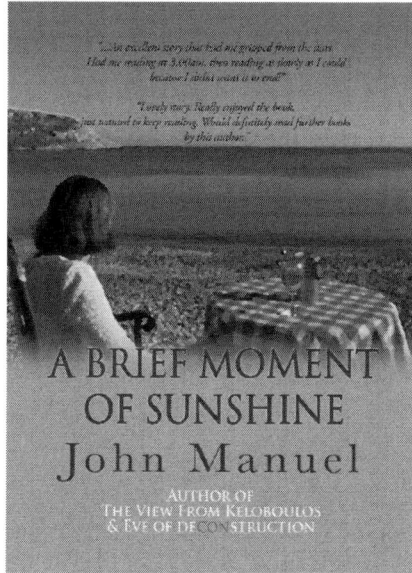

John Manuel was born in Bath, UK during the 1950's. He was educated at the City of Bath Boys' School and primarily excelled in the arts. He has always maintained a deep interest in music and writing, whilst having pursued a career as a graphic designer after having attended Gloucester College of Art and Design.

His wife's mother was born in Athens and his own love affair with the country of Greece eventually blossomed into his first published work, *"Feta Compli!"* He wrote several articles for the now defunct "Greece" magazine and has also had a piece published in the in-flight magazine of EasyJet, the European budget airline.

He now lives with his wife in a quiet area toward the south of the Greek island of Rhodes and, since the death of his mother in July 2013, only occasionally visits the UK.

Both John and his wife are enthusiastic gardeners and walkers.

John Manuel

1.

FETA COMPLI!

2.

MOUSSAKA TO MY EARS

A must for all Grecophiles, the **Ramblings From Rhodes** series of four travel memoirs traces the author's own story, from first meeting a half-Greek girl in the UK several decades ago, through visits with her family and holidays in her mother's country of origin to their eventually moving to Rhodes in 2005.

John Manuel writes in a witty, fast-moving style that has many readers falling about at some of the accounts in these sparklingly fresh Greek-themed books.

As the title of the series suggests, these are ramblings from all over Greece and her islands, with most chapters telling a short tale in themselves. There is a kind of chronology to the four volumes, but don't go looking too closely. Rather, these are books to be delved into much like that favourite chocolate assortment.

Read and savour each tale and be transported to the land of goats, olive oil, gods and golden sunny summer days.

3.
TZATZIKI FOR YOU TO SAY

4.
A PLETHORA OF POSTS

"I recommend them to everyone who is off to Greece, and Rhodes in particular. Very funny, laugh out loud, and I am actually wanting to read them again on this year's holiday."

"Another great, feel-good book which I thoroughly enjoyed."

"I'll certainly be buying other books in the series."

"This author is a breath of fresh air. His work in uplifting and entertaining. I downloaded several of his books to read on holiday but have already read them. I'll just have to hope that he writes some more soon."

•

ALL BOOKS AVAILABLE FROM AMAZON WORLDWIDE IN BOTH PAPERBACK AND KINDLE FORMAT.

FOLLOW JOHN MANUEL'S ONGOING GREEK ADVENTURES ON HIS BLOG:
HTTP://RAMBLINGSFROMRHODES.BLOGSPOT.COM/

Printed in Great Britain
by Amazon